POPPA

A FICTIONAL BIOGRAPHY OF JOSEPH OF NAZARETH

C. K. MCKENNA

 A publication of Bible Spinoffs, Palm Coast, FL 32137

Copyright © 2018 by C. K. McKenna

ISBN 978-1-7323260-1-9 Hard Cover

ISBN 978-1-7323260-2-6 Paperback

ISBN 978-1-7323260-3-3 E-book

Library of Congress Control Number: 2018943562

❀ Created with Vellum

DEDICATION

To the men and women
who are Poppa and Mama
to children born of other parents

ACKNOWLEDGEMENTS

Thank you, all you have provided encouragement, ideas and criticism.

Special thanks and love to Kathleen, my wife and companion in our life as Poppa and Mama, as well as my chief editor and supporter;

My heartfelt appreciation --

- For her insights and direction, to Lauren Andrews, whom I met at Daytona Beach's "City Island Fiction Writers," where I learned lots;
- For her thoughtful questioning and comments via a myriad of emails, to Rebecca Moon Ruark, whom I met online through The Maryland Writers Association's "Novel Manuscript Exchange" – an invaluable service;
- To Good Shepherd School in Inwood, Manhattan,

where I wrote my first paragraph and enjoyed bible stories;

- To All Hallows High School in The Bronx, where we read much, wrote some, and studied The Way, The Truth and The Life.
- For the cover art, to Michael Gleason, Palm Coast, FL.
- For the cover design, to M.H.Pasindu Lakshan, Sri Lanka

CHAPTER 1

"*I*t is a blessing to have a Jewish king," Joseph said to his father, Jacob. "That's what the men at the marketplace say."

Now all of ten years old, Joseph could hardly contain his excitement as he walked beside his father to his first day as a cutter, building Herod's new theater in Sepphoris, the largest city of Galilee.

Jacob had described the magnificent stone arches, the engraved artwork on the heavy cypress doors and the carved lentils fitted around every portal; then he had assured his son that any description fell short of the theater itself. For the past two years Joseph had worked the saw and blades, the hammer and chisel, until his fingers numbed and his forearms burned, developing his craft in preparation for this day.

Jacob looked around, as if to see if others had heard his son's remark. "That's market talk." He lowered his voice to a whisper, "At the synagogue you hear a different story: 'This man is not of our people so he cannot be our king.'" He shifted his leather sack of tools to the other shoulder.

Joseph said, "They both can't be right. Which is it, Poppa?" He carried his basket of wood-chisels, blades and a hammer over a strong shoulder as if they weighed fifteen ounces instead of fifteen pounds.

"I'll tell you later," muttered his Poppa.

The sandy, dusty trail between shy Nazareth and blooming Sepphoris was becoming more of a road each day as the dozen or so workers trod back and forth. So early did they start each morning that they neither saw nor heard a bird until half way to Sepphoris, the city set high on a hill five miles northwest of their little village.

The craftsmen passed the two-hour walk each day conversing about the happenings in their one-synagogue village and sharing lessons from the Torah and stories from the writings. During the first hour they talked and prayed together. As they approached Sepphoris, they formed groups of two or three because of Herod's prohibition against gatherings.

Now separated from the others, Jacob whispered to Joseph, "Our rabbis say, 'His father was not one of us, so he is not one of us, much less from the House of David from whence come all our kings. If we had our way, he would not be our king, but even in our own land we do not have our way.' On the other hand, the sellers in the market are happy to remind us we are well off to have a job. They say, 'So what if his father was a foreigner, an Idumean no less. His mother was one of us and that's close enough. Besides, he hires our craftsmen.' And the sellers in the market are pleased to take whatever the workers earn."

"If he's not really one of our own people, how did he

become our king?" His voice rose with anticipation. "Tell me, Poppa."

Jacob pulled his son close to him. "Not so loud, Joseph. After Herod was king for six years, the foreign Emperor died. Many of our people hoped the new emperor would install a Jewish ruler, but Augustus confirmed Herod as king." He spat on the ground, looked around and assumed the tone he used when he taught Joseph his lessons. "Joseph, tell me, when did Augustus became the Emperor?"

"That's easy, Poppa. The year I was born to you and the family of David." He laughed.

Jacob tousled his hair and again whispered. "Do you know why we walk in small bunches when we get close to Sepphoris?" Jacob did not wait for an answer. "Even with all his power and soldiers to protect him, the king is jealous of anyone who might be a threat. We are proud to be of the House of David but it is wise to keep our pride a secret when Herod's people might hear. A wicked ruler deserves no trust."

When they arrived in Sepphoris the workers moved by one's and two's to the section of the theater where they would spend the day. This theater was one in a long string of building projects undertaken by Herod. Jacob, and now Joseph with him, worked in the inner courtyard, chipping and shaping stones so that when placed together they would form firm walls or symmetrical arches ready for the door sills and lintels they would construct on another day. Few cutters had the talent for stone as well as wood, and to these few were given the task of working on the most visible and adorned sections of a project.

Picking up the hammer and chisel at the start of each day, Jacob prayed, "Unless the Lord builds the house," and Joseph replied, "They labor in vain who build it."

A foreign overseer walked from site to site. A leather belt around his short tunic held a dagger with a curved end and a length of fine hemp attached to a notched stone. "You're new here," he said to Joseph. He stepped closer as if inspecting his eyes and nose and lips. "What is this? This child should be with the women and the babies." He grabbed Joseph by his shoulders. Joseph flexed his arms as he felt the man squeeze. The overseer's hands moved down his biceps and forearms, squeezing and relaxing. He released him.

Jacob looked into the man's eyes and then lowered his head. "He knows his craft well. Test him if you like."

The overseer directed Joseph to pick up a nearly round stone about eight inches in diameter. "I will watch you shape this stone as if you want it for the keystone for that arch." He pointed to the half-built arch in front of them.

Joseph picked up the stone, turned it in his hands and examined it, without looking at Jacob for help. His Poppa had warned him that he might have to demonstrate that he was prepared for this job. Other boys Joseph's age worked with their fathers but most of them carried water or tools or shimmied into nooks too small for a man to fit in. Now holding the stone out in front of him, Joseph took a step toward the overseer and with a nod of his head pointed to one side of the stone. "I would not use this rock for the keystone. The swirls in the grain will make it break round. The keystone needs flat sides and must hold up under the force of the arch itself as well as the structure above." He put down the stone and picked up another. "In the hands of the right mason this one will fit."

"So you say. I'll be back another day to watch you shape it." He walked on to another pair of men.

With a smile in his eyes, Joseph nodded to Jacob. "Good

4

fortune for me that I had the right teacher." His hammer clanged against the chisel as they returned to their task.

With no prescribed meal time, workers ate between tasks, taking bread or dried fish or a few figs from their bundles. By midday their ears rang from the constant hammering, their fingers bled from sharp slivers of stone and ragged edges of hand-hammered nails, and their mouths and nostrils filled with sand and stone dust. At the end of a long day the workers gathered their tools for the return trip home where they would have a proper evening meal, provided there was someone to prepare it for them.

After putting their tools into their sacks, Joseph looked around their work area for a hiding place. "Poppa, there must be somewhere we can leave our tools." Although his arms and shoulders and back ached from the day's labor, he wanted his Poppa to know he would not shrink from carrying his sack, so he added, "That way we can walk faster."

"If you know where to hide treasure or tools, someone else knows where to find them."

Joseph understood Poppa's caution but he could not concede without another attempt.

"Before we go home let me visit some of the synagogues. Surely someone there will be trustworthy." Much larger than Nazareth, Sepphoris had four synagogues, each presided over by several rabbis.

Before Jacob could answer, Joseph dropped his sack and ran down one of Sepphoris's precisely laid out streets.

"Come back, Joseph. We must start for home."

Joseph heard the urgency in Poppa's voice but he continued running. After a short distance, he stopped and turned around. "Poppa, let me try one synagogue. Please, Poppa."

Jacob nodded and picked up both their sacks of tools. Joseph ran back and relieved Jacob of the smaller sack. Jacob's silence at Joseph's disobedient determination dampened the high spirits Joseph had felt the whole day.

While seeking a synagogue, they came upon two men discoursing near a town well, one addressing the other as 'Rabbi.'" Jacob and Joseph paused, standing at a discrete distance.

When the man walked off, the rabbi approached Jacob. "You are not from this village but many times I have seen you on the road." His eyes were set deep in his head, his dark heavy beard hanging below his prayer shawl, a beard much darker and longer than Jacob's.

Jacob explained who they were and what brought them to Sepphoris every day.

The rabbi said, "My wife and I are in need of someone to build us a new room. All the local tektons are busy on this newest of the Idumean's projects." He pointed with his eyes toward the theater, and then, nodding to them, invited them to walk with him.

Jacob walked beside him, with Joseph right behind, along the perimeter of the theater work site. Within minutes they reached a far corner when they turned down a street of stone houses, like homes in Nazareth, but with more space between them. They stopped at the third house on the street, putting it about sixty paces from the theater wall. They entered the house. Inside were two girls, both younger than Joseph, with ebony eyes like the rabbi's. Their laps held balls of wool yarn they were knitting into squares of fabric. A woman sat at a spindle. With considerable difficulty she stood when the rabbi and his visitors entered. She looked ready to give birth any moment. The girls looked at Joseph, nervous laughter making them giddy.

The rabbi turned to Jacob and Joseph and gestured toward the woman and the girls. "My family," he said. "My wife, Anna, and my daughters, Mary and Salome." To the girls he said, "Stand up like your mother. We have guests."

The girls stood, blushing. "Yes, Father Rabbi." They fidgeted with the balls of yarn.

"I am Joachim," said the rabbi.

In one corner of the room stood a set of shelves, holding scrolls and writing quills on the upper shelves and baskets of wool on the lower. Joseph saw neither hammer nor saw and guessed how this family spent its time. Two small sleeping mats leaned against a wall. A fire burned beneath a soup pot opposite the door. Two large and two small chairs stood around a table in the middle of the room.

Again following Joachim's nod, they walked through an opening into what looked like the beginning of an adjacent room. Four or five courses of stone described this room as an eight-foot square, with no door to the outside. Piles of unfinished stones lay nearby. Beyond the wall and adjacent to the house was a covered kitchen with a clay oven.

"This room will be for Mary and Salome after my wife gives birth. You can see we are a little tight as we are, and about to get tighter," said Joachim through a broad smile.

Joseph wondered if he and Jacob would build a second room in their own house if his mother were ever to have more children. He wasn't sure if he liked the idea of sleeping in a room set apart.

"Can you help us? Maybe after you finish your work on his monstrosity," asked Joachim.

Joseph saw in his Poppa's face sympathy for Joachim and other feelings toward both Herod's project, a huge theater that would dominate the flourishing and once-pretty village, and the builder-king who sought to dominate their lives.

Jacob said, "Your wife might deliver long before our work on the theater is finished."

Joachim's eyes opened wide as he gave a laugh. "No, no, I don't mean months from now or years from now when you finish with him. I mean for a few hours each day, before or after your work day."

Jacob's look to Joseph conveyed his distaste for adding to their already full day. He said, "My son is still a young boy. He has his limits."

Joseph shouted, "I am strong, Poppa. We should help this family get ready for their son, or even another girl." He stepped closer to his father and whispered, "Maybe we can leave our tools with them. We were looking for such a place."

In spite of Joseph's best efforts at secrecy, the rabbi heard him. "Yes, your tools will be safe with us. We will pay you as well."

Jacob consented, and agreed to stay at the home of Joachim and Anna during the week and return to Nazareth before the Sabbath. They would work on the room before and after their labor on the theater with the hope of completing the room before the baby's arrival.

That evening they set off for Nazareth well after dark. With the happy outcome of their visit, Joseph's lively step returned, even more buoyant than before. Poppa Jacob's continued silence portrayed neither anger, as when his eyes narrowed and his lips tightened at a troublesome client, nor fatigue, though Jacob and Joseph were both exhausted. Poppa was disappointed. Uneasy with a quiet Poppa, Joseph decided he should apologize.

Jacob broke the silence first. "Joseph, when we shape a

stone, it sometimes breaks crooked in spite of how careful we are." He paused.

"Yes, Poppa, it has happened to me."

"We do not say we have done something wrong, even though it does not end well."

"We take another stone and try again," said Joseph, certain that Poppa was talking about more than stone cutting.

"And sometimes we strike a careless blow and the stone splits just right in spite of us." He paused again.

Joseph's stomach tightened, his legs hesitated with each stride. He could not raise his eyes and let Poppa see inside him.

They walked, each in his own thoughts. Joseph had hurt Poppa, not only by disobeying but more by insisting, no, by demanding, that they build Rabbi Joachim's new room. Yes, helping another family was honorable but Poppa did not want to leave Mama alone from Sabbath to Sabbath. After a mile of silent sadness, Joseph said, "Poppa." The words wanted to stay inside him. "I should not have pushed for the extra work. I am sorry for disobeying you. Tomorrow I will find others to build their room."

"No, Joseph, we will do as we agreed. Perhaps your mama will find it easier not having to prepare meals every day. I hope today you have learned to chasten your need to fix everything by yourself." He pulled Joseph close and put a firm arm around him.

They continued walking in silence, a silence of relief.

As they approached their home, Rachel's joyful music welcomed them. "Shout with joy to the Lord, all the earth; break into song, sing praise," she sang.

Joseph ran the final steps to his home, delighted that his mother was playing and singing to greet them. In her songs

Joseph heard his mama's heart. Once inside the house he darted to her. She wrapped one arm around him and with the other enticed sweetness itself from her harp. He joined her in singing, "Sing praise to the Lord with the harp, with the harp and melodious song."

Jacob came in, stood by his wife and blew into an imaginary trumpet, his tightened lips mimicking the sound going up the scale. Rachel and Joseph continued their song, "With trumpets and the sound of the horn shout with joy to the Lord."

At their meal of lentil stew with flat bread and baked apples, Joseph told his mama all about his first day as a hired tekton. When Jacob boasted how Joseph had satisfied the overseer as well as the tektons from other villages, Rachel beamed and leaned into Joseph and gave him a hug. In the midst of the hug Joseph described their meeting Joachim and his family and the extra work he and Poppa had agreed to.

Rachel pulled back. "I hate it when your Poppa has to go away but I understand that is how he supports us. I will like it less now that both of you will be gone, but I will doubly look forward to the Sabbath when our house will glow with your presence. I hate to admit it to myself but my son is growing up, and he can't spend all his life in my courtyard."

Joseph read in her look that their family life was changing, one page turning to reveal the next. He would have less time with Mama and, at least while they worked for Joachim and his family, more with Poppa. He smiled at her, knowing she would greet them each Sabbath eve, and hoping that each greeting would find her as well as today.

DURING THE PRE-DAWN and evening hours that they had previously spent walking to Sepphoris, they now spent building a room. They split and chiseled stones in the evening before the family went to bed. The type of masonry that Jacob chose—Ashlar, the masons called it—meant they had to work each stone into a rectangle, with smooth faces on five sides. The sixth or front side they embellished with deft strokes from their smallest chisels. In the early morning while the family slept, they worked in silence, placing the cut stones smooth side to smooth side in even rows, which gave the walls stability and created a work of art.

Pointing to the tiny spaces between adjacent stones, Jacob said, "Joseph, here is where we see the benefit of all our work in smoothing the stones. We need little mortar and the stones press tight together."

He interrupted himself and said, "Listen."

Joseph imitated his Poppa and cocked his ear toward the house.

They heard someone inside the house ask, "Who was David?" Anna was speaking.

A girl answered, "Our greatest grandfather."

"And who appointed him?"

"Samuel appointed him, following God's command," said the older girl, Mary.

"So does that make Samuel a king too?" asked Salome.

Joseph wanted to shout out the answer but he kept his tongue.

Her older sister said, "No, silly. Samuel was the prophet that God used to set up our line of kings."

Their mother asked, "Who was Samuel's mother?"

Mary and Salome answered together, "Hannah was his mother and she gave us our special prayer."

Mother and daughters prayed together, in the rhythm that comes from repeating a familiar verse.

"My heart exults in God; my strength declares his power.

My enemies are vanquished; I delight in his strength.

No one is holy like our God;

No rock, no mountain is like him."

Anna hummed for a moment and then Mary and Salome repeated their prayer. Two or maybe all three of them – it was hard to tell how many – clapped in the joyful tempo of their prayer.

When the prayer ended, Joseph and Jacob continued laying stones. Over the next three weeks they made the walls grow taller, set a window facing east to greet the morning sun, affixed a strong roof with a channel to catch the rain, and joined Joachim's family for meals and evening prayer. With the roof now in place, they were able to sleep in the unfinished new room rather than in the covered kitchen.

What Joseph heard from Joachim's family prompted more questions as Joseph and Jacob journeyed to Nazareth in the late afternoon before the next Sabbath.

"We must be their cousins, if David is also their greatest grandfather," said Joseph.

Jacob said, "Yes, we are cousins since we are all of the house of David. Some cousins are close and some not so close."

"Could our family and theirs go to live in David's city and become close cousins?"

Jacob gave a laugh. "You have been to Bethlehem. Do you think everyone in the house of David would fit there?"

"I wasn't thinking of everyone in David's family, just us and Rabbi Joachim's family. Besides, he said the time is coming for a great son to be born to the House of David. We might get to see him if we move to Bethlehem. If Joachim wants his family to see him, too, we might become close cousins."

"We'll see, Joseph, we'll see. If God wants us all to live in Bethlehem, he'll let us know. Right now the sight of Nazareth and your mother in good health is all I want."

As they stepped up their pace for the final half mile to their home, Joseph thought about the next week and the end of their work for Joachim and Anna and their daughters, and wondered if he would see any of them again afterward. Not only were he and his father living up to their promise to have the room ready before the new arrival but their assigned work at Herod's theater was also nearing an end. He hoped he would get to see the baby before they left Sepphoris, maybe for good.

On their last morning in Joachim's house Joseph and Jacob rose earlier than usual to finish the new room for Joachim and Anna's daughters. They installed new sleeping platforms to keep Mary and Salome's mats high off the ground and a shelf to store the platforms during the day. With the roof now complete, father and son gathered their tools and pulled aside the curtain that led to the main room. Two women knelt beside Anna who lay on her mat; the rest of the family was nowhere in sight. Joseph and Jacob tiptoed out of the house and, as they walked toward the theater, they came upon Joachim.

"This is the day the Lord has made," said a cheerful Joachim.

"Let us rejoice and be glad," replied Joseph and Jacob.

"When you come this evening you will see who the Lord gives us." Joachim raised his eyes heavenward and added, "May it be your will."

Jacob said, "We have finished your new room none too soon, my friend. If it is still all right with you, we will leave our tools in your care at night."

"Yes, yes. Then we will be sure to see you again."

Joseph and Jacob went on to the theater work site.

As they reached their work place, Jacob said, "We will complete this job in a matter of days. Then we will not have the long journey each day."

Joseph said, "That is a mixed blessing for we will not see Rabbi Joachim again. I will miss them"

"I think Joseph will miss the daughters more than the good rabbi."

Joseph felt his face warm; he looked down as he dropped his tool sack. "Mary and Salome are pleasant to be with. They're different from the girls in our village."

The tiniest smile caressed one corner of Jacob's mouth. He lifted one end of a length of cedar. "We don't see fine wood like this in Nazareth."

Relieved to see a change in the topic of conversation, Joseph picked up the other end of the plank, probed it and admired it. "The grain in this wood is like a painting, Poppa. We must get some for our workshop in Nazareth."

"In Nazareth no one could afford to buy it, much less carry it all the way from Lebanon." Jacob made some markings on the wood. "I'll ask the overseer about buying the scraps, at least enough for you to carve something."

"Thank you, Poppa."

Joseph spent the day planing and smoothing and looking forward to their visit to Joachim's family before the trek back to Nazareth.

~

MARY AND SALOME had already moved their mats and shawls and yarn balls to their new room. Anna lay on a raised platform with an infant beside her. The two girls sat on either side of her.

Joachim welcomed Joseph and Jacob. "Come, see our new daughter. If the Lord doesn't send a son, there's no shame in a daughter."

The three of them approached the mat; the baby slept, her tiny hands poking her mother.

"She is precious in the eyes of the Lord and in our eyes, too. You may hold her if you wish," said Anna to Jacob.

Joachim picked up the baby girl and cradled her in his arms. "Mary. Her name is 'Mary.'" He handed her to Jacob, easing her from one cradle to another.

Salome said, "We're going to call her 'Little Mary' because we already have a Mary." As she looked toward her older sister she added, "And Mary isn't big enough for us to call her, 'Big Mary.'" The two girls giggled.

Joseph stepped toward them, surprising himself because he would not have done so a few weeks earlier. "Mary is a lovely name."

The older Mary looked down as she blushed.

Joachim looked into the baby's face, a smile playing on his lips, and maybe on Little Mary's as well. As he looked toward Joseph, he said "Joseph, do you want to ...."

"Yes, Rabbi Joachim." Joseph's heart raced. He formed a crib with his arms the way Joachim had, the way his mother had taught him whenever he held a neighbor's baby.

The baby's perfect face astonished Joseph as she looked at him. Her eyes were dark like her father's and her sisters', but hers had tiny flecks of gold that made them sparkle. The bit of hair on her head sat in little mahogany waves, framing her forehead and ears. Little Mary took a deep breath and wrapped one precious hand around Joseph's thumb. While worry over dropping tiny neighbor children had kept him from enjoying holding them, Little Mary gave him confidence that he would not let her fall. More than that, she would not let go of him. As little as she was, she drew him to her; their hearts linked in a first encounter. He studied her face.

"She has eyebrows," he blurted out.

The adults laughed while Mary and Salome leapt closer to get a better look. "She does. He's right," they said in unison.

Joachim extended his arms toward Joseph, who cuddled the infant closer to his chest. He studied her once more and then returned the baby to her father.

He looked at his own father, wanting to marvel but unsure of what to say.

Jacob helped him. "Autumn night comes early. We must be on our way."

As they walked toward home, Joseph's thoughts left no room for words. He had not experienced anything quite like this day. Mesmerized, and Jacob did not intrude. Eventually Joseph said, "She looks different from any baby I've ever seen, like she's a gift or something." He felt a tear coming, so he took a deep breath, and said, "I wish we could see them for more than the next few days."

"I wish the same but you know after we finish our work on the theater, we might not go back to Sepphoris for a long time." Jacob stopped, took down the large sack he had tied to his back and reached into it. "I brought something for your Sepphoris memories." Opening the folds of a woolen cloth, he revealed a piece of polished cedar, a foot and a half wide by two feet long and almost an inch thick. "It was the largest piece of scrap wood in the pile."

Joseph took it, turned it in his hands and explored the curls and coils of its grain and pressed his face against it, savoring its aroma. "Poppa, it is beautiful. I will save it for the right person and the right time." He wrapped the cedar in the cloth, returned it to the sack, and struggled with Poppa's help to tie it on his own back. "Thank you, Poppa."

The image came back to him: her beautiful face. Eyes that embraced him, small dark brown waves popping out all around her face, and tiny hands so powerful in their softness.

"Poppa, do Rabbi Joachim and Anna have a special way of mating to be able to make a baby like Little Mary?"

"They mate like any couple and then wait to see what God chooses to send them."

Joseph had wondered if Mama and Poppa wanted him to have a sister or brother.

As if reading Joseph's thoughts, Jacob continued, "Many times a couple mates and there is no baby."

Maybe they did want to have a sister or brother for him but God had not sent one, at least not yet.

"Poppa, the older boys tell us they sneak into the tents of the daughters of the traveling traders. The girls let them exercise their manhood. Do you think they might make a baby and then never get to see her when the traders move on?"

"Yes, that happens. Too often."

Joseph reflected on this, and thought again of what the boys had talked about. "If many boys lay with the same daughter, how would she know which mating gave her the baby?" He had seen the shepherds swab berry juice or saffron water on the chests of the rams. The reds and purples and golden yellows on the backs of the ewes announced which ram had sired each lamb.

"You have great wisdom to pose such questions, my son. You are quite right; the girl would not know which boy had fathered her child."

For a while Joseph thought about rams and boys and lambs and babies.

"I don't know which is more dreadful, Poppa, the boy who has a child like Little Mary and never knows her, or the girl who does not know the baby's father."

"Joseph, sometimes people bring dreadful things to themselves, but other times one person does something that brings the dread to someone else."

"What do you mean, Poppa?"

"A trader might force his daughter to do what she does so he can collect coins from the boys. If she becomes pregnant, her family will put her out, so she suffers banishment while her father gets shekels and the boys puff out their chests."

Joseph thought of the older boys in the village, of Little Mary and her sisters, of his Mama and Poppa. He shifted the sack of tools to the other shoulder and rearranged the slice of cedar tied to his back. "The boys never talk about the baby part of it."

CHAPTER 2

*W*eeks and months passed. With no daily trips to Sepphoris, Joseph spent the short winter evenings reading and re-reading imaginative psalms and favorite stories that came to life.

He enjoyed Joseph with his special coat and his generosity to his brothers even after they sold him off. He felt David's power and confidence against Goliath, and marveled over and over at how Moses remained true to his mission of leadership. Abraham remained his favorite. It was beyond his imagination that a man could have faith so strong that he lay his own son down to be sacrificed, all the time believing that God would provide a different offering. "Oh, give me faith so fervent!" he prayed.

When he was not at work with Jacob or doing chores for Mama Rachel, he whittled and carved and sanded. Several scraps of cedar sat on the bench before him, their scent filling the workshop. He had fashioned one small chunk into a doll's head and on it carved a nose, a mouth, and ears. Bits of onyx that he picked off the ground became eyes.

Other pieces of cedar he turned into a body, legs and feet, arms and hands. With deft handling of his awls and blades, he created tabs on some pieces and punched holes in others, so that the pieces fit together. With a few snips of his own light brown hair, he covered the wooden baby's head. Rachel gave him scraps of cloth that became swaddling and cloaks and shawls. In its playmate's hands, the baby could stand, sit or lie down.

Joseph had made the doll with scraps of cedar, imagination, a few tools, some patience and much love. That was the easy part. Getting the doll to Little Mary in Sepphoris before she outgrew it presented a greater challenge.

~

THE COMING of another spring brought plans for the family to travel to Jerusalem for Passover. Each year they made the plans, but many years they did not make the long journey. Spring time brought greater than usual difficulty to Rachel when each breath brought fits of coughing that racked her and left her exhausted and unable to travel.

This year like last year and the year before, Joseph hoped they would meet up with Joachim and his family early in the trip and be able to journey beside them.

Jacob decided that Rachel should not undertake the trip. Joseph, now thirteen years old and almost as tall as Jacob, persuaded his parents to let him join his neighbors in a caravan that had come south from the low hills near Cana and through Sepphoris. All along the way, pilgrims joined the procession until it covered a mile or more, and included thousands by the time it reached Bethel and Ephraim and the final day of the pilgrimage. To his sack of food, prayer shawl, and a water skin to be refilled at every opportunity,

Joseph added the cedar doll with the sparkly eyes. This would be his chance to give it to Little Mary.

Within an hour after he and the other pilgrims left Nazareth, Joseph discovered that Joachim and his family were not among them.

"I have not seen Rabbi Joachim for the past week. He and his family must have already gone to Jerusalem," someone told him when he inquired.

He assumed the whole family had gone; the girls would not go alone but it was possible that only the Rabbi went. The fellow traveler did say the *family* must have already gone, so he would look for them in the Holy City.

The caravan wound its way down the winding trails out of the hill country around Nazareth, south across the bumpy land approaching the mountain on which sat the village of Nain and then east to a route that paralleled the Jordan River, heading south as far as Jericho and then west to Jerusalem. Along the route, groups of boys Joseph's age left the caravan for hours at a time. When they rejoined their families at the evening meal, they told tales of running in the river, grabbing at giant fish and throwing smooth stones at them. None brought back a fish for the fire, not even the boy who had a small fishing net. If his friend Efron had gone to the river, Joseph would have gone with him, but his parents wanted Efron to stay with the caravan proper.

Once in Jerusalem, Joseph searched the inns and camps for Rabbi Joachim from Sepphoris. "He, too, is of the House of David," he said.

No one had seen him or even knew of him. Several snickered. "House of David," they said in mock seriousness. "That narrows it down to a few thousand people." A derisive laugh followed.

Joseph found this bewildering. With the faith that it took

to travel this far, and for such an occasion of remembrance and prayer, why should they belittle anyone? He had no answer.

Joseph appreciated the invitation from Efron's family to join them in the Passover ritual of storytelling, offering sacrifices in the Great Temple and sharing the special meal. On the last day of the week-long festival, Joseph found someone who helped him with his search.

"Sepphoris. Yes, we are from Sepphoris. At least we were," said a man, surrounded by a woman and four children.

"Do you know Rabbi Joachim? He has a wife Anna, and three daughters. I am searching for them."

The man explained that Joachim and his family had not come to Jerusalem this year. He did not know why. He told Joseph that Herod was taking the land near the new theater right from under the people, something about turning Sepphoris into another Herodium, a city known for its opulent excesses. "We will not return to Sepphoris but will go to live in Jericho. My brother lives there, near the river," said the man.

Joseph thanked him and walked away. What if Joachim and his family also moved from Sepphoris! He'd never know where they went! He thought about Moses, how he kept the faith, how he led the Jews, often not knowing what would happen next. "Oh, that I, too, would have such a fervent faith!"

As the caravan began to move out of Jerusalem, Joseph worked his way to the front with the hope of getting home sooner. He could not imagine a bleaker Passover. At least the caravan planned to travel back north by way of Bethel and through the middle of Samaria, instead of the eastern route near the Jordan river, thereby saving a day of walking.

Now that he had journeyed by himself, he decided to ask Jacob and Rachel if he could go to Sepphoris. He felt more determined than ever to find Little Mary to give her the cedar baby. "God will provide," he said to himself, unsure whether as a prayer of trust or an attempt to persuade himself.

~

IN THE FAMILY courtyard that doubled as a workplace for larger projects, Joseph and Jacob pieced together the framework of a pergola. A visitor stopped and got their attention. "I'm looking for the two Nazareth cutters, Jacob and his son."

Joseph and Jacob set down a long saw they had been wielding. "We are cutters, as you can see. Who is looking for us?"

The visitor explained he had come to arrange for the father and son from Nazareth to go to Cana. "Our synagogue has a leaking roof and also needs cabinets for our new scrolls." He paused and gestured, mimicking rain with one hand and protecting scrolls with the other. "To keep our scrolls dry."

Joseph turned away to hide a laugh at the visitor's comic gestures.

"Surely you have carpenters in Cana," Jacob said.

"A plasterer in our village worked on Herod's theater in Sepphoris. He saw your work. Our Cana carpenters made repairs last year but the roof became a home to worms. And it still leaks." He shook his head. "They call themselves carpenters; I have other titles for them."

They agreed on the details of the assignment, the type of wood—sycamore, treated to assure no worms—, the duration of the project, living arrangements and costs. The visitor departed.

Jacob and Joseph redoubled their attention to the pergola. Upon its completion, Jacob said, "Joseph, gather our tools."

Rachel prepared a sack of bread, dried fish and fruit for their journey. "Be sure to take your short tunic. If a long one catches your heel, you'll be on the ground and the synagogue's roof will keep its leaks and its worms." Before her husband and son set off from their home, she held Jacob and caressed his face with hers, and hugged her son close to her. Without another word she ran into her room. At the familiar farewell, Joseph and his Poppa exchanged a knowing glance. She had not let them see her cry.

Each time Joseph accompanied Jacob to a work site he hoped they would at least pass through Sepphoris. He now was approaching 14 years, so Mary was 12 and Salome 10. Little Mary at four was not so little anymore. After he packed his tool basket and his sack, he wrapped the cedar baby and tucked it into the sack. Perhaps it was already too late to give it to her.

"Cana is near Sepphoris, isn't it, Poppa?"

"Sepphoris lies about halfway between Cana and Nazareth. It is a flat path from Sepphoris to Cana, but at the end we must climb high hills when our legs are already tired. We will stop to rest in Sepphoris and still be in Cana before the sun sets." He looked up and whispered aloud, "May it be your will."

THE STREETS of Sepphoris no longer had a welcoming noise about them. No one stood around the well where Joseph and Jacob had first met Joachim. Where four years ago a row of stone houses had stood now lay a field of rubble, with the foundation for walls and a network of scaffolds marching across the land.

As soon as they saw Joachim's house from twenty paces away they knew it stood empty. Someone had knocked the lintels off the doorway. They had no need to go closer but asked about it when they saw a woman tending a pot outside a nearby house.

"Where are Joachim and his family?" asked Jacob, standing in the middle of the street.

"Where the whole city goes: somewhere else." Her shoulders were hunched and taut as if every movement of her stirring stick drained more of whatever spirit she had left.

"Do you know where they went?" asked Joseph. The woman's lack of energy sapped his own.

"Some to Cana, some to Jericho, some to some place I don't know."

Cana! Joseph brightened at the possibility of a coincidence. "I mean Joachim's family in particular. Where did they go?"

"Two days ago they joined a small caravan going to Jerusalem." She now stood up straighter and peered at them, eyeing their tools and clothing. "You're not from this village but you are Galileans."

Jerusalem! Wrong direction! Disappointment replaced Joseph's joy.

Jacob said, "We are traveling to Cana for work. Our home is in Nazareth."

For a moment her eyes sparkled. "Anna told me they had to tend to Temple affairs in Jerusalem. After that they will go to live in Nazareth. You will see them there." She took a labored step toward them, still holding her stirring stick.

"You have walked a long way. Come, have a cup of water." She turned and reached for a jug and handed it to Joseph. "I have no cakes to offer you because I have no oil."

Joseph took the jug, and poured a little water into their goatskin. They would fill it later at the well. "Here." He handed her a loaf of their bread and a bunch of grapes. "We have more than we need. Cana is not far and we will have a meal there."

Jacob blessed her and they went on their way.

"Poppa, did you hear what she said? Rabbi Joachim is coming to live in our village."

"Yes, Joseph, I heard. I am not sure I believe it. The woman was uncertain of where her neighbors had gone to live."

"But, Poppa, she had no reason to lie to us. She knows the family. Anna would have told her where they were going."

"She didn't lie but sometimes people who are uncertain about one thing can be uncertain about other things, even when they think they are sure."

They walked in silence for some time, each alone in thought. As they reached the first hills below Cana, Joseph said, "Poppa, I will get to see Rabbi Joachim's family again when we return to Nazareth. I am certain of it."

Jacob put his hand on his son's back. "Maybe you have so great a feeling for the family because it has been so hard for you to get to see them. I hope you won't be disappointed again, either because they do not come to live in our village or because they do come but they seem less extraordinary than your longing has made them."

"Poppa, this is a strange thought but I feel it is true. I have held babies before but never have I held one who shone like her. Like Little Mary. Heaven must already be inside her and draws everyone to her."

"If not everyone, you for sure. I admire the way you have not given up your hope of seeing that tiny baby again."

"She is not still a baby after all these years. Do you think she will like the cedar baby I made for her?"

"She will like it better now because she is old enough to enjoy it and you will find even greater delight in the look on her face because you have had to wait. Sometimes life keeps us from getting what we want to make it sweeter when we get it."

Joseph tried to recall a story of someone having to wait a long time for something. He couldn't remember which one.

Knowing his son so well, Jacob asked him, "Do you remember how Laban made the first Jacob work for seven years to be allowed to marry his daughter Rachel?"

"Yes, Poppa. Then he tricked him into working seven more. That's a long time. You don't think I will have to wait seven years, do you?" He thought for a moment and then said, "No, the first Jacob had to wait fourteen years." He paused in thought again and added, "But he wanted to marry her. I'm just giving her a wooden doll. That's different."

CHAPTER 3

*J*oseph and Jacob spent one week repairing the synagogue in Cana. From the village potter they obtained baked clay roofing tiles to replace several broken ones and to cover the new roof extension that went beyond the outer edges of the synagogue walls.

"Poppa, why did the builders put up a roof that did not cover the tops of the walls?"

"Maybe they didn't have planks long enough or maybe they didn't know what they were doing."

They packed their tools into their sacks. Joseph heard Jacob mumble, "They didn't know what they were doing."

Joseph took the repetition as a sign that he should not ask again.

When the rabbi came to inspect the synagogue, Jacob agreed to return if the roof leaked after the next rainfall.

As they walked down the steep hills leading away from Cana, Joseph looked out over the plain. "Here and in Sepphoris we can see far away across the land. In Nazareth we can see only as far as the nearest hill. I like our village better; it feels more like home. Now that Rabbi Joachim's family has moved out of Sepphoris, I feel something bad is going to happen there."

"It is a blessing that just because you feel that way doesn't make it so."

As Joseph and Jacob neared Nazareth they passed a patch of hyacinths and tulips on the low hillsides. Joseph ran ahead and broke off a spray, poured water from his goatskin onto a cloth and wrapped it around their stems. As they came close to their home and heard Rachel singing and playing her harp, both broke into a run.

Rachel hugged her husband and son. "Come, you must eat. What a long time you have been gone!"

"We did fine work in Cana. Your son's work has attracted the eye of many traders and sellers. Hunger will be no guest in his home," Jacob said, raising his eyes in silent prayer.

Rachel drew Joseph to herself and hugged him again. "I missed my big son, now almost as tall as his father."

Joseph hugged his mother back, with pride in his work and joy in his becoming a man, at least in his mother's eyes. "We brought these for you, Mama." He handed her the flowers.

She unwrapped them. "They are beautiful, Joseph." She set them into a jug and added water. "Come, sit, both of you."

She brought basins of water and towels for their faces and hands and feet, and sat with them. "Tell me, Joseph, how did the little girl like the cedar baby?"

Joseph told her what the woman in Sepphoris had said. "Can you believe it, Mama? They are moving here, to Nazareth. They could be here already. Have you seen them or heard of them."

"No, I haven't. Joseph. I would have heard if they were here. Nazareth is not so big." She held her son's face in her hands and looked into his eyes. "Why would Rabbi Joachim come here? We already have more rabbis than we have questions to ask them."

Joseph held his mother's fond look. "The woman told us everyone's moving somewhere else. That's what she said." He looked away from Rachel. "Maybe she didn't know. That's what Poppa said." In spite of Mama's encouragement Joseph feared his Poppa was right.

"They will come. The rabbi hasn't finished his temple business yet, that's all." Rachel put her arms around her son. "You'll see." He felt her heart speak with his as she held him.

Each day Joseph visited around the little village and inquired of his neighbors. Each day he received the same response. Weeks later a neighbor woman came to their home. "Rachel, have you heard? The rabbi your Joseph goes around looking for, he is here in Nazareth. Rabbi Joachim is his name. His whole family is with him."

Joseph found out where they were living, took the cedar baby from its basket on a high shelf and set off to welcome their new neighbors. His legs tried to run but his heart held them back. He considered asking his Mama to find out if Little Mary and the whole family had indeed come to Nazareth. Yes, that would forestall disappointment if the neighbor woman had made a mistake but it would diminish the excitement of seeing Little Mary for the first time in years if the family had come. He walked with a new lamb's tentative steps.

Anna greeted him. "Come in, Joseph, you are so tall I would not have known you." She raised her voice. "Mary, Salome, we have a visitor."

The two girls came in from the rear of the house;

Salome stood behind her mother, her gaze cast down, while Mary stood in front, also looking down. They, too, had gotten tall. But where was Little Mary? Joseph waited a moment, looking toward the back room, hoping. No one else came into the room.

To ask directly about Little Mary would be too forward, since it had been years since he and the girls had first become friends and then lost touch. "How was your visit to the Holy City?" he asked.

Anna looked surprised. "We arrived in Nazareth before sunset yesterday and already you know we visited Jerusalem. You must have a special messenger."

Joseph, dumbfounded at first, waited, and then said "I didn't mean..."

"You should not worry, Joseph, we are honored that word of our travels found you before you found us."

Joseph relaxed, still lost for words, and unsure about showing them the cedar baby.

"Sit with us. We will have tea and cakes that Mary made." She nodded at her daughters, who disappeared for a moment and returned carrying a plate of cakes and a jug. Salome retrieved some bowls from a basket on the floor. Anna said, "We have not put our things away yet after our long journey."

As they ate, Anna told Joseph of their visit to the Temple in Jerusalem. "We went to the Women's Court of the Temple, the real reason for our visit." At this, Mary's and Salome's faces registered a hint of sadness; their chewing slowed and then stopped, their eyes focused miles away.

Anna continued. "We always believed Little Mary was God's special gift to us, and, as with all special gifts, we had to give part of the gift back where it came from."

Mary said, "Little Mary knows what we mean. I don't

mean she understands everything like a big girl, but in her heart she knows she is a special gift." She paused, tilting her head, looking for the right way to say what she was thinking. "She knows deep down a gift is special not because of something the gift does but because the giver loves someone a whole lot." She looked to her mother and then to an attentive Salome.

"I know what it means but I can't 'splain it very well," said Salome.

Their pause made Joseph's heart pause. Finally he asked, "Where is Little Mary? Is she ...?" He could not bring himself to finish the question because he feared the answer.

With understanding in her eyes, Anna said, "Our Little Mary is fine and happy with other girls in the Court of Women in the Great Temple. With our blessing she has given herself in service to the Lord with the Daughters of Sion." Her face looked happy like his mother's when she was singing or sewing with the family all together, and, at the same time, sad, like his mother's when Poppa was traveling by himself through Samaria or the dangerous regions of the hill country.

In his synagogue classes Joseph had heard of girls going in service to the Lord but he never knew what it looked like, how it differed from the way ordinary people serve the Lord in the way they live their lives. He never knew anyone who went in service at the great Temple. Perhaps the stories were the happy beginnings of things that didn't work out. The first Joseph had gone in service of the Lord and was treated badly by his brothers. The story of Abraham and his son Isaac came to him; he shuddered as he thought of what service of the Lord might demand.

"Will Little Mary ever come home?" he asked. He fingered the cedar baby hidden in its blanket on his lap.

"Yes, she will come home after three years. After that she will either return to the Temple or she will serve the Lord within her family."

Joseph's shoulders slumped and his chest sagged. Three more years would make a total of seven! He tried to hide his disappointment but he knew that Anna sensed it. He slowly lifted his bundle, placed it on the table, and undid the wrapping corner by corner. "I hoped we would get back to Sepphoris long ago and Little Mary would like to play with this cedar baby." He demonstrated how one could move its limbs and make it sit and stand. Salome's eyes looked ready to leap from her head. He moved the cedar baby to the center of the table and looked to the two girls. "You should play with it so its arms and legs don't get locked in place. Would you keep it for her, for when she comes home?"

CHAPTER 4

*W*ithin a year Joseph saw changes in his mother. At first he heard her being sick, like him when he ate too many Passover figs before their time. Then he saw subtle changes to her shape.

One day in the workshop Jacob said, "Joseph, your mother will soon bring forth a baby." Jacob's shoulders leaned back a mite farther than usual, his chin held higher. "It has been many years since she bore you so we will have to take special care of her."

This confirmed Joseph's guess. He sang out with excitement. "We will have a baby in our house, Poppa." He recalled his few visits to Little Mary. "Oh, the things I will make for him."

His father looked at him, ready to ask a question.

Joseph guessed the question and added, "or her." He laughed, shaking his head in amused, imaginative wonder. "Will I be a good big brother, Poppa?"

"Yes, you will. But first you will be a good son to your Mama, a watchful son."

~

THE FIRST MONTHS of his being a watchful son passed easily. Jacob and Joseph made a new raised sleeping platform, assembled new shelves, bartered with the traders for a new larger jug and several baking flats and bowls. They chiseled and replaced mortar where it had deteriorated around the window on the western side of the house. "There's no hiding when a storm from the Great Sea comes to visit," Jacob said in his instructive tone.

Rachel teased them, "How easily we get busy when we have a new reason." She made new woolen curtains, and softened swaddling they got from a weaver neighbor. She filled the house with her harp and her song even more than usual.

As her time grew closer she covered her harp with a linen cloth, her singing stopped and she spent more time in her room. Joseph brought her leek soup, chamomile tea and flat bread that a neighbor had baked. Several times he saw her washing blood from her robe and the sleeping cloths on her mat. Unsure whether to offer to do it for her, he asked Jacob about it.

Jacob dropped the tools he had in his hands and ran into Rachel's room, mumbling, "I didn't know. What can this be? I didn't know."

Poppa and Mama talked for a long time. Poppa had left the curtain open when he went into her room.

"You should not worry, Jacob. I am fine, just older than when I bore Joseph," she said in soft, calm tones.

"You must tell me when any of this happens," he said in a louder, worried voice.

"This is woman's work, Jacob. You provide for us. I bear

35

your sons. I am fine. You must show Joseph how you trust in the Lord."

When Jacob came back into the main room, he told Joseph to ask Miriam the midwife to come. She brought with her two older women. They conferred with Rachel, then with one another, and finally with Jacob.

For the remainder of her time Rachel spent most of the day on her mat, Miriam visited every morning and anxiety hung in the air while Jacob grew quieter. Joseph did most of their wood work. While Miriam visited his Mama, he found reasons to stay inside the house. At first he heard muffled words, like "some difficulty," "might be turned" and "so tired." After some weeks the hushed expressions became more dire: "too much blood," "maybe soon," "pressing here" and "maybe too soon." Joseph put it all together and decided there was only one thing he could do. "I trust in your faithfulness. Grant my heart joy in your help, that I may sing of the Lord, 'How good our God has been to me.'"

When he greeted neighbors they responded in a somber tone, asked for Rachel and parted with a mumbled prayer, "Out of the depths, deliver me, O lord," or some other plea from dark and painful places.

One mid-day while Jacob was at synagogue Joseph heard a scream from his Mama.

"Get Miriam! Hurry!" Fear and pain punctuated every word.

"Yes, Mama," shouted Joseph as he ran from the house.

Miriam told Joseph to fetch the other women, the same two who had accompanied her a month earlier. When he returned to the house, Miriam told him to go tell Jacob it was time. "He'll know better than to come before he should. Stay with him; you're a man, too." Her tone said as much as her words: Joseph should stay away until told otherwise.

Rachel's husband and son spent the afternoon going in and out of the synagogue, going in to ask for favors of the Lord, going out to hear encouragement from other men. A jumbled kind of support, men sharing their own experiences: the many strong children that were given them, how their wives had suffered hour after hour, and, from one, how a wife's painful labor lasting a whole long day ended with a dead baby.

The third hour passed as they walked in and out. The sun settled toward the sixth hour. Jacob said to Joseph. "Come, we will wait nearer our home. That way when they call us we can go in quickly."

One of Miriam's helpers stepped out of the house as they approached. Without being summoned, Jacob and Joseph ran to her. Her eyes and the tilt of her head spoke volumes. To Jacob she said, "Go in. Rachel is too tired to speak but she will hear you." To Joseph she said, "Go, fetch Chava."

Joseph did as the woman instructed. The three women with his mother had much experience, each having several children and helping others to have more. Chava, on the other hand, had her first child, a boy, days ago. She was only a year older than he. How could she help his mother?

Chava came with Joseph, leaving her son with her mother. As Joseph was about to follow Chava into his home, Jacob stopped him and beckoned him aside.

Jacob said, "You have a brother." There was no great joy in his voice at this wonderful news. Where was the 'mazel-tov' Joseph expected? "Sons are a gift from the Lord, a blessing, the fruit of the womb."

Joseph waited, sure that more news would follow. When Jacob stayed quiet for a while, Joseph blurted out, "Can I see Mama? Where is the baby? Why are we out here?"

Jacob enveloped his son. "Your mother is having trouble finishing the birth. Miriam and the other women are tending to her."

Joseph had seen animals give birth. He knew it involved more than delivering an offspring and also knew that mothers often struggled before, during and after the delivery. If she battled a long time afterward, she was fortunate if there was someone to care for the newborn. "Who has the baby?" he asked.

"Chava. She will suckle the baby." He paused and reflected, then added, "Until your Mama ...."

A scream came from inside. Mama's scream. Jacob turned to go in toward her. Chava met him at the door, pressing one hand against his chest while holding the swaddled infant with the other. She stepped outside and held the baby for him to see. A smile broke on Jacob's face.

"James. We will name him James." He turned to Joseph.

Joseph reached to take the baby from Chava.

She pulled back. "Not yet. He is tiny, no bigger than a chick," she said to Joseph.

"I've held a baby before, a baby as small as James." He had not let his arms drop to his sides, still reaching toward the infant.

"You can talk to him." She eased the swaddling back, revealing a delicate face with closed eyes and wisps of light brown hair. "Miriam said I should hold him but I could let you see him, the two of you." She turned to Jacob. "He might be tiny, but he is as lovely as a baby can be."

Joseph put his hands together in front of him and bent to the baby. "James, this is your big brother, Joseph."

James had no interest in looking up as his little mouth continued sucking at the air. As Joseph focused on his brother, Chava asked, "What little baby did you hold?"

"Rabbi Joachim's daughter Mary. Little Mary."

She cocked her head in disbelief. "When they moved here, she was already too big for you to hold."

Before Joseph had a chance to utter a word, she said, "The baby is hungry. I will take him inside." She disappeared, only to be replaced by one of the older women.

"Jacob, again the Lord has smiled on you this day. Rachel is giving you another baby."

Jacob's mouth opened but not a sound came out. Joseph said, "Two babies! Maybe a brother and a sister."

Jacob finally took a breath. "Praise God, the Lord has showered us with abundance."

The woman had more to say. "Jacob, the Lord has also frowned on you. Rachel is working hard and suffering much. Miriam is trying to stop the bleeding but there is only so much we can do."

Jacob's shoulders fell. He nodded to the woman as she turned and went back inside. His head hung as if tied to a millstone.

He turned back to Joseph, hugged him, cheek to cheek, dripping tears onto his neck. After a while he stood, motionless, as if not sure of where to go or what to do.

Poppa's feelings poured into Joseph. Joy and fear tore at his heart. Excitement and worry turned his legs to jelly. What of Mama? He must go and sing to her. James? He could hold James. Poppa? Never had he seen him with no spirit, no purpose. He would take him to the workshop where a broken plow sat waiting patiently for their skillful hands. This newest one? He could—what? Do what? For now Miriam and Chava's commands and the sadness in their looks rescued him from having to decide to do anything. Except press even tighter to Poppa.

The evening had turned to night, bringing a chill they

had not felt before. Father and son walked toward the synagogue. An oil lamp burned in every home. Smells of home and family came to them: lamb roasted with garlic—at least one family would have meat tonight, not a daily ration in Nazareth; sweet and spicy apples wrapped in horseradish paste; and hot bread. The aroma of warm cakes provided dessert to their uneaten meal.

At the synagogue they stopped. Jacob looked skyward, pleas running from his lips. To Joseph and to himself he muttered his thoughts. "Trust in the Lord marks a devout man; trust in times of dire need marks a faithful one." He reached out and put a hand on Joseph's shoulders but remained looking up. "Joseph, pray with me for alone I cannot pray and I find no consolation. Praise the Lord with me; together we will exalt his name."

Joseph recalled what Mama had taught him. "When you can't pray for anything else put yourself in his care," she had said. Now into Jacob's ear he whispered, "Into your hands I commend my spirit."

After some time they retraced their steps to their home; no one beckoned them inside. As they ambled back toward the synagogue, Chava passed them, a shawl pulled tight around her shoulders.

"News, you have some news?" Jacob asked.

"Not yet, Jacob, but soon. Soon someone will bring word. I am going home to nurse my son and I will come back within the hour."

They sat outside the synagogue, the night dragging on. Clouds moving from the west hid the stars. Chava came from her home. The three walked back toward where new life had begun a few hours earlier.

"We have heard nothing. Soon did not come as soon as we hoped," Jacob said.

Chava said, "I will go in and let you know what is happening."

Minutes later she reappeared holding a baby. This time she had little to say as she held the infant toward his father. "Another boy."

Jacob repeated his prayer from several hours earlier. "Sons are a gift from the Lord, a blessing, the fruit of the womb." He paused and added, "Two blessings from the Lord on one day." Jacob peered down at the infant, smaller than James. "Joses, our little Joses." With a soft laugh he turned to Joseph. "Your Mama and I could not make up our minds. Do we name a boy baby James or Joses? Your Mama in all her wisdom took care of that."

"Mama always finds a way," Joseph said.

Joseph, not reaching for the baby but peering close to him, said, "Joses, this is your big brother, Joseph."

Jacob looked at Chava, waiting for her to say something about Rachel.

"Miriam will come out soon," she said. Her face foretold what Miriam would say.

In minutes that seemed like hours Miriam came out and took a few steps away from the house. Jacob and Joseph followed her. She drew a deep breath. More than fatigue showed on her face and in the arch in her back and shoulders.

Jacob said, "Miriam …."

She raised her hand for him to stop. "She has given you two fine boys. Chava is wearing herself out suckling them and she has her own son. Thank God she is young and strong."

"I can go in to Rachel now? Yes?" said Jacob.

"First, Jacob, I need to tell you something. Rachel is sleeping and it may be more than sleeping."

"What do you mean, more than sleeping?"

"She had to bear down hard to deliver the second child. Afterward she sighed with the sound of a great wind and slept. I do not know if she will wake up."

"What can … is there … should I…?"

"Jacob, hold her hand, tell her what you want to tell her and ask God to let your sons keep their mother."

Joseph said, "I will go to Mama with you, Poppa."

The three went inside. Chava dozed on a mat in a corner of the room while one of the women lifted a sleeping infant from her breast. The other woman sat in a chair holding the other sleeping baby. Miriam put her fingers to her lips, as if to remind them to relish and preserve this quiet moment.

Jacob knelt beside a sleeping Rachel and took her hand. Joseph knelt at her other side, half resting his hands on one arm and half caressing it. Her shallow breathing made the air stand still.

Each flicker of her eyelids brought Joseph back to another time. He heard Mama's harp sprinkle notes of joy that always drew a song from inside him; he tasted her spicy soup that warmed him after a long trek on a chilly evening; he felt her good-bye embrace given every time he and Poppa left with their tool sacks; he saw the tear she clung to until he and Poppa were out of sight.

Her shallow breathing stopped.

Jacob bent and brushed her lips with his as the finality of a last kiss wracked his body and his spirit.

Joseph could not let go of her. No more would he enjoy her scent or voice or look. He let her touch engrave itself on his memory. Unable to fix her, he lowered his head and let his tears fall onto her chest. "Out of the depths I call to you, O Lord. May your ears be attentive to my cry for mercy."

~

THE WOMEN who had attended to Rachel in her last hours prepared her body for burial later that same day. With Jacob's approval they covered her with her better tunic and robe and veil. Joachim led the prayerful procession to a village burial cave high on one of Nazareth's many hills.

Chava and Miriam offered care and affection for James and Joses in the days and months that followed. They comforted Jacob and instructed Joseph in the care of his brothers. Other villagers, Joachim and Anna in particular, shared special meals and celebrations with them. Now in his fifteenth year, Joseph had friends not much older who had children of their own to care for, or at least to provide for.

On the eighth day after their birth—the day after Jacob extinguished the seven-day candle that had burned for light for Rachel's departed soul—he announced for all of Nazareth to hear: "James is his name," and as he turned to the other infant, continued, "Joses is his name." Joseph winced when they screamed as Rabbi Joachim cut them and made them bleed. He had attended many circumcisions and had taken for granted the pain inflicted on the babies. Today the pain and the bleeding and the screams became personal.

"Poppa," Joseph asked Jacob later in the evening, "how can the law require babies to bear such pain? They have done nothing to deserve it."

"The rabbi circumcises our boys not in punishment but in keeping with our tradition. Go back and read again the first scroll, the long one. Open it down to the story of Abraham."

Joseph took the longest scroll down from the high shelf. So familiar was he with Abraham's story that he unraveled the scroll to the right section. After he read from it he said, "Yes, it says cutting the foreskin shall be a sign of the covenant between the Lord and our people. But why can't we wait for the baby to be bigger and better able to bear the pain?"

The blood drained from Jacob's face, turning even the sand on his face a bleached gray. He turned his head away and looked sideways at his eldest son. "I don't believe what I am hearing." He turned back around. "Joseph, read a little for reflection; read ..."

Joseph had heard this before. He nodded and said along with his Poppa, "Read the whole for understanding."

Again Joseph picked up the scroll and continued reading. As if it were the first time he read about Abraham, Joseph spoke with renewed belief. "Yes, it really tells us, that every one of our boys shall be circumcised when he is *eight days* old. If he is not, he is cut off from our people."

Jacob nodded and said not a word.

Joseph said, "Now I understand."

CHAVA CONTINUED to nurse the twins along with her own son until all three graduated to goats' milk and then crushed boiled lentils and apples. Jacob and Joseph scheduled their thriving tekton business so Joseph could stay in Nazareth and Jacob seldom left for more than a few days at a time, days when his three sons took their evening meal in a neighbor's home. In time the family that Rachel had left established a new routine, a way around her absence for Joseph and Jacob, the only way for James and Joses. Although Joseph missed the sound of the harp filling their home, he sang to his brothers. "Sing praise to the Lord with the harp, with the harp and melodious song. With trumpets and the sound of the horn, shout joyfully to the Lord." When they grew older, perhaps one of them would uncover her harp.

Joseph took his turn reading scripture in the synagogue and discussing its principles and proverbs with the rabbis and village elders. None of them lacked self-assurance, so much so that Joseph was reluctant to share his thoughts with them. He considered Rabbi Joachim more as the father of his friends than as his rabbi, so conversations with him were of family. Jacob, most of all, welcomed his thoughts, however ill-formed they were.

"We have the Law and the Writings to show us the way, and the psalms to sustain us when days are dark and nights are long," said Jacob.

The supper long over, he and Joseph sat at their table taking turns reading from their few scrolls by the light of an oil lamp. The twins slept on their mat, entwined like twin lambs without a mother. Joseph had fashioned a pair of gates that formed a protected sleep and play area in a corner of the room.

"And we have the words of the rabbis when the Writings are unclear or the Torah lacking," said Joseph.

Jacob bristled at what Joseph thought was a simple observation. "Nothing is lacking in the Torah. We have the stories and their meanings as God wanted us to know them. What is unclear?"

Joseph grasped for what he so often wanted to say to the rabbis. "The stories have not ended, Poppa; somewhere new stories happen. God's word to us did not stop with the Torah, Poppa. More is yet to be revealed, I don't know what, but I believe it will surpass the words of the wisest rabbis and the commands of the sharpest Pharisees."

Jacob's face softened. "What have you hidden from me, Joseph? What do you know?" He spoke kindly to his son, as if seeking enlightenment.

"Poppa, you have told me of our ancestors and our Jewish kings."

"Yes, I have. You know the difference between them and the pretenders."

"Yes, Poppa. The true kings are in our line, as you and I are in David's line, and we await the Messiah who will come from this line, from our family."

"You pay good attention; you are a fine student, Joseph. You are also an excellent big brother." Jacob's contentment with his oldest son shone in his casual praise. "James and Joses prepare you for your own children."

"Thank you, Poppa. You have taught me to study the Torah and the Writings. We live with the hope that comes alive in every pregnant woman. With every boy who is born, we say, 'This is the one, he will lead us, he will be our Messiah.' James and Joses make me remember that."

Jacob closed the scroll and placed it back on the shelf. "At least we are not wandering in some awful place while we wait. 'I have brought you out of the land of Egypt, that you should not be slaves.'"

"Yes, Poppa. There are worse things than waiting in Nazareth. I have been thinking ..."

One of the twins stirred on their mat. Joseph and Jacob stayed silent until the child regained his quiet sleep.

"I am torn, Poppa. On one hand I see girls at synagogue. I see Efron and other young men, now proud fathers, happy with their families."

"What is there for the other hand?"

"Rabbi Joachim and Anna told us how they presented Little Mary in service to the Lord. How would I do such a thing? Would I go to live in the temple in Jerusalem? And not take a wife? Tell me, Poppa."

Jacob leaned back, gathering his thoughts. He pulled two scrolls off the shelf and selected the long one they had been reading from. "Here, in the Torah, 'A man leaves his father and mother, takes a wife and they become one flesh.' I see nothing about the other hand."

"It puzzles me, Poppa. I know what I read there and I understand what it commands. Inside me I am pulled to something else and I can't see what."

"It's part of being your age, Joseph. Don't waste your time with all this pulling and puzzling. Nothing is unclear about this Torah command or any other. A man takes a wife, raises his sons—daughters, too, if God chooses to bless him in such a way. Is that man not dedicated to the service of the Lord?" His voice grew louder. "No man alive would say he is not." He covered his mouth, looked to the twins and saw they slept undisturbed. He let out a breath, turned back to Joseph and lowered his voice. "Nothing is unclear."

"Before Efron married, the rabbis read from that same scroll and explained to us how it is the will of God for all of our people to take a wife, and more so for those who are blessed to be in the line of David. Like us."

"It is our blessing to be of the house of David. Suppose you are the man, the man chosen by God, to whom the Messiah will be born. If you decide not to take a wife you deny the House of David what God promised long ago. Would you deny this to our people?"

The same should apply to the women who give themselves in service at the Temple. What if God had chosen one of them to bear the Messiah but she chose not to marry? She would not know this but our people would miss the chance to have the Messiah come.

These women believe God has chosen them to do something differ-
ent. Couldn't the same apply to a man?

He tried to put these thoughts into words. "Poppa,
suppose I am not that man and God has chosen me to dedicate myself to him in some other way. To not take a wife
and to ....." He stopped. He had no words for the muddle in
his mind. After a while he shrugged. "Just because I don't
know what it is doesn't mean nothing's there."

EVERY AFTERNOON JOSEPH played with his three-year old
brothers. Rachel would have laughed to see them frolicking
so. One twin would run to hide behind a tree or a stone or
in a neighbor's doorway, and Joseph and the other twin
would search for him. One day as they ran past Rabbi
Joachim's house, Anna called to them from the little garden
beside her house. They interrupted their game and ran
to her.

"I want you all to meet someone," she said.

Joseph hoped but braced himself for another disappointment. Mary and Salome came out of the house into the
garden. Both had grown into young women whom Joseph
often saw at synagogue as well as when their two families
shared a meal.

Out came Little Mary, now the age that the older Mary
had been when they all first met. Joseph recognized the
infant of long ago in her big girl face with the same hair,
brown so dark it looked almost black, and lots more of it
than he remembered. He stepped closer, pleased to find that
her eyes had the same gold sparkles under the same full
dark eyebrows.

"Shalom," he said. He introduced his brothers and himself.

"I know who you are. Mother told me when she saw you coming this way."

Anna said, "Come in, boys. Salome made some special cakes with honey to welcome her sister home."

The three boys knew the house well. They sat at the table that Joseph had made for the family, a table large enough to seat both families. Joseph scanned the room. The cedar baby was not on the high shelf.

Little Mary went into the rear room, a room that Jacob and Joseph had built, similar to the one they built years ago in Sepphoris, eight years ago, one long year more than the seven years of waiting he had dreaded. She returned carrying the cedar baby. "I named him, 'Noah.'" She held it out for him to see. "He was safe all these years in the fabric basket, like being in an ark." She smiled at Noah and then at Joseph. "Thank you. I keep him with my shawl when I'm not playing with him."

"I hope you will like living in Nazareth," he said. "I look forward to seeing you at synagogue." *I hope you don't go back to Jerusalem. And we get to know each other better.*

CHAPTER 5

$\mathcal{B}$usy in the courtyard workshop, Joseph kept James and Joses near at hand.

James sat close to him with a set of small square boxes of various sizes that Joseph had made, putting one inside the other. Joses ran from one end of the courtyard to the other, trying to get a young lamb to follow him. "I've named him, 'Other Way,'" he said. "When I call him, that's where he goes." Seldom did he succeed in having a follower but was often the recipient of a head butt to his bottom.

Now five years old, the boys showed their differences. James stood several inches taller, took his broad build from his father, liked playing with any tool or piece of wood that Joseph or Jacob allowed, and was as happy inside the house as out. Joses, like his mother, had fairer skin and a slight build. Neither heavy rain nor chilly wind could keep him inside. He reveled in getting an animal of any description to tag along. So far his hobby was limited to chickens, village dogs, and small sheep and goats.

A simple stew of onions, beans, spicy roots and sliced,

flamed eggplant simmered in a pot on the fire pit. Barley bread from a neighbor's oven would complete their dinner. Rachel would have served a minced pomegranate sauce or crushed berries to balance the sharp tastes. Joseph and his Poppa learned to do without and the twins did not miss what they had never known.

Joseph expected Jacob to be home long before the sun set, but already shadows had lengthened.

"Poppa not coming?" asked Joses.

"He said he would be here for the evening meal," James said.

"Sometimes the stones break in the wrong way and we have to cut many stones until we get them right." Joseph assured his brothers more than he could assure himself. The day before, Jacob had gone by himself to cut and lay stones for the archway of a small house. Exaloth was only an hour's walk to the southeast, where the hills around Nazareth become a moundy plain.

"He leads me on right paths. Even if I walk through the darkest valley, I do not fear, for you are beside me," Joseph prayed.

THE SUN HAD STARTED its climb when James crawled from his mat to Joseph's and closed his eyes as he snuggled against him. Autumn mornings brought breezes from the Great Sea within an hour of first light, an ideal time for sharing a mat. Joseph looked across the room and saw Jacob's mat empty. Of course it was empty; Jacob would not have come home in the middle of the night. Moments later Joses made three on Joseph's mat.

"I hungry," Joses said.

"Joses is always hungry," Joseph said as he ruffled Joses' hair. He added, "This is the day the Lord has made."

The twins answered, "We rejoice and are glad in it."

Bread and berries started the brothers' day. By mid-morning Joseph had led them in their lessons. Jacob had still not returned. Building a small arch would never take more than two days.

"Let's run up to the synagogue," Joseph said to his brothers. He hoped to leave them with the first neighbor who spoke to them. Chava greeted them within minutes.

After Joseph explained his plight, he was relieved when Chava offered to keep the twins for the day and Efron volunteered to go with him.

Joseph and his friend brought a sack of cloths and oil, as well as food and a goatskin of water. Jacob might need any or all of these things when they met him in Exaloth or along the way. The two young men reached the neighboring village in less time than Jacob would have taken carrying his tools. They inquired at the first inn they reached, inside the village's gateless entrance.

"We had a small caravan here last night. They left at sunrise for Capernaum," said the innkeeper. "No one else stayed here."

Joseph and Efron went to the next inn, and to the third, another inn by name but a small house by right, that brought them to the well in the center of Exaloth. They inquired of people gathered there for water and talk.

"A new arch! Yes, I will take you to the potter's house where they are building the new arch," responded a woman filling two jugs.

In front of the potter's house they saw large pieces of stone and enough thin shards to fill a cart. Jacob's tools lay near them. The arch, supported by a network of timbers and a beam, was complete except for the keystone, the foreign intrusion that Jacob detested in a Jewish home! Joseph shouted into the house.

A man in a potter's apron hurried to the door, his clothes bloodied. "Have you come about the cutter?"

"My father. Where is he?" Joseph said.

The potter motioned Joseph to follow. Inside the door lay Jacob with blood-soaked cloths packed around his neck. His arms lay motionless at his side. Joseph knelt beside him with waning hope. He peeled back the cloths, revealing a gash across his throat, a slash that had surely gushed until replaced by this trickle.

"What happened?" asked Joseph, even as he drew his own conclusion.

"Jacob said the grain in the stones made them shatter under the blow of the hammer. He had to throw away most of them. He said he would use only the stones that stayed sound after he shaped them." The potter shook his head and shut his eyes for a long pause before he continued. "When it got dark last evening, he decided to wait and finish this morning. Today, while the sun was low in the sky, his first hammer-blow threw a sharp slice of stone up to his neck and …." He stopped and waved a hand toward Jacob. "I am sorry."

"Is there a physician here in Exaloth?" Joseph asked. With or without a physician Joseph knew Jacob was beyond medical aid.

"We have no physician. The midwife brought cloths and oils and hyssop. She did what she could."

Joseph looked at his bleeding Poppa. As he knelt beside him, he fought to keep the utter helplessness at bay. *Behold I will treat and assuage your wounds: I will heal you and reveal to you an abundance of lasting peace.*

Jacob's eyelids fluttered, his mouth opened. Joseph said to the potter, "Get me a clean cloth; soak it in wine and hyssop." He bent his ear to his father.

With great effort Jacob said, "Love my sons. My James and Joses. No longer ... big brother, now you must be ... Poppa." He took a breath, shallow and difficult. His shoulders heaved with the effort. "Keep them out of travelers' tents. Raise them faithful sons of David."

"I will care for them as you have cared for me, Poppa. Blessed be the Lord." He thought of all the changes since the birth of the twins. Not long ago he worked and learned beside Poppa, while beside Mama he shared songs and the dreams of his heart.

Again he felt the frustration of being unable to do anything. And again the fabric of life was taking on a different hue. Poppa was struggling to raise his hand. Knowing why, Joseph lifted it for him, bowed his head and placed Poppa's hand on his head.

Jacob gurgled a blessing already familiar to Joseph. "The Lord God helps you, God Almighty blesses you; breasts and womb, fresh grain and blossoms, mountains and hills: may they rest on your head, a prince among his brothers." He took a broken breath as his hand slid from Joseph's head. A second breath brought a shudder to his chest. His lips parted with great effort. "Into your hands ...."

"I commend my spirit," Joseph finished the prayer. Five years earlier he had lost the woman who held his heart; now he lost the man who secured his trust and enlivened his faith.

Joseph stood, watching his Poppa, waiting for him to move or speak or breathe. Nothing. "Are James and Joses next?" he cried out. "What have I done, what have I thought, have I doubted you?" He looked around, seeing only a blur.

"Where do I put my trust? In God, in myself, in anyone? Abraham, Abraham, show me how you trusted." He could not hold his head up any longer. With Efron's arms around him he let his tears fall and his body quiver until he had energy for neither.

As Efron released him, he knelt again at Poppa's side and saw his eyes closed in a final sleep. Joseph held his father's hands, feeling the fingers adjust in the stiffness of death. After some time he felt them cool. He stood, with Efron and the potter beside him. "The souls of the just are in the hands of God, and no torment shall touch them." *No more will the blade rip his palm.* "They seemed to be dead but they are in peace." *Nor the hammer strike his thumb.*

With resignation Joseph said, "We must take my father home to prepare him before sunset."

"Did you come with an ox or a donkey?" asked the potter.

Joseph shook his head.

"I have a donkey. You may borrow it."

The three men wrapped Jacob's body in large cloths the midwife had left and laid him across the donkey. As Joseph gathered Jacob's tools, he said to the man, "When I return your donkey I will finish the arch."

Joseph and Efron walked in silence. Joseph thought and prayed. *Keep me true to Abraham and David. In the name of Jacob and Rachel help me be Poppa to their sons.* All that Poppa Jacob had taught him came to him: how to plane timbers and pump the sanding stone, to care for pregnant Mama Rachel and the twins, to read whole passages from the Torah and the prophets, to praise God and marry a wife.

Halfway home they paused to water the donkey and themselves. Joseph said, "You are a good friend to come with me."

"You would do no less for me. I heard you promise Jacob you would raise his sons faithful to the covenant. We are your family, Joseph, so ask of us what you need."

"Making such a promise is easy. Keeping it will require a family. I embrace your offer."

As they started again Joseph asked, "Efron, how did you know you were to marry Chava?"

He looked at Joseph as if he had proposed splitting the road in front of them. "How? My parents told me I would marry Chava, her parents told her she would marry me, and that was that."

"I thought you might say that."

"I couldn't have made a better choice. Chava is a holy woman and a caring wife. What more is there?"

"Did you ever think of not marrying?"

"Not marry? What would I do, grow old alone? Never."

Now that he was to be Poppa to two five-year old boys, perhaps this was what the Lord had in mind for him, that he would not take a wife but would raise his brothers.

Efron interrupted his thoughts. "Now that you have boys to raise, a wife would be a true gift. It is no secret, Joseph; you are close to Rabbi Joachim and his family."

"They are true friends."

"Now might be the time for you to talk to Joachim about his daughter Mary. She is the right age."

Joseph nodded. "Mary will make a fine wife, but she will soon marry Clopas."

"Clopas? Are you sure?"

"Efron, yesterday I was sure my father would be home for dinner. What good was it to be sure?"

"If not Mary, Salome then. She, too, is a proper age."

"No, Efron. If I were to ask Joachim for one of his daughters I would choose Little Mary. You have seen her.

She has a way about her that strikes joy into the heart of all who know her. I learn more from her gentle silence than from the words of the wisest rabbi."

"I know her. They call her Mary the Younger for a good reason. She is very young."

"And I am very patient."

THE PRESCRIPTIONS for Jewish burial aided Joseph as they had sustained him and his Poppa when his Mama died. The close knit structure of the small village supported him again in practical ways. More food came to the home than he and his brothers could eat. Neighbor women took care of the twins while Joseph arranged with Joachim for Jacob's burial and afterward when Joseph had to continue to provide for the boys. For the second time in five years, Jacob and Rachel's sons had to remake their family.

MONTHS AND SEASONS PASSED. Each Spring and Passover arrived before the memory of the prior ones vanished. Joseph and his brothers stayed busy in the common court-yard behind their home. Table legs, board and top sat on the workbench ready for Joseph's skill and James' lesson. Joses sat on the ground watching a neighbor and learning how to shear a sheep. All of a sudden he popped up and ran to Joseph, looking toward the edge of the courtyard.

A woman stood in the shadow of the olive tree.

Joseph looked in her direction and then returned his attention to James and planks and saws. Joses stood behind

Joseph, tugging at his tunic. Joseph looked around and saw Joses still staring at the woman.

She looked like she wanted to come to talk to him but no woman would enter a courtyard uninvited, even a common courtyard that served as space for many homes and families.

Joseph walked toward her. He did not recognize her. Before he said anything she said, "I am looking for Joseph the Tekton."

"I am Joseph." He took another few steps.

Her dark woolen shawl hid her hair, exposing not a single strand. She had a pleasant face, pale, younger than Anna but older than Chava. The tiny lines around her eyes showed weather and kindness, not age. "People say what you build stays built. And at a fair price."

He walked to her. James watched from the workbench; Joses eased halfway toward Joseph.

"I need four raised sleeping platforms that can be used as needed or set aside and stored easily." She paused, her eyes on Joseph. "Wider than the usual ones."

He had made and repaired sleeping platforms of every description: cedar sleeping board with an inlaid headboard —perhaps the most expensive; cypress frame with a taut cloth instead of wooden board—popular, the least expensive and least durable. "Where do you want them?" She was not from Nazareth.

"In my home where I live with my ...." She hesitated. "With my friends."

Not many women ordered sleeping platforms, much less four at a time. Women did not live with their friends, several in the same house. This sizable work order would provide meals for his family for many weeks. He needed more information. "Where is your home?"

"We live in Japha."

Japha! Joseph had heard of it, could find it if he had a reason to, but had never had a reason. He knew no one who had been there.

The weary feet of laborers and craftsmen produced the road to Sepphoris; caravans traveling between Sepphoris and Jerusalem generated the rutted road between Nazareth and Nain; no one had fashioned a path to Japha. "When do you need them?"

They agreed on the physical details of the platforms, the price and the schedule.

The woman reached into a fold in her cloak that covered a long dress and drew out a cloth bag of coins. "If you agree, I will hand over the balance when you deliver the platforms."

Joseph nodded.

The woman turned and left.

"Wait," Joseph said louder than he had been speaking to her. "What is your name?"

"Deborah. I am the only Deborah in Japha and Japha is tiny. Call out my name and you will find me."

DEBORAH'S SCHEDULE allowed Joseph to continue a routine that included lessons for the twins and completion of tekton projects previously promised. When he hammered the last dowel for the fourth sleeping platform, he announced to the twins, "Tomorrow we're going to Japha."

They jumped up and down, hugged each other and Joseph, and then said, "What is Japha?"

Joses' eyes brightened. "I remember! That woman, the one who stood under the olive tree. She lives in Japha. She's the one you built the sleeping platforms for."

James corrected him. "*We* built the platforms for."

"You're both right," said Joseph.

Early the next morning Joseph borrowed Joachim's ox and two-wheeled cart. "I made this cart for you and I use it more than you do," he said to his rabbi friend.

Their route took them on paths that were not paths at all, winding over and around the low hills southwest of Nazareth.

"Quiet now," whispered Joseph.

Joses slowed the ox to a crawl. "Easy, Hoofy."

As they came around a hill they saw a clearing with a stream running through it. On the far side of the stream stood a doe with a tiny fawn, both standing stock still. The mother's eyes locked on the forest visitors. When the ox swayed its head against Joses' restraint, the pair vanished into the woods ahead.

"How did you know they were here?" asked Joses.

"I've seen deer drinking here before. The cool water draws them from near and far."

They approached the stream, turned right and walked along it until they arrived at a low cave out of which gurgled the steady flow. Guiding the ox up and around the cave, they then walked on the opposite side of the stream back the way they had come.

"Why didn't we walk through the water?" asked James when they arrived at the spot where the deer had been drinking.

"The bottom of the stream has sand so fine that even your feet would sink into it. We'd never get the ox out." Joseph peered into the distance. "I'm not sure but I think we have to go beyond the largest of those three hills and we'll be there." With no paths, he relied on advice from friends who often walked in these woods.

Japha appeared out of nowhere when they reached the top of the last of the hills. In minutes they were in the village. Smaller by far than Nazareth, it had not more than a dozen homes, each separated from its neighbor by thirty feet or more. Like Nazareth it had neither gate nor wall, nor apparently any great need for protection. Poverty drew no thieves from afar.

As Deborah had promised, Joseph found her house by calling her name.

"Here. Over here," she shouted. She raised her hands for him to see her.

They stopped in front of her small house. Eyes wide, Joses held the ox's tether. James stood by the cart.

"Come. I will show you where to put the platforms." She turned to the house and shouted in, "Susanna! Ruth! Rebekah! Come see what we've been waiting for!"

Joseph followed Deborah into the house, almost bumping into the women coming out.

"These are my friends," said Deborah. Three young women! Rebekah, seeming the youngest, was no older than Mary, not Little Mary, and about the same size. Susanna, the eldest, was about his age or younger. Ruth, taller than the others and taller than Deborah as well, walked with difficulty, bent at her waist with her hands pressing into her lower back, ready to deliver a baby any moment.

He saw why the platforms had to be wider than usual.

Joseph nodded to James and Joses who then shouted their names to Deborah.

What looked from the outside like a small house consisted of three rooms, more than most homes in Nazareth. The main room held a large table with six chairs around it, another smaller table against a windowless wall, and one sleeping platform in a corner. A second doorway

led out the back of the house, and two other smaller open-
ings, covered with strings of beads, led to two smaller
rooms. One room had two straw mats on the floor near
opposing walls and the other had a single mat. Joseph
wondered how Ruth would manage to get herself down
onto a mat without tipping over. And then, have to get back
up. Deborah was wise to provide raised platforms.

"Here?" asked Joseph.

Deborah nodded. "I will help but I don't want my friends
carrying anything heavy."

Joseph said, "James and Joses are strong helpers."

At this the boys ran to the cart, untied the ropes that
secured the platforms and carried the first platform into the
house. Joseph showed Deborah how to remove the dowels
that kept the legs folded against a board, then to unfold the
legs and finally to replace the dowels. The now open
sleeping board was ready for use. He tugged on the leg,
demonstrating its strength. As soon as he set the first platform in place, Susanna covered the board with a large
ivory-colored linen cloth. The other girls did likewise as
their platforms were set in place.

On the wall nearest each platform, Joseph secured a shelf
thigh high. He placed the unopened platform on it and
secured it against the wall. "Store a platform here so it won't
take up floor space."

"What they say is true; you do fine work," said Deborah.

James looked at Joseph with a twinkle in his eye.

"*We* do fine work," Joseph said as he drew James against
him.

The young women prepared tea and offered the three
brothers small cakes. With Joseph's approval James and
Joses sat at the large table and enjoyed the unaccustomed
treat.

Deborah pointed toward the back of the house. Joseph followed her out into a courtyard, half of which was devoted to a vegetable garden that used every inch of the space allotted to it.

"Your friends have a contented glow about them," Joseph said.

She handed him several coins. "Not everyone sees them like that. Most would not take the time to see them at all."

"How did all of this come to be?" He gestured to the house and the courtyard and to her.

"Some months ago the tallest girl came to me."

"Ruth," offered Joseph.

"Yes, Ruth. Not only do you see the girls, but you show an interest in them. Most people would not bother to remember their names."

Joseph nodded and shifted his weight. She was not looking for a comment.

She said, "Ruth came to me. She had not eaten in a week and was sick every morning. There was nothing to throw up and that made it worse. Her family had cast her out; they even burned a seven day candle for her. No one in Nain would help or even recognize her."

"No one except you, it looks like."

"I took her in and the people—my friends and neighbors —stopped talking to me. They refused to let me buy food at the market in Nain. Japha is a strange place." She walked toward the garden area and inspected the neat rows. "I had heard the people here leave you alone so I moved into this empty house. I had some money after my husband died."

He assumed Ruth's story was true also for Susanna and Rebekah. Deborah had found a way to serve the Lord in spite of what the Law or her people said. "How do the women find out about you and your house?"

63

"Gossip sometimes serves a purpose." She bent and pulled out a weed.

"What will you do if more women come to you?"

"I will go back to Nazareth for more sleeping platforms." She smiled. "Other than that I will rely on the Lord who always listens to the cry of his servant."

"And after the babies are born?"

"I don't have an answer to that. Not yet, but I will."

Mama Rachel had Jacob. Chava has Efron. Every pregnant woman needs someone. "In the meantime, you give a young pregnant woman what no one else will."

They walked through the house and out to the front. Joses held a bucket of water for the ox while James secured the ropes and covers inside the cart.

"Your sons are well trained," said Deborah, loud enough that the twins heard.

James broke into a fit of laughter. "Can I ride in the empty cart, *Poppa?*" he asked.

"Me, too, *Poppa?*" Joses joined him.

Joseph felt his face warm. He nodded to the boys and did not correct Deborah. "Poppa" sounded comfortable coming from the lips of his eight-year-old "sons."

JOSEPH APPROACHED Joachim as they walked from the synagogue. "Rabbi Joachim, I wish to talk to you about your daughter."

"Joseph, I have three daughters." His smile said he knew which daughter Joseph had in mind.

"I mean Little Mary. I wish to take her as my wife with your blessing, Rabbi. For many years you have taken me into your family. You must have seen how I have been taken with her."

"You surprise me, Joseph. I thought at one time you might want to take Mary for a wife. She is now married to Clopas. A good man, Clopas."

Joseph nodded. "Yes, a good man, Clopas."

Joachim knew Joseph was aware of Mary's marriage. In mentioning her, Joachim reminded Joseph that he had never inquired about Mary and that there was another unmarried daughter, Salome, older than Little Mary. Birth order mattered.

Joachim let his point sink in. Joseph must compensate him, but later.

Joseph broke the silence. "Clopas is a good man who married a great woman. Your daughter Salome, she, too, is a devout woman. But Rabbi Joachim, your daughter Little Mary —she is extraordinary. Never have I seen a girl, a woman, a person, so compelling. More beautiful than the moon, resplendent beyond the sun! From the first day I saw her, she drew me to her the way a cool stream draws thirsty deer. In a way I cannot explain, she drew me to God at the same time. Rabbi Joachim, my friend, you have lived your life with Anna. You and she serve God with your lives. That's the way I want to live my life, serving the Lord with Little Mary as my wife."

Joachim paused, stopped walking and regarded Joseph eye to eye. "God gave Little Mary to us as a special gift when we thought we would have only two daughters. Somehow she comprehended this. Just a child, she insisted on giving herself to the Daughters of Sion at the Temple as a return gift to the Lord. In the years since she rejoined our family she has remained steadfast in her dedication. Little Mary has chosen to spend her life giving herself to the Lord, leaving herself open to his will. As for giving herself to a man as well, she ...." He paused. "I will speak with Anna first, Little Mary next. Then I will decide."

∼

IN THE MONTHS after Joachim announced the betrothal of his youngest daughter, Joseph took pleasure in opportunities to talk to Mary while her parents stood or worked at a discrete distance. Meals shared with Joachim and his family provided opportunities to see Mary in their home and to learn more of what she liked, what she did, what she valued.

"See the cedar baby," Mary said to him, pointing upward.

Joseph looked up at the doll sitting on a shelf.

"It reminds me you have loved me for a long time," she said.

"The first time I held you I felt it was the other way around, that you were holding me."

"What an image! A little baby holding a big man! You make me laugh."

He laughed with her. "Or even holding a ten-year old boy."

"I don't remember it, of course, but I wish I did." She smiled.

"It would not surprise me if you did remember. Your sisters told me you were aware of things you weren't old enough to understand."

"I remember that not everything made sense to me. Did you believe Mary and Salome when they told you that?"

"Yes, I believed them. I was ready to believe anything about you. Then you disappeared."

"Joseph, I never disappeared." She laughed again.

"Yes, you did." He nodded, a smile creeping onto his face.

"It took years before you reappeared; it felt like a lifetime." He felt the power of her pull, drawing him to her. He so wanted to wrap his arms around her.

"I know how you feel, Joseph and I know that you want to dedicate your life to the Lord. So do I."

"My parents lived their lives serving the Lord, both their *individual* lives and their *together* lives. Your parents, too. I believe God wants me to serve him and at the same time share my life with you. I don't know how to work that out, not yet."

"You and I will find a way to give ourselves completely to God *together*."

"We have a few months to figure out how."

JOSEPH CAME from the vine grower's with a selection of pieces of cut vine, some gnarled and angular, others plain and straight. At his work bench he selected thick pieces, naturally bent, to form the legs and back of a chair, which he fastened together with strong, green vines. He braided thinner strips of vine into a seat and tied a woven woolen cover around the seat to add comfort and durability.

James sawed and drilled and hammered beside Joseph. With some persuasion Joses agreed to spend some hours indoors to help prepare their house for the new family member. They put a roof with oak beams and turpentine planking over what had been an open upper room. The twins had already moved their mats and tunics there. An opening in the ceiling of the main room allowed passage to the new upper room. Connected by a doorway from the main room, a new stone-walled sleeping room was similar to the room Joseph and Jacob had built fifteen years earlier.

When outfitted with the new raised sleeping platform and the new chair, the room would be ready for the first woman to live in the house in ten years. Joseph replaced the oak dowels and braces in Rachel's spindle that would welcome Mary into her new home. New shelves on two adjacent walls would hold the baskets of wool and flax that she would bring with her.

~

As THE TIME of their wedding approached, Joseph sensed a change in Mary. He had told her of how he and his brothers were preparing their house for her. She and her mother had made new curtains. Her father selected a psalm for their wedding ceremony; her sisters and their friends planned a suitable feast of roast lamb, roots boiled with onions, a thick soup of lentils and barley, and sweet cakes and sauces from every fruit they could find. Mary said not a word about anything bothering her or out of the ordinary but Joseph could not help feeling something was happening, something he knew nothing about.

As Joseph collected bread and vegetables at the village market one day, threads of gossip from women caught his attention: *betrothed to the tekton with the two boys; might be with child; the rabbi's youngest daughter.* If he put these snippets together, they would explain his sense of foreboding. He could not believe such things of Mary, his Mary, his betrothed. Then he saw her some distance away, without her mother or a sister, selecting something from the fruit seller. As much as he wanted to approach her, he could not because she was alone. He watched her bend and stretch and drop some plums into her basket. He looked more closely; her shape had indeed changed, if only a little, unless gossip had sparked his imagination. Where she once was slim, her reaching now revealed a soft mound at her belly. Joseph turned away. He would not let her see him. Hoping he had been mistaken, he stole a last fleeting look. There had been no mistake.

Joseph returned to his house, went to his outdoor workshop, sat at his bench, held his head in his hands and prayed. "Hear me, Lord, and answer me. Lord, hear my prayer; let my cry come to you. Teach me your way that I may walk in your truth."

Of all the village rabbis the one he would choose for counsel happened to be the father of his betrothed. That would not do. To speak to anyone else might leave the woman open to ridicule, or worse. He remembered a reading from the Torah. Before his friend Efron's wedding, a rabbi used the passage to give instruction. The guidance of that day now seemed to fit. He went to the main room, took down the scroll and searched for the passage, knowing and fearing what he would read. He heard his Poppa's oft repeated belief: "Nothing is unclear about this Torah command or any other." He read the passage. *If there is no evidence of the girl's virginity at the time of her marriage, they shall bring the girl to the entrance of her father's house where the townsmen shall stone her to death.*

CHAPTER 6

*J*oseph felt Jacob's presence. The Torah scrolls lay across one side of the table, songs of David on the other. He again heard his Poppa. "We have the Torah and the Writings, and the psalms sustain us until the Messiah comes."

The Torah had the answer for every dilemma, or at least the rabbis taught them so they fit every aspect of daily life. Joseph found in the Torah precisely what he feared. And it applied to Mary! His Mary! Whether it suited him or repulsed him, he must abide by it. But he could not bring himself to initiate the law's prescription in her regard. There must be more to it.

"God will provide" had been his hope and his prayer since childhood. He knew Abraham as the father he was, a father who had come so close to sacrificing his son. Perhaps he only *seemed* to come close, knowing all the time God would provide the offering in due course. Joseph drew a deep breath. "Lord God, remind me of how our greatest grandpoppa Abraham faced his dilemma, how he stayed steadfast, never believing his son Isaac was in danger, and how he climbed the mountain knowing your will was at the summit. Guide me to find a way to keep your law and my love for you, and to protect my other love."

Jacob was advising him again. "Read a little for reflection; read the whole for understanding."

Joseph opened the scroll again, found the grim passage, and read before it and beyond it.

If a man, after marrying a woman and having relations with her, makes monstrous charges against her and defames her by saying, 'I married this woman but when I first had relations with her I did not find her a virgin,' if this charge is true and if there is no evidence of the girl's virginity at the time of her marriage, they shall bring the girl to the entrance of her father's house where the townsmen shall stone her to death because she has committed a crime against Israel.

The understanding that Poppa had promised did not come. Staring at the rolled scrolls offered no help either. He returned to the workshop. There he saw boards and strips and dowels left over from the four sleeping platforms he and James had made for Deborah. In his mind he put the pieces together and decided he had what was needed for a fifth platform. Even without James' assistance he could finish it by the end of the day.

He sawed, planed and hammered. He gripped the length of rough oak that would become four legs, pressed it against the spinning sandstone, back and forth, back and forth, giving it a smooth polished look. When he finished with this piece he would cut it in four, shape the pieces and be ready to assemble the platform and deliver it to Japha the next day. Deborah had not ordered it but Joseph was sure she would put the gift to good use. And building it gave him something to do.

71

This repetitious, almost mindless phase of furniture construction allowed Joseph the chance to ponder the words he had read. Jacob's advice to read the whole must have meant that he decipher as well as read, for the reading itself had done little for him.

His thoughts rearranged themselves as he pressed the oak plank back and forth, back and forth. Mary was his betrothed, not his wife. The dictate applied to a man who has already married. Joseph concluded that since Mary was not yet his wife, he had no obligation under the law to denounce her for her infidelity. But by the same dictate, he could not go through with the marriage knowing Mary was pregnant by another. Back and forth, back and forth, getting closer to completion.

Deborah and her pregnant girls! That was it. While certain there was more to all of this than he knew, he would speak to Deborah about Mary when he delivered the platform to her. Then before too long he would take Mary to her. She and her baby would be safe. He would secure a writ of divorce from a rabbi in Sepphoris and by the time Mary's baby was born he would know what to do next.

"Thank you, Poppa," he said aloud.

He turned to his project with renewed faith in himself and in God's providence. As for Mary, he recalled his Poppa's caution not to judge harshly the traders' daughters. He set to the final step, putting the parts together and hammering the dowels and thoughts into place.

A man entered his workshop. The color of his cloak, like a cloudless sky, identified him as a stranger to Nazareth. He nodded to Joseph, looked over the workbench and ran his hand along the oak legs Joseph had fashioned.

"You do fine work, Joseph," said the stranger.

Surprised at the man calling him by name, Joseph nodded his thanks but stayed silent.

"What I see in your workshop mirrors what people say." He held each leg up to the sunshine, admiring its base, chiseled to match the fine curve of a deer hoof. "I can see the trouble in your soul does not derive from your handiwork."

Stunned at the stranger's insight, Joseph studied his face for some sign. Was he a messenger from Joachim? Did this have something to do with Mary? "What ...," he paused as he realized his voice was quivering. He steadied himself. "What makes you think my soul is troubled?"

"Joseph, you have nothing to fear from me. God is well pleased with you." The visitor spoke with confidence, as if he often engaged in this kind of conversation.

Poppa and Mama often spoke of God being pleased with him. He wondered on what authority this stranger spoke, thinking it rude to ask. "It is generous of you to say that. I have confidence in God's goodness," Joseph said.

"You should have confidence in Mary, too. I assure you she has remained faithful to you even as she is with child." He picked up a handful of dowels, poured them from one hand to the other, and put them back down.

Whatever his authority, he knew of Mary's condition.

"What do you know of Mary?" asked Joseph.

"I know Deborah in Japha will appreciate your craftsmanship in creating another platform worthy of God's children."

Joseph had told no one, not even James and Joses, about this platform. He eyed his guest. His sandals were free of sand and dust in spite of the ground around them.

The visitor examined the platform braces and set them down again on the work bench. Moving away from the collection of wooden parts, he sat in a chair toward the center of the room. He had a joyful countenance, radiating the pleasure one feels with a task well done.

Joseph walked to the edge of his outdoor workshop and faced the courtyard he shared with his neighbors. As he gathered his thoughts, clouds rolling in from the west and the Great Sea signaled the coming of evening. Joseph decided to invite the man for a meal. He closed his eyes for a brief moment, took a breath and turned to him. The workshop was empty. The completed platform sat beside the workbench. He was unsure whether he had had a visitor or a dream.

Joses burst into the room holding a little lamb. "Poppa, I found a stray with no mama. I named him 'Wander.' Can we keep him?"

Joseph sat down and wondered at the happy commotion of his life: one ten-year old 'son' a budding tekton, another with a growing flock, a knowing but disappearing stranger and a faithful but pregnant betrothed.

IN THE MORNING the twins helped Joseph load the new platform onto the back of his donkey.

"Why don't you take Hoofy instead of Ears?" asked Joses.

Puzzled, Joseph looked at him and then at James. As Joses was about to explain, Joseph remembered Joses' names for Rabbi Joachim's ox and their donkey. "The donkey can carry one sleeping platform with no trouble. I'll also get there and back faster than with the ox." *I am not ready to meet Rabbi Joachim until I have my dilemma figured out.*

Joses put blankets under the platform to ease the burden on the animal.

Joseph walked to Japha in what seemed like less time

than was possible while his head spun with possibilities. Deborah greeted him with surprise and gratitude. She helped him carry the platform into one of the small rooms off the main room. The four platforms Joseph had delivered months earlier were in use, two in each room. Beside one of them lay a small mat enclosed by a wall of swaddling. On a shelf lay two or three additional mats of various sizes. If all the mats were in use at the same time they would cover the floor. An unbleached woolen curtain filled the small window. Deborah had been busy at many things since his last visit.

In the main room a woman he had not met on his earlier visit sat at a spindle that was also new to the house. Beside her lay a baby gumming its thumb while watching his every move. Deborah explained that Joanna had joined them several weeks earlier, just in time to give birth a week after Ruth.

"Your girls keep you busy."

Nodding, she led him to their courtyard. She kept her voice low. "Most of them have no fault in how they wind up here. Many were assaulted, some by respected Jews they knew, others by Roman soldiers or other foreigners, men who know the women they dishonor will have no recourse. Some, more than you would guess, have no choice but to offer themselves for shekels or drachmas. For them it is only a matter of time before they reap what others sow.

"They are lucky to have you. Rather, they are blessed to have you."

"Yes. The lucky ones—or the blessed, as you say it—find their way to me or someone else when their families throw them out. The unlucky? They're delivered to the Pharisees, our holy leaders who see only the broken laws. They say they have no choice but to carry out the atrocious punishment written in the Torah." Her face flamed. "Malicious vipers!" She spat on the ground.

She walked toward the vegetable garden; her face resumed its usual amber shade.

Joseph said, "It is not easy to balance the two: on one hand, to obey the law as it is written, and on the other, to love someone caught in a web of another's spinning."

She turned to face him. "I prefer to tip the scale toward those in the web. If I am wrong, let it be on my head." She looked at him, the way a woman looked at her brother or father. "I see her in your eyes, Joseph. You are speaking of someone close to you who is caught in this web, as you say it. A sister perhaps? Or a cousin who fears the reproach of her family as well as the harsh hand of the Pharisee?"

"You are wise."

"Or you are transparent," Deborah said.

"Either way, you are right. Someone I love is caught in a web I know little of, a devout and beautiful woman."

"The details of her web won't matter here. Whatever she wants us to know, she will tell us."

Relief must have shown on his face or in his demeanor because she encouraged him with her eyes and gentle manner.

"Joseph, it looks like you found a way to handle love and the Law, at least in the interest of one woman." She walked toward the door into the house. "Like the other girls, she will be safe with me—safe, quiet and busy. This combination helps them to have healthy babies." She entered the house and continued toward the front door. "Now you must go. You have a distressing task before you and I have meals to prepare."

They agreed that the pregnant woman from Nazareth would stay with Deborah until she gave birth and Joseph would provide Deborah with funds to care for her and her newborn. He had until then to figure out the rest.

～

ON THE WAY back to Nazareth Joseph prayed for guidance, hoping he was choosing wisely. "Make known to me your ways, O Lord; teach me your paths. Guide me in your truth and teach me, for you are God my savior."

After some time he sensed someone walking near him. He looked up, startled to see him.

"I didn't realize you were there," he said to the familiar and still unknown blue-cloaked stranger. "Have you been here the whole way from Japha?"

"Hilly and green it is from Japha to Nazareth."

Joseph wondered where the stranger had come from, for he had passed no crossroad since leaving Japha.

The traveler stepped closer to Joseph. "Do not be afraid to take Mary into your house as your wife."

Joseph wanted to take Mary into his house but he was also determined to remain faithful to the Law. Doing as this man said would achieve the first part. But at what price? Joseph hoped this man was not one of Palestine's many charlatans or messiahs. A simple test would make it easier to believe him. "What arrangement did I make today in Japha?"

"I don't play guessing games."

Joseph flinched at the retort. The donkey brayed and gave a sharp pull on the tether. Joseph stroked his neck and rested his chest and shoulders against the animal's back, calming him. When Joseph raised his head the blue-cloaked stranger had vanished, if he had been there at all.

~

JAMES AND JOSES ran to him as he entered his village.

"Come, Poppa, see what I finished," said James. He took one of Joseph's hands, encouraging him to walk faster.

Joses took Ears' tether in one hand and Joseph's hand in the other. "Remember Wander, you know, the stray baby lamb?" He did not wait for an answer. "He found a new mama. The ewe Simon gave me feeds him right along with her own baby even if he's not hers. They keep her busy. I wish I could help her."

"You can help her by bringing food to her so she doesn't have to spend her energy grazing," said Joseph.

"Yes, Poppa, I will do that."

They reached the house. In the courtyard Joses pointed to the ewe lying on her side being nuzzled by two balls of wool.

"Which one is hers?" asked James.

Joses replied, "She doesn't care." He thought for a moment, watching the ewe nuzzle the lambs in return. "I guess you don't have to be a mother to be a mother." He looked at Joseph, puzzled at himself. "I mean …."

"I know exactly what you mean, Joses," said Joseph.

James led Joseph to the workbench beside the house. He picked up the box that Joseph had begun to make. He turned it in his hands, displaying each side, and pointing out the specks of onyx embedded in the lid. The joy of a completed scroll box shone on his face and the uncertainty about its reception cast in his eyes.

"Thank you, James, it is beautiful. I got it started but, without you, we'd still have pieces of wood and stone chips. Because of you we have a lovely treasure to give Mary." It dawned on him that he was not the only one who would be sorely disappointed if events did not turn out the way he hoped.

The deeds of the day lingered with him well into the night. He knew his boys as if they were his sons: their origin, their thoughts, their talents and their prayers. Today they had shown him the future they wanted to share with him. He had also come to know Deborah better and the life she had built for herself. If only the stranger's message were as clear.

Mary's time would not stand still. He would have to find a time to speak with her. With her image before him and his prayers on his lips, he slept an interrupted sleep.

JOSEPH LAY CURLED on his mat, unsure if he was looking at or was dreaming of the familiar stranger.

"Why have you returned?" Joseph sat up, pulling his blanket around him.

"Joseph, you strive to be a trusting son of David. Complete trust means trusting when you do not understand."

"Tell me if it is possible to remain faithful to the Law if I take Mary as my wife."

"It is through the Holy Spirit that this child has been conceived in her."

David had written of the spirit of God giving life to creation. People and animals being conceived in their mothers by their fathers was an everyday occurrence. Joseph did not see how the spirit of God fit with the conceiving of a child. "Tell me more."

"Have faith. You need neither question me nor fear me."

Joseph bowed his head. *Father Abraham, lead me to trust.* After a moment he looked up at the visitor.

"Mary will bear a son and you, Joseph, are to name him Yeshua, because he will save his people from their sins."

How would this happen? What did Mary know of this? Why was he chosen? Before he could put words to his questions, he awoke, curled on his mat, as bright sunlight played on his face.

Joseph thought about the stranger's messages over the past few days: Mary was pregnant by the Spirit of God, pregnant with a child who is the son of God, a child who will save his people from their sins, and he, Joseph, will have a role in it all. Yes, he was going to need the trust he had prayed for all his life.

SOME MONTHS earlier Mary sat in the main room of her family's home, lengths of newly woven wool on her lap, a feather needle plying slender thread through the wool, joining the pieces the way breezes nudge two clouds into one. She had first softened the wool by washing and pressing it, and then selected pieces suitable for a man six inches taller than her father. This inner tunic would provide Joseph with warmth and comfort. Her father had gone to synagogue, her mother and her sister Salome had gone to the village market, leaving Mary to work in quiet solitude. The stillness of the air matched the silence until the curtains swayed, catching her attention. She looked around the room, saw nothing and no one. She was astonished when the curtains fluttered again.

"Hail, favored one. The Lord is with you," said a voice coming from the now still curtain.

Mary looked again and could still not see where the voice was coming from. The quiver of her hands echoed the flutter in her heart.

"Do not be afraid, Mary."

He or she or it knew her name and sensed her growing fear.

"You have found favor with God."

If she had found favor with God, why did this encounter worry her?

"You will conceive and bear a son, and you shall name him Yeshua."

The voice had come to the wrong house, for giving birth was not in her future.

"Your son will be magnificent and will be called Son of the Most High. The Lord God will give him the throne of David his father."

She had better stop him before his error went too far.

"He will rule over the house of Jacob forever, and of his kingdom there will be no end."

She could delay no longer. "How can this be, since I have relations with no man?" *And I do not intend to.*

"The holy Spirit will come upon you and the power of the Most High will impregnate you."

She did not comprehend it, but she did hear the voice.

"Therefore the child to be born will be called holy, the son of God."

It started to sink in that God was arranging something for her, something she had thought was out of the question.

"And besides this, your aged cousin Elizabeth has also conceived a son; she who was considered barren is in her sixth month."

Elizabeth pregnant! She would not have believed it.

"Nothing is impossible with God."

Since her childhood, Mary had tried to believe that. If Elizabeth were pregnant at her age, then it was no less reasonable that Mary was pregnant without a man.

The voice had stopped. No, not a voice, a messenger from God.

"I am the Lord's maid servant." She could not let him go without her consent. "May it be done to me according to the Lord's word."

The curtain fluttered and the room became silent again.

Mary deliberated on these words of the messenger during every waking moment, considering what they might mean and what they implied for her future. Pondering and praying about them from rising to lying down again kept the thoughts blooming in her dreams. One morning she heard her mother say to her father, "That girl is in another world! Thinking about her wedding has absorbed more of her than it did her sister."

She thought about confiding in her mother and her Rabbi father, but wondered how to explain a visitor who informed her she would have a baby. She could not ignore an arrival her people had longed for from generation to generation. She had given her consent to be an instrument of God's will. If the Lord could send her a visitor, he could send one to her parents or to anyone who should know about it. She had no need to tell anyone.

Except Joseph! She had to tell Joseph. Just not right away.

WHEN MARY DESCRIBED all this for Joseph months later, he surprised her with his matter-of-fact acceptance, and his relief that her expectations lined up with his.

"Joseph, I didn't know if I had dreamed it all or if it really happened."

"Just because you dreamt it doesn't mean it didn't happen."

"I sensed something come alive inside me. Oh, Joseph, the power of God drew the breath right out of me and my words followed. 'Yes,' I said, 'yes.' I wanted you with me, Joseph. God is choosing you and me for his own reason. I also choose you. Because I love you."

Joseph restrained himself from holding her, from letting his touch tell her what was in his heart. He turned and looked through the doorway to the courtyard. "Your mother is working in the garden. Let's join her." They greeted Anna and went to the far corner of the little garden and sat on two beches under a fig tree.

"I am with you, Mary, and will be with you as your husband. If you had come to me earlier, I would have borne your secret with you." Joseph's whisper set the tone for them.

"I wanted to but I feared you would think me too forward to speak of the changes inside me while we were still far from our marriage." With her gaze she drew him to herself as she had when he held her in the cradle of his arms.

"If you had told me right after your visit, I would not have known what to think." He paused to re-capture the hopes and prayers they already shared. "Mary, I, too, had a visitor—or maybe a dream—and he—or maybe it—overwhelmed me, too." He told her of the visits from the blue-cloaked stranger and his quandary at deciphering them.

He continued, "When you and I first talked of marriage, we told each other we believed the Lord would provide a way for us. Now he has sent us a messenger, or two messengers, to let us know he is providing a way, and more than a way, he has a plan for the two of us."

Anxiety replaced the wonder that had filled her face while she recounted the events for Joseph and then listened to his description of his encounter. With a hint of uncertainty in her voice, she said, "If I am to be your wife and you my husband, the law says we must consummate our marriage." She took a breath, giving the thought a chance to form on her lips. "We have both promised ...."

Joseph interrupted her. "Yes, we promised to dedicate ourselves to God even as we embark on a life together. God has provided a way for us to do this. The son of God growing in you and in us as a family gives us the holy intimacy we need to consummate our marriage and our lives."

"I can't imagine any of our rabbis, not even my father, agreeing with you."

"Poppa Jacob explained to me the reason for all of our people to marry. It is to hold open the possibility that any woman might become the mother of the Messiah." He pleaded in his voice for her understanding. "Mary, for you no longer is it just a possibility. You are the one who will bear the son of God. That is sufficient."

"You give me strength. You are my cedar, my cypress." She inhaled, a breath slow and long. "My sachet of myrrh."

They let the power of the moment linger.

Joseph told her about building the platforms for Deborah and about his arranging for Deborah to care for her. "Now with God's plan, you will not need her care."

Mary said, "The messenger from God told me something else. My cousin Elizabeth is going to have a son. She will need me; she has no other family near her."

"God works his will as we do not expect. Her pregnancy must have shocked her and her husband."

"They have prayed all their lives that God would bless them and now he has. It won't be easy for her because she is not young, but it is a blessing."

"When will you go to her?"

"By now she is in her eighth month. Right after our wedding I will go."

"Yes, provided you can join a caravan."

"If James or Joses comes with me we won't have to wait for a caravan." She hesitated. "Nain is not more than three hours away."

Joseph sensed Mary's unease, either because she would leave him so soon after they married or because she would be traveling while pregnant herself.

"How long will you stay?" he asked.

"I will stay several weeks after the birth. There's no sense going if I don't stay." Her concern was for her cousin not herself.

"Mary, that's two months. How do you know they will have room for you as well as their new son?"

"As a priest serving in the temple in Jerusalem, Zechariah opens his home to priests from every temple district. His home in Nain has more than enough room for a handful of guests."

Each of the priests in the twenty-six temple districts took a two-week turn serving in the Great Temple. They offered one another hospitality on their travels to and from Jerusalem.

"In that case the four of us will go. I will bring tools and supplies, you and I will not be apart and the twins will get to see Nain and cousins they didn't know they had."

Mary nodded. "But first, our wedding."

CHAPTER 7

*N*azareth neighbors needed no invitation. Their gifts to the new couple filled the tables for the wedding feast with jugs of wine, platters of raisin cakes and warm loaves of every variety, pottery bowls of spiced olives and onions, and salted locusts with dipping bowls of honey.

According to custom, a groom gave the father of the bride a gift, the so-called bride's price. The day before the wedding Joseph brought to Joachim an oak pigeon-hole cabinet, taller by a hand's length than Joachim himself and nearly as wide as it was tall. "Every scroll of the Law, the Writings and the Psalms will have has its own place," Joseph said.

"Every time we take a scroll from the cabinet we will think of the tekton who made it." Joachim caressed the cabinet, ran his fingers along the embedded onyx on the face of a shelf exactly at the height of his eyes. He smiled and shared a knowing look with Joseph. Joachim reached up to a shelf on the wall and took down the longest and fattest scroll, and slid it into one of the larger holes of the new cabinet. He exclaimed with prayerful joy, "The precepts of the Lord are right; keeping them brings great reward." He looked and looked again at every corner and nook.

"You know me long, Joseph, and you know me well. How long? Since Little Mary opened her eyes. How well? Well enough to help me keep the word of the Lord from falling to the floor, may the Lord forgive me." He raised his gaze in prayer.

To acknowledge he had bypassed Salome, Joachim's older unmarried daughter, Joseph offered a second gift: a polished cedar reading board, two feet long and wider than any scroll, with hinged fasteners at top and bottom that would hold an open scroll in place. It could stand on a table or a shelf.

Joachim smiled again. "Now I will read until my eyes tire, not my arms."

On the wedding morning Joachim honored the other side of the custom. For the bride's dowry he gave Joseph his ox and cart. "For carting the stones and trees and all the things you make from them. No longer will you have to borrow my ox. It is now your ox. May the Lord bless the beast's strength and may he stay strong into his old age." He gave Joseph a warm embrace and added, "Into your old age as well."

Joseph wore his new wool tunic, a gift from his bride. Embroidered on an inner fold he read, "Set me as a seal on your heart, as a seal on your arm." Mary wore the gift from her mother, a cloak of finely spun wool, washed and whitened, with a matching veil that covered her head and shoulders. Into the belt of the inner tunic Anna had sewn well-worn tassels. "Many years ago I attached these to your father's wedding tunic. They will remind you of our love for each other and our love for you," she said as she helped Mary put it on.

The wedding garments of bride and groom and guests soon absorbed the dust and sand stirred up by a hundred feet coming into the common courtyard behind Joseph's house. A man played music on a harp, reminding Joseph of his Mama and the first harp he heard. Joachim poured a cup of thick, dark purple wine from a jug on the table. Anna looked at it, smelled it, wrinkled her nose and turned away. "There will be no marriage, for your daughter will be unable to drink it. Maybe Joseph, too." Joachim replaced it with pink wine from the jug next to it.

Mary followed Joachim as he walked toward Joseph who stood at the edge of his outdoor workshop beside his home, Jacob and Rachel's home before him. Rabbi Joachim raised the cup and prayed aloud, "Blessed are those who fear the Lord, who walk in his ways; your wife shall be like a fruitful vine in the heart of your house, your children like olive shoots around your table." He handed the cup to Joseph who sipped from it, and then to Mary who did the same. With a proud smile and with his arms raised, Joachim proclaimed, "I give my youngest daughter Mary to Joseph, son of Jacob, the Tekton from Nazareth." The music, which had paused while the couple shared the cup, now started up again with the men singing in loud chorus. They filled their cups and plates from the table and sat on chairs, stones or the ground on one side of the courtyard. Then the women took their food and found a place on the opposite side.

As Joseph led Mary into his house, a guest shouted a blessing, "May the Lord increase your number."

The couple smiled at each other, a smile and a look that carried their shared secret. Joseph showed Mary the new room with the new chair and sleeping platform. "In peace shall you lie down and sleep."

"How lovely your dwelling: a home for the sparrow, a place for the swallow to nest her young." She sighed and her sigh became a word of love and gratitude. "The Lord has sent me a thoughtful, loving man."

As they turned, Mary saw on the wall opposite her sleeping platform an engraved fragment of cedar, shaped like a cloud of no particular description and polished to a sheen. She read the engraving: "My heart exults in the Lord, my horn exalts in my God. He gives to the vower his vow and blesses the sleep of the just."

"It is more beautiful than any urn of gold or silver, embedded with all the jewels of the earth," she said.

Joseph smiled and stepped closer to her. "Sixteen years ago Poppa Jacob and I worked in Sepphoris."

She smiled the smile of one who is ready to enjoy a familiar story again.

"He bought this section of cedar and gave it to me to make something for someone I loved."

"I never heard that part of the story," she said.

"Nor the next part: I hoped even then that it would be a gift from me to you."

"And here it is, more than a gift: a song, a poem, a refrain that recalls the first prayer of my childhood."

"The first time I heard Hannah's poem, Poppa and I were building your sisters' new room and you were still the unborn that your family waited for."

"Now we have our own unborn that everyone has waited for." As she looked at Joseph, her eyes invited him to look inside her, and see there the love she had reserved for him.

After a quiet moment, they stepped back into the

main room.

"I will do all I can for you and the child you bear." He nodded toward the table. They sat facing each other. He took hold of one of her hands. She wrapped her other hand around his. Each drew in the power of the other. In silence they let their hearts listen to their unspoken prayers and hopes and promises.

He felt more than saw her nod, coming back to the moment. Joseph said, "Many were the days I thought I would never see you again, that the Lord had separate plans for you and me, designs that would take us to different dwellings rather than bring us to begin our together life."

"So much has happened." She managed to hold a mood at once joyful and pensive. "Yesterday I was Little Mary." She paused, smiled with her whole face and looked at Joseph.

He read her thoughts. "Little Mary. The only Little Mary I have known. The Little Mary I have always loved."

"And now, my dear husband, I have married the man I love." Mary had a way of being excited and calm at the same time. "I am the wife of Joseph the Tekton and I carry the son of God in my womb. We have to believe that God will take care of him and of us. I know no other way."

"There is no other way." He stood, still holding her hands in his. They walked toward the courtyard. "Our friends are waiting," he said.

She peered outside. "Joseph, don't be silly. They are enjoying themselves too much to be waiting for anyone." She gave his hands a squeeze, let go and then walked outside to where her mother and sisters stood with neighbors.

Joseph went to the gathering of men and watched James and Joses enjoying their first wedding dance. Each of the boys laughed and frowned at the same time: laughed in the sheer delight of the bouncing, turning, kicking, holding onto neighbors, one with each arm; frowned with concentration to leap when others leapt and kick when others kicked.

Joseph treasured his Poppa's blessing that bestowed on him the duty and the power to be Poppa to his Poppa's sons. He recalled his Poppa telling him that in caring for his brothers, he was preparing to be Poppa to his own children. How well had it prepared him to be Poppa to the son of God?

∾

Two days after Mary slept her first sleep in her new home, she and Joseph, along with James and Joses, packed clothes, supplies and tools into the ox cart.

Joses set the yoke comfortably in front of the ox's shoulders. After Joachim gave the ox to Joseph, Joses spent much of his time fastening a leather lining to the wooden yoke so it would ride more easily on the animal. "Simon let me put my sheep into one of his fields. They'll wait for me there until we come home." He arranged the donkey seat for Mary and was ready to go, now that all his creatures were accounted for.

The way from Nazareth to Nain followed a path made by the frequent caravans traveling between Sepphoris in the north and Jerusalem in the south. Once the travelers walked down out of the hills around Nazareth they had level land to traverse. Even a family traveling with most of their possessions could cover the journey in a few hours.

As they came within sight of their cousins' home, Joses said, "This must be the biggest house in all Galilee."

"Biggest in the whole world," said James.

"Many priests stay with our cousins on their way to Jerusalem for their Temple service," Mary told them as Joseph helped her off the donkey.

Joseph asked the boys, "How often must a priest travel to Jerusalem to offer sacrifice in the Great Temple?"

Vying to be the first to answer, the boys shouted in unison. "Two times a year."

Joseph was about to applaud them when an elderly couple came out of the house, their arms raised in greeting.

Thrilled at seeing her cousins, Mary hurried to greet them.

Elizabeth shouted out to her, "Blessed are you among women."

Mary embraced her. "You, Elizabeth, are blessed among all of us."

Elizabeth continued, "Blessed is the child in your womb." She took Mary's face in her hands, and kissed her eyes, her cheeks, her forehead. Her own eyes were wide and moist, her mouth open in praise. "How does this happen to me that you come here!"

"Since the day I first heard of your blessing, I have longed to come to you."

Elizabeth's excitement grew with each pause and each phrase. "You, the mother of my Lord, have come to me!" She gasped and reached for a breath, as if she could find no air. Her fingers stroked her abdomen as she calmed herself. "At the moment your greeting reached my ears, the infant in my womb leapt for joy." She held Mary again. "Let me look at you, you dear child. You are blessed because you believed. You knew what was told to you by the Lord would come to pass." She closed her eyes and raised her hands in prayer. "My son knows his Lord."

Mary took Elizabeth's hands and pressed them to her chest. "Elizabeth, feel my heart for it exults in your good favor."

The women, so delighted in each other and in the special blessings they bore, seemed to forget they were not alone.

"My mother, your cousin Anna, taught us to honor the gifts from the Lord as Hannah did. 'My heart exults in God; my strength declares his power. My enemies are vanquished; I delight in his strength. God my savior has looked with favor on me, his lowly servant. My spirit rejoices in him.'"

"Our sons' generation will bless you," Elizabeth said.

"More than their generation, from this day all generations will call me blessed because of the great things the Almighty has done for me; holy is his Name."

"The Lord's mercy has touched you."

"He has mercy on all who fear him, in every generation."

"Mary, look at me, a woman long beyond child bearing." Elizabeth looked down at her protruding belly, pressed it and then raised her hands over her head, praying as she talked to Mary. "I am a sign of the Lord's contradiction."

"The Lord's power bubbles over with contradictions." Mary gestured with both arms toward her cousin, the way a neighbor gestures when she has many things to say. "He scatters the proud in their conceit; he casts down the mighty from their thrones; he lifts up the lowly."

"He has blessed the womb of an old woman and gladdens her heart with a child," Elizabeth said, showing her gratitude for one of the Lord's contradictions.

"His blessing surrounds us; he fills the hungry with good things and the rich he sends away empty," Mary replied.

"He has blessed our nation, our family," said Elizabeth,

coming to tears, short of breath and waving her arms in search of support.

Mary embraced her, steadying her. "Yes," Mary sang out, "he comes to the help of his servant Israel for he always remembers his promise of mercy, the promise he made to our fathers, to Abraham and his children."

A man as old as Elizabeth came and stood beside her, sharing in her joy as Joseph shared in Mary's. When he had everyone's attention, he gestured to them, inviting them into his home.

Elizabeth motioned toward him. "My husband, Zechariah, has also found favor with God, although at first, he was less sure that the wonders of the Lord will come to pass. As he offered sacrifice in the Temple, a messenger of the Lord approached him and told him we will have a son who will be filled with the holy Spirit and will turn the people of Israel to the Lord and we should name him, 'John.' Since then Zechariah speaks with signs, not his tongue. You can imagine the difficulty he had telling me about the messenger in the Temple. Then he came to me and we conceived."

EIGHT DAYS after Elizabeth delivered her son, neighbors gathered for the boy's circumcision.

"We shall name him Zechariah," said a neighbor woman to Elizabeth, as if the baby's father had vanished.

"No," Elizabeth said, "we shall name him, 'John.'"

A man standing with the woman said, "Elizabeth, you have no one in your family named John. You don't want your son to be without a family bond. Zechariah it should be, like his father." The neighbor nodded toward Zechariah.

"John it is. You can add 'bar Zechariah' if you must but his name is *John*." Elizabeth stamped a fist into her other hand, and directed their attention to her husband with a pronounced nod of her head.

The neighbors gestured their protest to Zechariah.

He took a scroll and wrote, "His name is John."

As soon as he wrote the name, he was again able to speak. "His name is John," he proclaimed.

Mary tugged at Joseph's sleeve and whispered. "I think Yeshua heard him and drummed his hands against my insides." Her look told him it had not hurt.

Joseph stepped closer to her. "Our Yeshua can't wait to meet his cousin. They will be friends."

Zechariah shouted out like any man who had not spoken in months. "Blessed be the Lord, the God of Israel; He has come to His people and set them free."

The neighbors looked to one another for an explanation.

"What then is this child to become if he is to set anyone free?" they asked.

Zechariah directed their attention to Mary and the child she carried. "The Lord has raised up for us a mighty Savior, to be born of the house of His servant David."

Friends and neighbors who had gathered for John's rite of initiation looked from Zechariah to Elizabeth to Mary, inquiring of one another what Zechariah was talking about.

Zechariah walked among the crowd as he might have done in a synagogue lesson. "Ages ago he promised through his holy prophets that he would save us from our enemies." He turned from one neighbor to the next. "He promised to show mercy to our fathers. To set us free to worship Him." He pounded his fists against the air and repeated with renewed emphasis, "To set us free to worship without fear."

He looked across the gathering toward his infant son

and drew their attention to him. "The days of the prophets have not ended."

He walked to his son with arms outstretched. "You, my child, shall be called the prophet of the Most High." He took him from Elizabeth and walked over to Mary and Joseph. He cradled him and spoke to him so all could hear. "You will go before the son of God to prepare His way. You will teach his people about salvation through the forgiveness of their sins."

Mary and Joseph stood with the others, listening to Zechariah, wondering what it all could mean, questioning whether Zechariah knew more of it than they. Mary said to Joseph, "John and Yeshua will be more than friends."

SOME WEEKS after John's circumcision, Joseph and Mary, along with James and Joses, returned home, looking forward to the birth of their son in Nazareth. During the next several months the family continued preparing their home for the new arrival with extra attention on Mary's room. Beside her raised sleeping platform now lay a smaller version.

One of the wall shelves held a bundle of new softened swaddling, two tiny robes and a bag of cloths for his bottom. "As soft as a cloud," Mary said as she rearranged everything on the shelf.

On the topmost shelf sat a clay bowl that held a growing collection of coins. Joseph set aside some of his tekton earnings for the Temple offering of a lamb for the child's presentation and Mary's purification. They planned to travel to Jerusalem for this ritual, the second rite of initiation, a month after the infant's circumcision.

"Poppa, come, come." James came running into the house one day. "Soldiers are in the market and people are shouting and crying out."

"How many soldiers? What are they saying?" Joseph ran to the door bumping into Joses who was coming in. "Joses, what have you heard?"

Joses said, "Some men said they weren't going to move and the soldier with all the metal on his clothes said they better if they valued their life."

Joseph thought of the people of Sepphoris who had to find a new place to live whether they wanted to or not. He looked back to Mary. "It wouldn't surprise me if Herod was behind this. His compulsion with building is how your family wound up in Nazareth."

"I am happy Herod's compulsion brought my family to the village where you live," Mary said. "You'd better go and find out what is going on. Be safe, dear husband."

Two soldiers on horseback, one with a scroll unfurled, had moved the fifty feet from the market stands to the well. "Emperor Caesar Augustus has decreed that all people everywhere will be registered in their tribal home. All you people from somewhere else will make haste to do as he commands."

Before the soldiers moved along to their next crying stop, Joseph pushed his way through the small but immovable gathering. "Sir," he said to the lead soldier. "My wife is heavy with child. My family is of the house of David, of the town of Bethlehem. She is in no condition to travel such a distance. It presents great danger to the mother and the child."

"What is that to us? If you are of Bethlehem, then to Bethlehem you go."

"The child she carries will have a special mission." Even

though he did not want to leave her, he preferred doing so to having her make the long journey. "I will go by myself to register for my wife and my children." By this time, as far as the law was concerned, James and Joses were Joseph's children.

The soldier without the scroll shouted at Joseph. "You people think every baby will have a special mission. Who cares about your mission?" With the horse whip held across his chest he left no doubt he would enforce the decree.

The first soldier bellowed in a voice taut with threat, "The decree says, 'all people.' It does not say, 'all men.'" Having made the decree clear, both soldiers spurred their horses, setting them galloping.

Joseph turned around and found James and Joses standing in his shadow.

"What will we do, Poppa?" Joses asked, worry redefining his features.

"We packed and traveled to visit your Mama's cousin in Nain; we will do the same for Bethlehem." He jostled their heads. "I'll race you home."

DURING THE NEXT few days Simon added most of Nazareth's sheep to his own flock. Families packed what they could from their larder and their beds under the watchful eyes of the soldiers who had made camp at the edge of the village. "Make haste," they shouted and showed they meant it.

Joseph and the twins again packed their tunics, supplies and Joseph's tools. Mary took what she could from the little bed they had prepared and bundled it into the ox cart. She carried water skins and two loaves on their donkey.

Haphazard caravans formed as families headed for places like Magdala to the east; Capernaum to the east and north along the banks of the Sea of Galilee. "Tell my sister Mary and her husband Clopas we send our love," she told someone heading there. No one traveled to Sepphoris for it was too new to be anyone's ancestral home.

Families going to Jericho traveled east to the Jordan River and then south along its banks. Those headed for Jerusalem and Bethlehem could also go south along the Jordan and then head back west to their destination or they could save a day's travel by going directly south past Nain and down through the hills of Samaria. Joseph chose the route near Nain with hopes of meeting up with Zechariah and Elizabeth.

When the caravan approached Nain, Joseph led his family off the main way to Zechariah's house. A neighbor informed them that he and Elizabeth had already gone with their baby to Jerusalem for Zechariah's turn to offer sacrifice in the temple. Afterward they planned to go to Bethlehem to register for the census.

Joseph and Mary chose not to stay the night in their cousins' empty house in Nain but to make good use of the remaining half day of sunlight. "We will see your cousin when we get to Jerusalem or even in Bethlehem. Perhaps they will have found a place to stay that will have a room where you can deliver our son," Joseph said.

"The Lord will take care of us. I hope we can visit while the new cousins are still babies."

Mary got off the donkey, and flexed and straightened her back as she walked beside it. Fine sand stirred up by the pilgrims' parade stung their eyes and dried their mouths. The dust in the air settled like a dark cloud on the spindly trees and thirsty brush.

Joseph held the ox's tether while the boys skipped ahead or wandered to one side or the other, looking at birds in trees and locusts on the ground. He said to Mary, "We will have to pay innkeepers for six nights or more. That will take much of the money we saved for an offering for Yeshua's presentation."

"We will still have enough for an offering, won't we?"

"Yes, maybe something less than the lamb we planned on."

"The Lord expects us to offer what we have, not what we don't. You provide well for us, Joseph, so don't concern yourself with what matters not one tittle in the Lord's eyes." She caught his gaze and smiled a smile of reassurance, as he did when she needed one.

Joseph said, "Perhaps the census is God's way of having us live in Bethlehem. Your family and mine are of David's house. This may be the time for us to move. Herod's building plans for Jerusalem assures plenty of work for every willing tekton." He nodded toward his sack of tools in the cart.

A handful of years after Augustus became Emperor, Herod turned his attention to rebuilding and expanding the Great Temple. Projects like the Temple and the theater in Sepphoris became a monument to his power and wealth; in addition, the Temple project appeased the people of Judea who had mixed feelings toward Herod. Now, twenty years later, the reconstruction continued, giving jobs to workers and a place of worship and sacrifice to the faithful. During that time Herod's work enhanced the empire, thus ingratiating him further with the foreign rulers.

"Whether we stay in Bethlehem for long or for short, we will be close to Jerusalem for Yeshua's presentation in the Great Temple," Mary said.

"The Lord will let us know where we shall raise the son of God."

After half an hour Mary got back on the donkey. "The midwife in Nazareth told me to walk a few minutes every couple of hours but now I am tired."

By evening the first day they had lost sight of their fellow travelers because of their slower pace. They came upon a camp of four tents near the River Jezreel, a small stream that flowed into the Jordan half a day's walk to the east. Three men, one a generation older than the other two, sat in front of the largest of the tents, the only one made of strong braided black goat hair. Two women tended a fire in the space between two smaller tents. Children's voices came from a field beyond the tents.

"Have we caught up to someone from our village?" James asked with hope in his voice.

"No, James. The ground around the tent pegs hasn't been disturbed for a long time. This is a permanent camp."

Joseph left his family at the edge of the camp circle, approached the men and inquired about spending the night.

The eldest responded, "We have room in the men's tent for you, your wife can stay with the women, the boys with the children." He tilted his head, looked at Joseph, and then added, "For one shekel."

One of the younger men said, "If your wife spends the night in the little tent you won't have to pay the shekel." His eyes widened and he sneered at his own imaginings.

The eldest man raised his hand and brought it down hard across the man's face. "Oaf, even from here you can see the woman is heavy with child. Do not insult the man or his wife."

Joseph looked to his family as they bristled at the rough discipline. Joses moved to the far side of the donkey and stroked the animal's neck. James stepped closer to Mary who rested her hand on his shoulder. Joseph said to the elder, "The night is clear. My family will sleep together." He pointed to an outcropping of rocks near where Mary and the twins now stood. "There."

"Sleep where you wish. For one shekel."

Joseph looked at him and thought about arguing over the payment but decided the shekel might save harassment.

As if reading his thoughts the elder said, "We will keep you safe for the shekel and you can drink from our river."

Their river? Joseph emptied his purse onto the palm of his own hand. Three coins fell out; he picked up one and handed it to the camp elder.

"Welcome to our village," the elder said as the coin disappeared into the folds of his cloak.

"Bless the Lord," Joseph replied.

A protruding rock ledge provided shelter for their sacks and blankets. Joseph helped Mary from the donkey and guided her to a large stone that provided her a place to sit when she was ready.

She walked around, stretching and bending, and then set their provisions on a mat.

"James, Joses, take our skins and fill them," Joseph said as he relieved the donkey of its saddle. Joses unhitched the ox cart.

James carried the skins and Joses led the animals to the stream. When the boys and the beasts walked back to Joseph, the animals found a patch of grass, more gray than green. Joses secured them to an old and full cypress tree.

"Come, we have fish and olives." Mary handed around the food sacks and took a round of flat bread and gave it to Joseph. He broke it and divided it among them.

Joseph offered a blessing. "Praise the God of heaven. He frees us from foes and gives food to all flesh."

As he picked up a piece of fish, James said, "If we eat a lot we will have a lighter load tomorrow."

Joseph laughed as he looked at him. "That's true, but we will be hungry again tomorrow."

After the meal the boys returned to the stream and skipped flat stones across the surface. Joseph watched them from their improvised camp site, recalling other streams and rivers in Galilee where he had gathered stones and skipped them toward the other side. What he pictured in his mind's eye was lush compared with this desolate spot, with not a vine or olive tree in sight, and he wondered if this rugged family group depended on passing traders for oil and grain and lentils and everything else. At least the stream would provide them with fish. A joyful shout from Joses brought him back to the moment. He replaced the shekel he had taken from the little purse with one from a leather folder secured inside his wide cloth belt. He hadn't planned on having to pay to sleep outside and now hoped he had enough shekels to last several weeks.

THE SIXTH DAY of their journey brought Joseph and his family to a crowded Jerusalem. Streets and markets, wells and inns, all became gathering places for the enormous number of census-registrants traveling from their homes to their ancestral villages, along with worshipers coming to the Great Temple, and the usual horde of traders plying the routes through Jerusalem that connected Egypt with the nations to the East.

Joseph and his family went first to the Temple, or as

close to it as they could manage. Outside the gate to the Court of Gentiles they asked anyone who would listen if they knew of Zechariah. Leaving the boys with the animals, Joseph and Mary pushed their way toward a middle court, the Court of Women, inquiring as they went.

After an hour of futility they found three priests coming from the Court of Men. "Do you know of Zechariah, a priest of Nain, or his wife Elizabeth? Have you seen them?" Joseph asked.

One of the priests answered, "I saw Zechariah, yes, not Elizabeth." He paused, looked at Joseph and Mary, and bowed his head.

"What is it? What's wrong?" Mary asked.

"The wife came with the priest. Like him she was long in years." He took his time, as if looking for the right words. "I have offered sacrifice with Zechariah many times in our periods of sacrifice." His eyes smiled a sad smile. "I am not so young myself. Now when I come to Jerusalem I leave my wife at home. Traveling is not so easy these days." He looked to his fellow priests who nodded agreement but appeared relieved that someone else was doing the talking.

Joseph said, "What do you mean, she *was* long in years. Tell us."

"Zechariah offered sacrifice two weeks ago. When he went back to where they were staying, he found his wife asleep in the middle of the day. He could not wake her. He sent to the Temple for a physician but when he arrived at their place the wife had still not awakened." He stopped.

"Do you mean she …?" Joseph asked.

The priest reached his hands toward Joseph, a quiet offer of compassion. "Zechariah arranged for her burial here in Jerusalem. So blessed to be buried in our Holy City!"

Mary's eyes filled. Joseph steadied her with an arm

around her shoulders.

"Out of the depths I cry to you, O Lord," Joseph prayed.

"Lord, hear my prayer," she replied.

The priest closed his eyes, out of sadness or fatigue or prayer.

"What of their son, still a baby?" Mary asked. She stepped from Joseph's arm, drawing a deep breath.

"Zechariah took him to Bethlehem to register, for he is of the house of David."

Mary brightened ever so little. "We shall see them then for we, too, are of the house of David."

"We are on our way to register." Joseph said.

"Register! Census! Even in our own land we must obey the foreigner." The priest spat, so only his companions and Joseph and Mary could see. "Be careful when you go there. Zechariah said it is another Babylon."

Mary looked puzzled.

Joseph asked, "You saw Zechariah after he went to Bethlehem?"

"Yes, Zechariah and his son came back through Jerusalem on his way back to Nain. He joined a caravan going north along the Jordan. The women in the caravan will help with the boy."

They thanked the priests and inched their way back through the jostling and shouting of the Court of Gentiles. Thinking Mary was not right behind him, Joseph stopped. As he turned, Mary bumped into him and grabbed his arm to keep from falling. He reached for her. She had been crying as they squeezed through the crowds. Now in this brief respite she took a breath and exhaled, took another, closed her eyes and eased out the air. She opened her eyes. "So much, so fast," she said. "Elizabeth dead and buried. Zechariah registered and gone. John, baby John, motherless and..." She paused, tired and bewildered. "And what? Motherless and yet an infant. I had so hoped..." Her thought went unfinished.

Joseph recalled his own disappointment when he arrived in Sepphoris and discovered Mary, Little Mary, had left, and, years later, even greater distress when he anticipated the arrival of her family only to learn she was not with them. Now holding her, he knew the hollow in her heart at losing her cousin and her frustration at not getting to see her cousin's son.

"Mary," he said, "on our way back to Nazareth we will visit them." His and Mary's decision about where to live after their son's birth nagged at them, pulling them to Nazareth and pushing them to Bethlehem.

"*If* we go back to Nazareth," Mary finished the thought.

They found their way back to the twins and out away from the Temple. In spite of the crowds Joseph found a room for them in an inn. Because of the crowds he paid three times the usual fee.

THE WALK from Jerusalem south to Bethlehem usually took less than half a day on the up-and-down narrow paths if there were few other travelers. The movement of so many throughout Judea for the census made passage slower on the narrowest parts of the trail as Joseph let others pass, those heading north as well as faster travelers going south like them. Mary told Joseph her time was close, "but you already know that," she said to him.

Joseph slowed their pace so the donkey jostled Mary less. They stopped often, employing a routine they had adopted: Joseph helped Mary from the donkey, she walked back and forth for awhile, James looked for wild berries and Joses gave the animals a drink.

As evening neared they saw their destination in the distance. "The home of our ancestors," Joseph announced to his family.

Outside the gates of the city a temporary caravansary had grown up. A dozen or more tents formed a large circle with open space inside the ring where camels, donkeys, oxen and goats slept or drank from troughs within reach of their tethers. Three fires scattered among the tents heated flat stones on which women baked bread and cooked soups and stews in pottery bowls. The smells of the spicy fare merged with the stench of close-quartered animals to turn stomachs and shut down lungs.

Mary's face had taken on the colorless hue of her veil. "I'm all right," she said to a concerned Joseph.

A man holding a stringed purse approached Joseph as the family paused on the outer edge of the site. "Welcome. We have space for two more groups, or three if they're thin." He laughed at what he thought was funny and pointed to open spaces between the pegs that held animal tethers and tents. There was nothing to keep the animals from sharing those spaces.

Joseph said, "My wife will give birth soon, tonight we believe. Do you know of a midwife nearby?"

"Not here; inside the city if you can find them. Compared to what you will find in there, this camp is a spacious palace fit for a king."

"Is there a tent or a place where my wife can have a little privacy?"

"The tents have two or three families in each, men and women together. Children, too. Look around. If you see a private space I will rent it to you."

"We will look inside the gates." Joseph led his family through the crowd. What had been streets the last time he had come to Bethlehem, had become a camp site. James and Joses looked wide-eyed at the crowds unlike anything they had ever seen. The family found its way from inn to inn until they reached one on the western edge of the city. It was arranged much like a caravansary they had stopped at, except instead of tents on the outer ring there was a series of rooms beneath a flat wooden roof. Tents and tentless sleeping spaces littered the roof.

Joseph said to Mary, "I will go and inquire. Sooner or later we will come to where God wants his son to be born." He went to the innkeeper while the rest of the family waited.

The innkeeper pointed to a corner of the inn. "We have one enclosed room in that corner." Ropes were wrapped around the posts and fastened to the roof beams in that section of the inn.

"I will take a look," Joseph said. He inspected the posts and the beams above them and returned to the keeper. "That section of roof will come tumbling down, if not tonight then soon. What other space do you have?" He explained Mary's imminent delivery and their desire for privacy and preference for having a midwife with them.

"You are welcome to stay wherever you find a space to your liking. As for a midwife, one used to live on the other side of the city."

"My wife is strong, but I don't want her to have to deliver in a crowd."

The innkeeper pulled his cloak closer around him to thwart the chill that came with a setting sun, took a few steps toward the inn's gate, and peered toward it. James and

Joses huddled close to Mary who leaned against the donkey. The man turned back to Joseph.

"Not more than two hundred feet from our outer wall I have a stable built into the hillside. It is not much but it is private and it is yours if you want to rent it. Move the sleepy cow you find there. The hens will come back if you shoo them away so don't waste your time."

Joseph thanked the keeper and led Mary and the twins in the direction the innkeeper pointed. Outside the inn was a cluster of homes, each joined to the next, some with windows and others without, with roofs of different heights and doors that didn't fit. An oil lamp burned in every window. Bethlehem indeed was crowded. What might have recently been an open courtyard now held a large three-sided stall in one half, and a dozen tents in the other.

"That place doesn't look as private as you said," Joses said as he peered into the stable as if studying its occupants.

Joseph said, "We have farther to go. He said to go to the stable built into the side of a hill."

Their stable was dark. Its open front allowed animals to wander in and, they hoped, smells to wander out. Joseph struck a flame and lit a lamp he took from their supplies. The twins repositioned the animals already there, brought their animals into one stall, spread clean straw in the stalls where the family would sleep, and fashioned a large mat of folded blankets and covers for Mary. At Mary's request, they cleaned and filled a feeding trough with more clean straw and a blanket from Mary's bundle, and set it next to Mary's mat. The hens flitted from stall to stall and flew or trudged up to rafters where they had a clear view of the stable's new tenants.

Mary reminded James where to find the food that was left. He divided it so everyone had something. Mary deferred. Before long he and Joses collapsed into their tunics and blankets in a small stall.

Mary lay down on the mat. Joseph put blankets under and over her and her cloak around her.

"Thank you, dear husband." She moved to one side of the mat and patted a spot beside her. "Here. I want you near me." She reminded him of what he was to do when the time came.

Joseph sat on the mat facing her and reached under the blanket, feeling for her feet. He held one by the heel, massaged its sole, flexed her toes and kneaded her instep and ankle.

She took a deep breath and exhaled through pursed lips. "You make the miles drift away." Her shoulders lay back, she clasped her hands on her stomach and continued to breathe deeply. "I should be caressing your feet; you walked all the way." She slid her foot from his hand and replaced it with her other foot. "One more and then you must sleep. Later you will be busy." She smiled her knowing smile.

"Bringing you comfort arouses my heart more than even your caress might." For the first time in days Joseph felt himself relax along with her.

He watched her gaze sweep the stable, from the simple roof, to the straw tied in bundles in the far corner, to the hens snuggled in nests wherever they chose. She cocked her ear at the deep snoring from the cow and the ox. They heard not a sound from James or Joses.

"Look," she said. A large pottery bowl near the twins' stall held a growing rock rose plant with thin branches stretching up. "Our couch, too, so green and lovely; our beams are cedars, our rafters cypresses."

She closed her eyes. The smile stayed on her lips.

As he watched her he recalled his Mama's screams at the

birth of his brothers, screams of pain and fear. Her pain did not end at James' birth; perhaps that was a signal to Miriam the midwife that she had to deliver yet again. After Joses' birth, he and his Poppa stood outside their house and they did not hear another cry or plea or joyful noise from her again, no doubt another sign, one less joyful.

Now he wondered if giving birth would make Mary cry out like his Mama did, or wail like Chava did when he stood with Efron outside the young couple's home. His Poppa was worried and brave and prayerful. Efron was frightened—and also seventeen. He became prayerful when Chava delivered their second and third and fourth.

How will he respond, he wondered. Without a midwife, a bride's mother, or even a neighbor, he had no choice. Mary had taught him and brought everything the midwife in Nazareth told her to bring. She had arranged it all on the extra tunic that lay beside them now.

He realized he was not looking at anything even though his eyes were open.

Mary took his hand. "My mother used to tell me I was preoccupied. Now I see I am not the only one."

Joseph nodded agreement. He got up and went to where the boys' were sleeping. Joses had thrown off his covers and had snuggled against James. Joseph rearranged the boys and their blankets to protect them against the cold night air that flowed into the open stable, uneasy that there was nothing else he could do.

He returned to her side.

Mary said, "We need not worry, Joseph. We are doing as the Lord directed. We have made all the preparations we could. Everything else is up to him. Any pain vanishes in this: we are giving birth to the son of God." She pointed to her heart. "Abide with me and all will be well."

CHAPTER 8

"Joseph," Mary whispered.

"I'm here, Mary."

"It is time."

Joseph rose, lit a lamp, saw that the twins slept undisturbed, rearranged for the third time the clean cloths just as the midwife had advised, and unsheathed his sharpest blade. He did what Mary had taught him.

No Miriam came. No Chava lived nearby. An open stable with straw bedding replaced the neat home with new wool curtains. Where Mama Rachel had come to childbirth after weeks of confinement and poor health, Mary glowed, still strong after a week on a donkey. No long wails of fear and pain, but short breaths of effort and longing.

Three hours later Joseph rejoiced at the birth of the son of God. "Sons are a gift from the Lord, a blessing, the fruit of the womb."

Joseph cleaned and wrapped the infant in the swaddling Mary had saved for this moment. The child had his mother's dark, cheerful eyes, waves of deep brown hair, and amber skin, but more than that he had her power to draw Joseph to himself. Joseph held him close before passing him to Mary as she lay on her makeshift mat, forming a cradle with her arm to support him while he nursed. For some time the infant alternated between sucking and sleeping until he was satisfied. When he stayed asleep with no more rooting at the air, Joseph eased him from Mary's side and laid him in the manger.

Mary spoke in whispers. "Joseph, we have a child. What we once thought was not our calling has come to pass."

"The Lord has blessed our consecration and made it a home for his son."

Their peaceful quiet became joyful noise as two men wearing sheepskin shawls appeared at the entrance to the stable. "Look. It is true," the taller one, holding a staff, said to the other, "just as they announced to us."

James and Joses awoke, wrapped themselves in their tunics, and crept close to Joseph as they flicked their gaze from the sleeping baby to the strangers.

The tall shepherd approached Joseph and Mary and the infant, while the other one went back to the stable entrance and waved. Seconds later a woman and three children appeared.

"They said a savior has been born ...," said the taller shepherd.

"And he'd be lying in a manger wrapped in swaddling," said the other.

The woman and children stepped close to the manger, behind the two men. Many more shepherds filled the entrance.

Joseph drew closer to the child, fearful for his safety as the growing throng crowded into the small stable.

Mary looked up at him. "Don't worry, Joseph. Our baby has come to us and also to all people."

Joseph relaxed. "It is hard for me to fathom it." He turned to the shepherds. "Who told you about the infant?"

"Voices from the clouds told us that in our city of David a newborn is the Messiah and Lord," said the tall shepherd.

The smallest child spoke up. "I heard it first. A single voice. When he got our attention there was a whole flock of them. All over the sky."

Another child said, "I heard the singing first. They sang, 'Glory to God in the Highest.' I was scared."

The smallest child peered into the manger. "He's awfully small to be a Messiah."

Joseph stepped closer to the little shepherd boy. "He won't always be so small."

The little child nodded in response while he kept looking at the infant.

The band of shepherds stayed for some time, mesmerized by the infant who, having awakened, cast his gaze from visitor to visitor.

The woman spoke to the others in a whisper. "The child needs sleep and his mother needs rest. Let us go."

The tall shepherd said, "We will go back to the fields and share the good news."

As the shepherds left, Mary motioned Joseph to come closer to her. "Dear husband, you have done a great thing this day."

"It is you who have done the great thing. You have given birth to the son of God who will save his people. What that means I'm not so sure." He tapped his heart.

"Yes, with the power of God I have brought his son to life, and you did this with me."

He watched the child sleep for a few moments and then stroked his wife's cheek. "Rest now, my sweet."

"We have done what the Lord asked of us." She looked deep into Joseph's eyes, the way she had done when he first held her in Sepphoris. "Today we have finished the easy part."

~

DURING THE NEXT week registrants went back to their homes and new arrivals replaced them in every inn and house in David's city. Joseph convinced the innkeeper that he should repair the damaged roof and posts in exchange for a stipend and the use of one of the houses behind the inn. By the end of the week Bethlehem eased toward normal.

On the eighth day after Yeshua's birth, the family's new neighbors came to witness the child's circumcision. As members of the house of David, neighbors were cousins, and cousins were brothers and sisters. They talked among themselves while all waited for the rabbi.

"Does another rabbi live nearby?" Joseph asked a few men whispering together.

"If we had another, he, too, would be here."

When Joseph told Mary what he had learned, she told him, "You have witnessed the ritual seventy times. We can wait no longer."

Joseph honed his best knife to a fine edge. Mary held the wide-awake infant as she watched Joseph prepare for the cutting. In an instant his steady hand sliced the skin. Mary winced at the blood dripping onto a cloth. The infant shuddered, held his breath for a moment, and wailed. Now that he had made the cut, Joseph's hands shook as he realized the pain he inflicted on a baby while fulfilling the law. The howl stopped as abruptly as it had started. Joseph saw in the baby's dark eyes forgiveness and understanding.

As the visitor had told him many months earlier, Joseph now declared, "His name is 'Yeshua.'" His gaze went from Yeshua to Mary whose look signaled a similar recollection: "Yeshua is his name."

In the weeks following, Joseph searched for work in and around their new city, James worked with him and Joses went to the fields to see the shepherd children who had come to the stable. "We live in a house now," Joseph heard him tell the children when they repaid his visit.

Mary baked and cooked what Joseph's labor earned, and delighted in watching the growing Yeshua. "He lets me know when he is hungry or wet," she told Joseph more than once.

As they prepared for the short trip to Jerusalem for Yeshua's upcoming presentation in the Great Temple, Mary said to Joseph, "David's City is good for us."

"On most days Bethlehem offers a peaceful security. We are getting to know more neighbors but I have found little work. Bethlehem has many masons and carpenters—good for Jerusalem, not encouraging for us."

"It will get easier as people see the quality of your work." She caressed his arm. "Living here in Bethlehem will mean we can go to Jerusalem for every feast. Yeshua won't always be a baby so traveling will get easier." Her tone conveyed less conviction than her words suggested.

She continued, "The Lord will provide for us whether we live in Bethlehem, Jerusalem or Nazareth."

"He provides for us by giving us the ability to provide

for ourselves," Joseph said. He read compassion and worry on her face. "Mary, I have the same concern as you."

"Zechariah and John?"

"Zechariah is not a young man. For him to have to care for the child...," he paused.

"For him, for both of them, we should return to Nazareth," Mary said.

"In case something happens to Zechariah, we must be near them. After we present Yeshua let us go directly to Nazareth."

She took Joseph's hand. "Your father named you 'Poppa' to two children. The Lord made you Poppa to a third. Who knows, John might become a fourth."

THE ROUTE from Bethlehem north to Jerusalem brought Joseph and his family back through hill country that grew steeper as they neared the Holy City. The Temple, standing high on Mount Moriah, drew travelers' attention even from a distance. With census registration now complete, the usual crowd of pilgrims and traders filled the areas outside the Temple's many gates and in its courts. In the noisy outer Court of Gentiles, larger by far than several village synagogues standing side by side, money changers shouted from behind their tables to get the attention of those going into the Temple. Joseph traded coins he had earned in exchange for Tyrian shekels that, according to the Law, he would have to use to purchase sacrificial animals.

Joseph bought two pigeons for the temple sacrifice from an animal seller. "Not what we planned," he whispered to Mary.

'We are fulfilling the Law as much as if we shed the blood of the perfect lamb," Mary said.

At that Joses cringed. Joseph's arm on his shoulder offered some comfort and steered him away from the animal sellers.

James carried the small wooden cage with the two birds. Mary held Yeshua who turned from left to right, from back to front, seeming to examine every corner and every passerby. The family moved through the crowds and into an inner court, far smaller than the first. In this Court of Women music and singing and shouts of praise came from every corner, the tenor and spirit of the sounds more joyful and uplifting than they had heard forty-one days earlier.

An old man approached them, with arms reaching forward. He looked on the infant and then at Mary and in an instant swept Yeshua from her into his arms, raised him aloft and then lowered him to his chest, holding him close.

As Joseph was about to protest, the man raised his eyes heavenward and prayed aloud, "Now, Lord, you may dismiss your servant in peace. My eyes have seen your salvation."

Moved from concerned to amazed, Joseph looked to Mary, whose face registered the same astonishment without the concern.

The man again held Yeshua high in his arms and turned his attention to Mary. "This child, this very child I tell you, is destined for the fall and the rise of many in Israel." He lowered the child. With kindly eyes he looked deep into Mary's being. "And, you my dear lady!" He interrupted himself with a silent prayer, turning from her and shaking his head as if not wanting to go on. As Joseph started toward him to regain Yeshua, he turned back to Mary. "A sword shall pierce your very soul." He hung his head.

Mary paled, looked at Yeshua and then at Joseph.

Joseph bristled at the thought of injury to Mary. He reached for Yeshua to return him to Mary. The old man relinquished him, looking on Mary with sorrow.

Joseph said, "What do you mean, 'a sword'? Is my wife to die by the sword?"

The man disappeared into the crowd.

Joseph huddled his family around him. The twins stood on either side of Mary, one arm around her, the other reaching up to Yeshua. They looked up to Joseph.

A group of women danced their way around the Court, pausing to sing praise. "All sheep and oxen, beasts of the field, birds of the air, fish of the sea." They stopped singing and continued their dance to the far side of the Court.

James and Joses now watched their every move, loosening their grip on Mary.

The women, now on the farthest side of the Court, interrupted their dance again. They sang out, "O Lord, our Lord, how awesome is your name through all the earth!"

"Stay close to Mary," Joseph said, looking down at his boys.

He turned to Mary and asked, "Do you think he does that to everyone?"

She shook her head. "He knew who was in my arms. 'The rise and fall of Israel' is all about the Messiah." She shook her head again, puzzling. "How could he have known about Yeshua?"

"We know Yeshua is the son of God. We'll find out what that means when we are supposed to. Perhaps Yeshua brought this on by his very presence," Joseph said.

"If you're right, we will see more of this." Her look said she was pondering what had happened. "That man and what he said frighten me."

119

"Me too. Not for myself but for you. I want to know what he meant. I abhor the thought of someone or something hurting you, of piercing your heart." He squeezed his family tighter, his arms around all of them.

A lone voice, a woman's voice, called from right behind Joseph. The family turned to her, an older woman, as she exhorted all the people in the Court, drawing attention to herself and then redirecting it to Yeshua. When the crowd had quieted, she exclaimed, "This child is for the redemption of Jerusalem. Blessed be the Lord."

Recalling their recent encounter, Joseph waited for a more dire pronouncement. None came. The smiling woman raised her face to the heavens, gave thanks and left them.

"Who else is coming?" asked James.

Joseph looked around the Court. The flute music and singing started up again. A few in the crowd continued looking at the family that had drawn the attention of the elderly woman.

"No one else," Joseph said.

Mary said, "What you said, Joseph—by his presence alone the people come to him. Is that possible?"

Joseph shrugged. "Some day we might know." He eased his grip on his family and guided them to the entrance to the Men's Court, smaller by half than the Court of Women. He reached for Yeshua and spoke to the twins. "One of you will stay here with Mary and one will come with me."

Joses stepped closer to Mary. "I'll stay."

With Yeshua in Joseph's arms and the cage with the pigeons in James's, they advanced through the Men's Court to the entrance to the Court of Priests. There a priest took the pigeons, prayed silently over Yeshua and entered where Joseph and James were not allowed. Joseph breathed out a sigh, pleased they had not drawn more attention to Yeshua.

~

AFTER THEY FULFILLED the law they walked exhausted to a house Joseph had rented outside the Temple district. He learned of a caravan going north along the Jordan four days hence. He said to Mary, "We have enough money for food and lodging. The boys and I can gather fruit along the way." He patted the backs of his growing fruit pickers.

The little house contained a narrow wooden door that did not quite fill the doorway, a window opening with a wool blanket covering it, one small table with four chairs and no sleeping mats. "We don't want to use someone else's sleeping mats anyway," said Mary. On the table sat a half-filled oil lamp, a half filled oil skin, a large empty water jug and three clay pots of different sizes, all blackened from use. "Good, we have pots for cooking and won't have to unpack everything we own." Behind the house was a common courtyard with a fire pit on which several clay pots sat steaming. "And a place to put the pots," she added.

They unloaded their blankets and sleeping covers.

After they had eaten their dinner, Joseph opened a scroll. James and Joses were staring at the doorway. There stood three men arrayed in splendor unlike anything Joseph had ever seen, either in the grandeur of Sepphoris or the magnificence of Jerusalem, the crossroads of their world. Adorned in silk robes and rich leather sandals, they entered and, without hesitation or question, they knelt and bowed their heads before Yeshua, who had fallen asleep on his cloth mat.

From their robes they brought out gifts which they left before the child: a jeweled box with vials of aromatic myrrh, a polished urn of frankincense, and a silk purse of gold coins. Joseph looked to Mary, whose look repeated what she had told him when the shepherds arrived: "Our baby has come to us and also to everyone else." The visitors stayed on their knees for some time.

When they stirred, Joseph asked, "How did you know where to find us?"

One of the visitors rose. "We consider the movement of the stars with great attention. During the past months a most unusual star arose in our western sky, growing brighter by the week. We chose to follow it, and as we did it moved farther west. The traders' caravans were noisy, but when we had to travel alone, the thought of bandits frightened me."

The other visitors also rose. A round little man, robed in a cloak as purple as a plum, took up their story. "We also study whatever writings we can acquire. I had read about a new king of the Jews who would be born in a stable in Bethlehem."

Mary and Joseph exchanged knowing looks, showing their shared astonishment.

The third visitor, covered in yellow and gold that glowed against his skin as dark as Mary's hair, said, "I put the two findings together. The star led us to Bethlehem as I expected."

The first visitor, adorned in the crimson of ripe pomegranates, continued, "In Bethlehem we inquired of many innkeepers. One told us of a family who stayed in his stable and the woman gave birth there, but he knew nothing of a newborn king of the Jews. He described your family and said you had come here to Jerusalem with your infant for a temple observance."

The purple-clad visitor said, "So we came here and inquired of the priests at the Temple. They, too, had not heard of a newborn king but they told us that when he comes he will be born in Bethlehem not Jerusalem. One of them recited a prophecy: 'And you little Bethlehem, too small to be among the clans of Judah, from you shall come one who is to be a ruler in Israel.' We told them we first traveled to Bethlehem following the star, and then followed the keeper's advice to come here to Jerusalem. While we were inquiring about you, your King Herod sent a courier with an invitation for us to visit him. We are to inform him where we found you so he can come and pay homage as well."

Mary motioned to Joseph to invite the men for a meal.

"We are most grateful," said the red-clad visitor. "It is already three days since we received the invitation and we dare not anger him who expects us to return to him."

Anger, indeed! Joseph recalled what his father had told him of the jealous and wicked Herod.

As their guests left, Joseph accompanied them to the doorway and watched them untether their camels and lead them away. Not far from the house, a man in a cloudless-blue tunic approached the three men. At whatever he told them, they shook their heads, raised their fists in the air and hunched their shoulders. When he departed from them, they mounted their camels, retraced their steps past Joseph's house and rode on in the opposite direction.

Joseph turned back to Mary and the three boys.

Mary said, "I remember my father read that prophecy to us, the one the visitors repeated."

"I heard it, too, in the synagogue." Like most of their Nazarene neighbors, Jacob's family had few scrolls: sections of the Torah and some of the writings and psalms. As a result, many of the stories came to them from lessons in the synagogue. Mary's father, like other rabbis, had accumulated a collection of scrolls.

"Salome asked Father if it meant that women in Nazareth and other villages throughout Judea could not bear the son of God because they lived in the wrong place. Father told her, 'If the Lord wants the savior born in Bethlehem, he will make sure his mother goes there.'"

Mary gave Joseph her knowing look.

"Yes, here we are. I shudder to think I tried to get the soldier's permission for you to stay in Nazareth," Joseph said.

"The Lord had other plans," said Mary.

Joseph gathered the gifts the visitors had brought. "Too bad we did not have these generous visitors before we came here to present Yeshua."

"Yes, we could have offered the gift we had planned on. But it is all right, Joseph. Now we have enough for the trip to Nazareth even if you don't find fruit along the way."

Joseph agreed. He could not get his father's warning out of his head.

"What troubles you, my husband?" Mary asked.

"Herod is not to be trusted. Thank God we will soon leave Jerusalem."

∾

TWO DAYS later James and Joses came into the house carrying a heavy jug they had filled at a nearby well.

James motioned to Joseph to come to help them with the jug. "Poppa," he whispered.

Joses blurted out, "People at the well were talking, Poppa. Scary talk." His lips quivered, his eyes squinted. Fear showed in his young, taut neck. "Yeshua, hide Yeshua," he shouted.

Joseph wrapped his arms around the two of them. "What is it?"

No longer able to speak in a whisper, James cried out, "All the people at the well said so. Herod's soldiers have sharpened their knives. They have set out to kill every boy baby."

CHAPTER 9

*J*n the main room of their little rented house in Jerusalem, Joseph demonstrated what he and the boys would do if the need arose. Mary and Yeshua had fallen asleep in the one small bedroom. The oil lamp stood unlit on the table for night had not fully come. Cooking smells and smoke hung in the still air. More sounds than usual in their neighborhood, the sounds of men running and speaking and breathing, made Joseph wonder if someone had already heard or seen soldiers in the village. Not yet, he decided, for he would have heard shouting as well.

"We tie up the blanket like this." Joseph tied the four corners of the blanket to one another and slung it on Joses' back. To James he said, "Put straw and swaddling into the blanket sack and then put the baby on top, like this." He put several stones into the sack. "We'll practice with these. They're about the same weight as Yeshua. Then we'll put a flat of bread on top of him to hide him; it won't hurt him."

They repeated the drill until James and Joses could do it

without any help from Joseph or any word spoken between them.

Night had come.

"Poppa, do you think we'll really have to do this with Yeshua?" Joses asked.

"I hope not but we will prepare ourselves and leave the rest in God's hands."

"What if Yeshua cries?" asked James.

"We can't do anything about that so we'll leave it with God."

Joseph rested his hands on the boys' shoulders and drew them close. "Tonight the three of us will take turns keeping watch. Herod's soldiers will try to frighten all of Jerusalem with their loud commands and shouted curses so we'll hear them coming. When we do hear them you two will put Yeshua in the blanket sack and carry him to the stable. Hide in the straw pile behind the cow. When the soldiers burst into our house they will find only a childless couple asleep."

"How long will we have to stay ready to do this?" asked James, struggling to hide his fear.

"Two nights here and then we'll join the caravan to Nazareth. The two of you might have to hide Yeshua along the way." To ease their fears he added, "And think, in a few days we'll be back in Nazareth."

Joses said, "I miss my sheep. I'm glad we're going home."

"Going home always feels right." Joseph released the boys. "Now get to sleep. I'll take the first watch."

He went to Mary and Yeshua, and watched them sleeping. *Rescue me from my enemies, my God; lift me out of the reach of my foes.* They had to keep this special baby safe from harm.

He set a chair inside the doorway. Before sitting on it he went outside. Dark clouds hid the stars and moon. Their

Jerusalem neighborhood slept, the quiet broken only by the howl of a wolf in the nearby hills. Perhaps it was all well talk, no more than a rumor. Could even Herod be so vile as to order the death of newborns? Joseph walked past the next house and the next and stopped, looked in every direction, and held his breath to listen without interference.

Nothing. No sound. No movement. No light. The jagged streets of Jerusalem, often ending at the side of a house or a stable, made it impossible to see beyond three or four houses. From what he could see, not a soul was about, so he turned back toward his house, stopping every few steps, listening, looking. He winced at the mental image of soldiers slicing babies. All of a sudden he felt someone behind him and turned, his hands flexed and ready to defend himself.

"Much has happened since last we talked," said the familiar stranger. Even a night like this could not dull the cloudless blue of his cloak.

"Much indeed." Joseph looked down, drew a deep breath, closed his eyes and eased out the breath. The stranger's past visits had taught him he could rely on what the messenger told him.

"Get yourselves up, take the child and his mother, and go to Egypt. Stay there until I tell you. Herod is searching for the child to kill him. Go now to the Great Sea and turn south along the coast. Stay away from Bethlehem; fly like the sun in the sky."

Joseph looked up to face his visitor. He had gone.

Joseph entered the house, went to his boys and woke them. "James, Joses, get up."

They stretched, rubbed their eyes and looked from Joseph to each other.

"We must go now," Joseph said.

"Did the soldiers come? Did they hurt Yeshua?" asked James as he pulled on his tunic.

"They haven't come, not yet anyway. A messenger warned us they are coming so we must get out. Bundle everything for the cart."

James picked up the blanket and started to fold it the way they had practiced.

"We don't need that yet. Put the blanket and our supplies into the cart. Joses, fetch the donkey and secure the cart to the ox. Quick and quiet."

Joseph entered the bedroom. Mary stirred. "What is it, Joseph?" She looked toward the still dark window.

Joseph related the messenger's warning. She rose, bundled up food and belongings and packed the gifts from the generous travelers in a leather bag, which she wrapped in a blanket. She picked up Yeshua, snuggling him against her and tying the sling that would keep him close to her.

Joseph helped Mary and Yeshua onto the donkey, put his tool sack into the cart and led the ox at the head of the group. Joses held the tether and stroked the donkey's neck every now and then. James walked at the rear. Joseph turned his head toward his family. "Lord, show us the way."

They responded in one voice, "Lead us on a level path because of our enemies."

The traders' route to Ashkelon and the Great Sea brought them southwest through the hills before it turned straight west across the coastal plains. The road to the south would have saved time getting to Egypt but the messenger had told Joseph which route to take to avoid Bethlehem.

By the time a muted sun rose behind them they had traveled ten hilly miles from Jerusalem. Toward mid-morning, as he guided the donkey around the last of the hills, Joses cried out, "Look, Poppa." He pointed west.

In the distance along the plain stood a caravansary, offering the promise of a midday rest and meal. As they came nearer, the smell of camels and open fires sickened and welcomed them. The open gates, symbolic of the safest and busiest hours of the day, gave them full view of the interior and its bustling commerce.

"Stop," said Joseph to his family. "Wait here." He walked forward forty paces or so, strained to get a better look and then returned to his apprehensive family. He said, "There are three horses standing inside the gate, not pack horses but saddled, but not Roman saddles." The pendants on the horses of Roman soldiers distinguished them just as the uniforms did the soldiers. Traders in a caravan rode on camels or donkeys unless the beasts had full loads, in which case the traders walked. Their own people and other peasants could not afford fast but hungry horses. That meant the three horses belonged to Herod's henchmen, whom they would have to pass whether they entered the caravansary or passed it by.

Joseph said, "James, prepare the blanket as we practiced."

James took the blanket from the sack in the ox-cart and spread in on the ground.

Mary caressed Yeshua's sleeping face. "Stay sleeping, my precious son." She handed him to Joseph and looked again at the baby. "Please," she whispered. She raised her eyes and prayed just loud enough for her family to hear. "When you lie down and sleep, may the Lord preserve you to rise again."

Joseph placed Yeshua on the straw and swaddling in the blanket. James covered him with another blanket and put two wide flats of bread on top, and then tied the blanket corners together. Joses gripped the knots in both hands and eased the sack onto his back.

"We will walk past the caravansary," directed Joseph as he took the donkey's tether and the long rope guiding the ox behind.

"Won't that get their attention?" Mary asked. "Doesn't everyone stop, at least for food or water?" Her dark eyes revealed a fear that comes from threat and a confidence that comes from trust.

Joses circled the donkey, following Joseph's hint that movement would help keep the infant asleep.

James walked beside Joses, ready to take his turn with the blanket bundle.

Joseph said, "They will notice us but we have no choice. If we turn back they will be even more suspicious. If we enter through the gates, they will wait for us to settle into place and then they will discover Yeshua." He took Mary's hand as he prodded the donkey. "We don't know what will come of this ruse, so we will leave it in God's hands."

They walked at their usual pace, the twins with their precious burden several yards in front of Mary on the donkey, with Joseph alongside her and the ox and cart in the rear. Fifty yards from the caravansary they could see individual people, not just a crowd. At thirty yards they stole glances at the dealing and eating. At twenty they could see the faces of three soldiers of Herod going from group to group, engaging in animated conversation. The shouted curses of the tallest one reached the family.

Mary said, "So angry. What can they be so afraid of?"

"They fear Herod," Joseph said. He nodded toward Joses' blanket sack. "And Herod fears a baby." He saw Mary try to hide her worry with a tender smile. He returned it.

"Our baby," she said.

"If Herod only knew he has nothing to fear."

They reached the gate, a gate so wide it seemed to take

hours to walk past it. Mary let out a breath as if she had not breathed for those same hours. They were beyond the gate when they heard a roar.

"Stop. You there!"

Joseph said to his family. "We must stop. Be brave. The God of our father Abraham is with us."

Joses looked like he was about to go back to Mary and Joseph. Joseph whispered, "Boys, stay as you are in front of us."

Three soldiers approached. Joseph turned the donkey so they could see that Mary carried nothing but a small food sack. Her robe hid the leather bag resting across the donkey's back.

"So great a hurry that you cannot rest?" asked the one whose angry shout they had heard.

Joseph picked up the leather sack and removed a hammer and a set of chisels. "I go to find work."

"You look for work? You are walking in the wrong direction. With all the building that goes on in Jerusalem you would find work there if you know how to use these tools." He studied Joseph and took the sack from him.

Joseph said, "True, Jerusalem has many building projects." He watched the soldier take his tools from the sack and one by one drop them to the ground. "Jerusalem also has many tektons."

The other two soldiers headed back to the caravansary.

The shouter looked toward the two boys and back to Joseph. "Be on your way."

Joseph bent to gather up his tools and watched the shouter disappear inside the gate.

James and Joses walked back, close to Joseph. Then from inside Joses' bundle came a cry.

Mary reached for Joses and the bundle, but then,

catching herself, dropped her hands to the donkey's withers. With every ounce of restraint she could muster, she turned toward Joseph and away from Yeshua.

Joseph slipped one foot behind James and pushed him, knocking him to the ground.

The shouter reappeared at the gate.

Joseph whispered to James, "Cry out." He pretended to wrestle James onto his back.

James gave out a cry, "No. Poppa, no."

The man at the gate gave a loud laugh and shouted. "Well done, mason. A boy's either coming from trouble or heading into it." He turned back and again disappeared.

Joseph helped James to his feet. "You did well, James."

Mary reached down and ruffled his hair. "James, you saved your baby brother."

Joseph led the family more quickly than they had walked all day. When they were far enough away from the caravansary and out of sight of its fearful visitors, he dug Yeshua out of the blanket sack and handed him up to Mary.

LATE THE THIRD DAY, tired and hungry, they reached the open city of Ashkelon on the Great Sea. The seaside market yielded fish large and small, fresh and salted; dates, whole and pureed; and pomegranates as well as finely ground wheat flour.

"Buy here. The last market with wheat. From here to Egypt nothing but barley," said the woman with the weights and the scale and two small children at her feet. She eagerly exchanged a large basket of food for one of the smaller coins given to Yeshua by the visitors from the East.

Opening onto the market was a large inn, with two

levels of rooms and tents in the open space, all within the protective walls. After three days of hard hiking, Joseph and the family enjoyed a day of rest in the inn. The fires and clay ovens in the courtyard allowed Mary to prepare food for an evening meal and for travel as she had not been able to do since they left Jerusalem. She soaked the salted fish in goat's milk to reduce the salt. Mary said, "This way Joses won't wrinkle his nose when he eats it. And the pureed dates will balance the salt that remains." With the fish immersed in milk, she rinsed a pot of seaweed in fresh water and kneaded a mixture of barley and wheat dough.

Even though the free city of Ashkelon provided legal protection from Herod, there was no deterrent to Herod's motivated killers dragging their prey beyond the city and there claim the authority to do their wicked deeds. Thus Joseph and his family made every effort to keep the infant quiet and hidden in their small corner room until the next day when they again packed their few belongings and cooing infant.

The road along the coast of the Great Sea ran southwest from Ashkelon past Gaza and Rafiah to where the coast turned westward to Pelusium, which a prophet had once dubbed 'the strength of Egypt.' In that old city they passed a synagogue and, recognizing a community of their own people, decided to spend the night.

Joseph saw a man coming out of the synagogue. The man stopped and struggled to pick up three long planks of turpentine lumber he apparently had left outside when he went to pray. Joseph approached him. "What are you building? Do you need a carpenter's help?"

"My roof is turning to mush, the sun and the rain come in. I have never fixed a roof before, so, yes, I need help."

Joseph showed the man his tools: a drill, a saw, a

hammer, a drop line, among others.

"If I could afford to pay for help, you're the man I would hire," said the man. "Either you know what to do or you do a good job pretending."

Joseph introduced himself and learned that Daniel and his family had come to Pelusium from Jericho a year earlier.

"We may never be wealthy here but we don't have a pretend king ready to take away the little we have."

They came to agreement that Joseph would repair Daniel's roof and in exchange he and his family would have a room in Daniel's house.

"Come, you will share our meal," said Daniel.

Staying with their own people provided a sense of security even though, like generations of their ancestors, they had become the foreigners.

JOSEPH COMPLETED the work on Daniel's house within a week, by which time he had other small jobs waiting for him. He rented a wooden house with two rooms that opened onto a large courtyard with a central fire pit and oven, all shared with a dozen other families. There with their children around them, a husband and his wife sat or stood together as they would not do outside the wall of the courtyard. In Nazareth or Bethlehem the courtyard was as public a place as the street. In Pelusium neighbors treated the courtyard as an extension of each family's home. Watching another couple or another family in the privacy of the courtyard was as forbidden as peering through a neighbor's window.

Although Joseph and Mary had not chosen Egypt, they settled into Pelusium and its different ways while they lived in wait. Their ancestors had handed down a talent for waiting.

As a one-year old, Yeshua followed whichever brother happened to be nearer. He laughed when they laughed. They tickled him just to watch him laugh, laugh so hard that he went from sitting on the ground to lying on it. He would roll over, get onto hands and knees and try to get himself up from all fours, only to wobble for a few seconds, freeze as if suspended in motion, and then collapse onto his rear. This gave James great fits of laughter, which in turn set Yeshua into a fit of his own. When they quieted down, Yeshua pleaded what sounded like, "Play me, Jah," until one of the big brothers tickled him and started the routine all over again. The exchange never failed to entertain Joseph and Mary.

"I wonder what has become of Zechariah and John. Life cannot be easy for them," Mary said to Joseph one evening.

"With no family near them they are on their own. I, too, wonder about them."

"I wonder about my family as well. No one knows where we are so they cannot send word when something happens."

"We don't know if Clopas and Mary have children, or if Salome has married, or if your parents still live in Nazareth. With Clopas and Mary in Capernaum, they might go there, too."

"So we leave them in God's hands," Mary said.

"Yeshua is well and safe. For that we are thankful."

"When we return to Nazareth we will see them all. In the meantime we raise our boys in Egypt."

"There is a great precedent for living in Egypt." Joseph worked his knife, whittling a grizzled stump of grapevine, turning branches into arms and a knot into a joyful face.

They became quiet. Joseph's concern centered on Mary

and Yeshua, James and Joses. He read in Mary's face that her thoughts had stayed with John and Zechariah.

She brushed wood shavings from his beard. "How long will we stay here?"

He thought for a while before answering. "There is great precedent for that as well." He paused to let her think about it, as he continued to whittle.

Her eyes widened: she shook her head. "Not forty years."

He looked at Mary out of the corner of his eye, pretending to hide a smile.

"Joseph, you're not serious." The arches of her brows rose along with her voice.

When Joseph did not reply she asked in a less confident tone, "Are you?"

He shook his head. "No, I'm not." He smiled and touched her hand.

"You can be such a tease. Did you and James inherit that from Jacob or from Rachel?"

"My Mama. She loved to tease my Poppa. I'm sorry she did not get to see how James takes after her."

After a while Joseph said, "We don't know how long we'll have to stay. Many of our people are waiting until the right time to go home."

Mary nodded toward the house at the far end of the courtyard. "Their five children were born here. They grow up knowing Egypt and only Egypt, except for what their parents teach them."

"Many of the children have never been to Jerusalem, not even for the great feast. They have never prayed, 'If I forget you, Jerusalem, may my right hand wither.' They have missed so much and it is not their fault." As he carved eyes into the knot, flecks of wood flew up and stuck to his tunic.

Mary dug the specks out of the fine weave of the fabric

with her finger nail. She said, "If they had someone to lead them, they'd return to our land, to their land. They need a 'Joseph' with or without a dreamy coat."

Joseph laughed. "Or a Moses with a rod," he said.

They both looked at Yeshua, sitting not far from them, entranced by James and Joses, who were spinning small carved gourds, transforming them into wedding dancers.

Mary turned to Joseph and lowered her voice. "Do you think this could be the son of God's mission, that he be the next leader to bring our people back from this foreign land?"

"Moses and Joseph were saviors. We know our Yeshua will be a savior. God has brought us here for some reason and I can think of no better reason than for Yeshua to lead our people home."

"Joseph, I wish I knew."

"So do I, but in the meantime we will await God's call. The messenger told me to trust even when we don't know."

"Perhaps he should have said, '*Especially* when we don't know.'"

As MONTHS PASSED, James joined other boys in walking the half-mile to the Great Sea, often returning with a basket of fish for an evening meal. He frequently spent the day watching the boats ply the coastal waters and return with a great haul. What attracted him more than the fisherman were their boats and the carpenters who built and repaired them. Every boat carpenter had boats waiting for his chisels, tar and oils, and most were eager to tell James about boat work and show him how to repair hulls and masts. And he was eager to share with Joseph all he saw and learned. He told Joseph he wanted to apply his carpentry skills in the boatyards of Pelusium. Many a boat carpenter would employ a twelve-year old apprentice eager to learn and willing to work.

Joses reported that Egyptian sheep had coarser and darker fleece than Nazarene sheep, a finding confirmed by Mary when she spun their wool. Joseph's craft provided well for his family, and here that meant a supply of fresh fish and fruit and spices. If they had chosen to, they could have enjoyed fine linen and silk that they could never acquire in Nazareth. For the first time in her short motherhood, Mary joined other mothers as they watched their toddlers running, flapping and bumping into things, and climbing and falling until they wore themselves out. A formation of four sandstones stood together in the courtyard, of the right size to invite smaller toddlers to climb onto the first and jump or fall back to the ground. Bigger toddlers and little boys pulled themselves up onto the next, until they reached the top of the tallest stone. Reaching this "pinnacle of the temple," as they named it, became a rite of passage from toddler-hood to boyhood.

The women used the stories of Abraham and Isaac, Moses in this very land, David the singing shepherd boy, and Joseph with his special coat, to keep the faith alive in the village's children. Mary shared with Joseph the experience of other women. "They are alone in sharing their faith in their own homes. Their husbands have lost interest in passing on their rites and traditions."

Joseph said, "I hear the same from the husbands. Egypt offers more opportunities to work and then trade for marvels for their ovens and tables, and for adornments for their walls and wives. The men have decided to get all of it."

"I see now what frustrated Moses. When life is easy we

forget our covenant with the Lord," said Mary.

"The one who today calls himself the king in Judea cannot live forever. When he dies our people here will be able to return to Israel and resume the faith of our fathers." Joseph paused in thought. "*If* they choose to return."

"The women say the men enjoy Egyptian life too much to return even to the Holy City."

"We will soon return to Nazareth and from there we will go every year to the Holy City."

Mary said, "We will visit Zechariah and John often so that Yeshua will grow up with his cousin."

If they haven't grown up before we return.

IN THEIR THIRD year in Pelusium, one day Joseph stood alone in the rear of the town's little synagogue. Their fore-fathers, wandering this land for forty years, must have lived with the same sense of anticipation that he now felt deep inside, hoping and trusting that Egypt provided them a temporary home only, all the while living their lives, raising their families, wondering how their homeland was changing in their absence. He had no shortage of work here; the fisherman who needed new oars or the seamstress with a bent spindle did not care whether the man with the tools hailed from Greece or Persia or anywhere in between as long as he shaped and shaved the timbers and bits with skill. He shared a home with the woman he had always loved, cared for the twins who had become his own, and nurtured the son of God; all this fashioned a life easy to appreciate wherever they lay their heads. "God of our fathers, give Zechariah and John the same simple pleasures!" All this and Jerusalem too, would be more than anyone should ask for.

"My soul yearns and pines for the courts of the Lord. Better one day in your courts than a thousand elsewhere."

He felt more than heard someone join him, perhaps a neighbor with the same hopes and prayers and who sought the same brief privacy. When the newcomer came closer, Joseph recognized the cloudless blue of his tunic.

"I've missed you," Joseph said.

"You didn't need me," said the visitor.

Joseph waited for a message. After a while he asked, "How is Yeshua's cousin?"

As in the past the visitor did not answer Joseph's question. "Herod has died. It is safe for you to return to Israel."

"Might we visit Jerusalem before returning to Nazareth?"

"I am a lowly messenger."

Before Joseph could respond the visitor stepped away. When Joseph went outside the synagogue, he shared the news with his neighbors. Some were elated, others reserved and most had something to say. Joseph listened.

"A pox on his house," cried one man.

"A pox is already on his house. How do you think he died?" said another.

"Israel is better off without him."

"Maybe not. Kindness does not exactly bloom in his sons."

"Neither does sanity."

One man added what he had heard from traders. "Old Herod still rules from the grave. At his request the Emperor has divided Israel among the three sons."

"Of course. Someone is always dividing Israel."

"Who rules what?"

"Archeleus the mad man controls Jerusalem, Bethlehem and all of Judea."

"If there was any doubt, the doubt has vanished; we're better off here in the land of fine linen and fresh fish."

Having heard enough, Joseph returned to his home. "Mary, Mary, listen. We can at long last return to the land of our ancestors."

"Jerusalem." She embraced him out of pure joy. "How good to celebrate our God in song. The Lord rebuilds Jerusalem, gathers the dispersed of Israel."

"Let's not forget the harp that goes with the song." They stood holding each other, enjoying a first moment of freedom.

Joseph said in a less joyful tone. "We can't go to Jerusalem. Spice merchants report that Judea is already in chaos, even before the dead king has gone cold. Zealots of every description shout their messages wherever three people gather, be it a well or a synagogue, and create ever greater turmoil among the people. We will return to Galilee where one of the other sons rules. They say Herod Antipas is civil, for the moment."

"*One* of the other sons? How many sons did he leave behind?" Mary asked.

"Three. Travelers say Herod Philip controls the land north and east of the Sea of Galilee, Herod Antipas rules Galilee and the region across the Jordan River, and Archeleus rules Samaria and Judea. The traders say Archeleus will help a friend and kill an enemy today and do the opposite tomorrow. Until the day comes when the Emperor banishes him, the people of Judea and Samaria will live an anxious life."

"Back we go to Nazareth. Do you think Zechariah and John still live in Nain?" She paused, lost for a moment in her thoughts. "May they both still be alive, somewhere! We will visit them, won't we?"

"If we can get to Nazareth, we can visit Nain."

Mary asked, "How will our life in Nazareth be different with Herod's son as ruler? We pray he won't be a threat to Yeshua."

"We won't expect much from him, poor man. They say he is weak and easily led. How could he be otherwise with that murderer for a father? He's more predictable than Archeleus, and has shown no sign of killing infants." He looked at Yeshua climbing the sandstones. "Nor toddlers either."

The family left Pelusium within days, waiting only for Joseph to complete projects he had promised. Although James put off becoming a boatman, he talked of it every time the family passed a boatyard as they journeyed along the coast back through Gaza and the free city of Ashkelon, and then north on the Coastal Plain of Sharon. Because Samaria's port city of Caesarea had grandeur that might attract Archeleus and the uncertainty of his whim, Joseph guided the family northeast away from the coast and across the Great Plain, finally traveling through the familiar hills outside Nazareth. With neither a pregnant Mary nor an infant Yeshua, the trek from Egypt to Nazareth took no longer than the sojourn from Nazareth to Bethlehem. The family that had left three years earlier as a young expectant couple with two young boys now arrived home as Poppa and Mama with two young men and a three-year old eager for the challenges of childhood.

"When the Lord restored the fortunes of Zion, we thought we were dreaming. Our mouths are filled with laughter; our tongues sing for joy," said Joseph, happy to be home.

Neighbors came to greet them as soon as they arrived, with stews and loaves, fruit and sweet cakes. Word spread.

One woman said to Mary, "I'm sorry you were not able to come home last year." She embraced Mary, brought a barley loaf to the table and left without giving Mary a chance to speak to her.

More to herself than to Joseph, Mary said, "I wonder what the neighbor meant." She turned to James, "Would you come walk with me?"

James accompanied Mary to her family's home. A woman with three small boys stood in the yard beside the house, pleased to meet another neighbor. Mary asked if she knew the people who had lived in her house before her.

"The husband, a rabbi, died shortly after we came to Nazareth. My husband helped the wife move to Capernaum and she told us to take over her house."

Mary reached for James, drew him to her and leaned on his strong young shoulders. The woman was still talking although Mary heard not another word. She thanked her, turned, and was in tears by the time she could tell Joseph.

Mary spoke through her sobs. "James, what else did the neighbor woman say?"

James said, "Your mother went to live with Salome and her husband, near her other daughter."

She leaned into Joseph. "And all that time we knew as much of them as they knew of us. My poor mother."

"Your father taught me how to love a child. His love for Mary and Salome and you showed in how he cared for you, in the way he looked at you." Joseph put his arms around Mary, held her close, quieted her sobs, and whispered to her. "His Little Mary became a greater gift with each breath she drew. He knew from the beginning that hers would be a singular life, a life not easy but loving."

She stayed in his arms until her strength returned. "Hear my words, O Lord; listen to my sighs."

CHAPTER 10

"We will go to Capernaum another time. First we must visit Zechariah and John. It would be terrible if they needed us and we did not know it." Mary's sense of urgency regarding her cousins increased after the family's return to Nazareth. As soon after resettling as they could manage, Joseph, Mary and Yeshua walked the six miles southeast to Nain, hoping their cousins still lived there. Their well-traveled donkey made the trip manageable for the young Yeshua.

James and Joses, now thirteen years old and growing in independence, remained at home in Nazareth. James worked with Joseph on plows, tables, chairs, spindles, outside walls, inside walls and whatever in Nazareth needed repair or replacement. It occurred to Joseph that all of a sudden the twins seemed eager to get on with lives of their own. If he and Mary did not have Yeshua, they would soon be alone. It must have been hard for couples like Elizabeth and Zechariah during the years they longed to share their lives and their empty homes with children.

Joses had started to rebuild his flock with the return of his sheep from Simon. Some had survived his three-year absence and Simon offered him several lambs in exchange for his help tending his own large flock. Joses said the shepherd psalm must have been written especially for him. "Shepherd of Israel, listen, the guide of Joseph's flock attends you."

Now Joseph pointed to the horizon in front of them, where a prominent hill appeared among all the lower hills "Look as far as you can see, Yeshua."

"What is it, Poppa? Is it a big hill?" Yeshua stretched as far up as he could on the back of the donkey.

"It is a hill, the Hill of Moreh," Joseph said.

Mary said, "When I was a little girl and my family came to visit Cousin Elizabeth and her husband, we called the hill 'Little Hermon.'"

Yeshua looked at her, brows furrowed and head tilted. "Is there a big Hermon, Mama?"

Mary hid a laugh. "Yes, Yeshua, there is. Mt. Hermon—we can call it Big Hermon—is far away and big and high."

Yeshua looked straight up. "Does it reach heaven?"

"If any mountain can reach heaven, Mt. Hermon can."

Yeshua seemed satisfied with that and went back to peering at the city on the horizon. "What are the white specks on the hill?" Yeshua looked from Joseph on his left, to Mary on his right, and back to the distant hill.

Joseph looked to Mary who gave him her knowing smile. He said to Yeshua, "I'll tell you if you want but it'll be more fun if you figure it out as we get closer."

"I'll keep looking," Yeshua said, eager for the challenge.

After some time Yeshua cried out, "They're not specks, they're houses. Houses I can see from far away."

"Good for you. All those houses make up the city of Nain. Your cousin John lives in one of them," Joseph said.

"Or at least we think he lives there," Mary added.

As they got closer Yeshua kept looking at the city on the slope of the Hill of Moreh. "I can see the whole city. There's no place to hide there."

This brought a smile from Joseph and Mary. She said, "You would have to hide behind the houses if you didn't want to be seen. We are still a mile away and we can see the city and its gate. It's not anything like Nazareth that hides itself from travelers until they're on top of it."

Yeshua thought for a moment. "So if you want to hide a city, you better not build it on a hill."

His parents marveled at his observation.

In a short time they passed through the gates of the city. They went to the house they had visited when Elizabeth was pregnant with John. John and his father were outside the house. The two little boys eyed each other, shifting their gaze from cousin to parent, eager but unsure. While Yeshua's hair had deep brown flowing waves like his mother's, John's close curls might have been rubbed with the reddest of wild flowers; later Yeshua said his cousin "had a head full of flames." As the cousins approached each other, Yeshua had to look up to maintain eye contact with John. John's already broad shoulders and sinewy legs held the promise of strength and speed while a selection of bruises and scrapes that colored his arms and legs said he spent much of his time climbing and crashing, jumping and falling. John took Yeshua's hand and led him to the rear doorway. Yeshua looked to Joseph, who nodded approval. Yeshua ran after his cousin.

The rectangular courtyard behind Zechariah's house was bounded on three sides by the walls of homes; the

147

fourth side opened to the rising slope of the Hill of Moreh. At the edge of the opening stood an old and busy oak tree. John ran toward it and when several feet away leapt up and grabbed onto a branch. From there he swung his feet up, grabbing the next higher branch with the backs of his knees. One spring upward and he was all but lost in the foliage.

Yeshua stood at the base of the oak as if wondering whether and how to follow.

John pointed to the knob where a branch had been cut off. "Step there." He then pointed to a low limb. "Grab that." He demonstrated for Yeshua by putting his hands on a branch above him. "Pull."

Yeshua did as John said, struggling and finally succeeding in reaching the branch below John's feet.

Joseph had followed the boys into the courtyard but did not interfere in their game.

Mary stood behind him. "Do you think he'll be all right up there?"

"Even if he falls, he won't fall far," Joseph said.

John climbed several feet higher and made a display of looking across the roofs of nearby houses and up the slope of the Hill. Yeshua watched him climb. Joseph wondered if he would follow. Mary relaxed as Yeshua stayed put.

"How we get down?" Yeshua asked.

"Watch." John shimmied along a high branch and let himself drop to a lower one. He repeated the move once more, and finished with a drop to the ground, landing in a squat. He looked up at Yeshua. "Throw yourself down. I'll catch you so you won't hurt your feet against the ground."

Yeshua let himself drop, landing on top of John and knocking both of them to the ground.

Mary rushed to the boys, hands outstretched in ready aid.

John popped up. "We're fine, Cousin Mary." He reached for Yeshua, who grabbed his hand and pulled himself up.

The boys chased each other from one corner of the courtyard to the next.

Mary walked back to Joseph and took his arm. "My family only had girls. James and Joses were ten years old by the time you and I married. I have a lot to learn about little boys."

Joseph rested his hand on hers. "John looks so much older than Yeshua, yet they behave like old pals."

She looked around, from the boys to Zechariah. "John might be left on his own a lot. If only Elizabeth had lived longer."

"Boys grow up fast when they're on their own. Something tells me the two of them will bear watching."

JOSEPH'S WORK gave him opportunities to hear what his clients heard. A split axle on the ox-cart of a trader on his way from Samaria past Nazareth to Sepphoris brought the trader to Joseph's workshop. Joseph, James and Yeshua went with the traveler and propped up his packed cart with a series of levers and heavy blocks, and then walked back to the workshop. The man waited and talked while they worked, bringing news not yet heard in Nazareth.

"What your people expected since his first day has come to pass after seven years. Weary of Archeleus's antics and cruelty, Caesar Augustus has replaced him with a Roman horse soldier. Coponius is his name. He has commanded other horse soldiers so that's the kind of rule we expect."

"It will be an improvement if he is consistent," said Joseph as he measured a log that would become the new axle. He saw a face full of questions on Yeshua and some interest from James. "How are the people of Samaria taking the change?" Joseph asked, as much for his sons' benefit as his own.

Yeshua listened to the conversation as he worked with James, smoothing the center hole of the wheel, preparing it for the new axle.

The trader said, "Like you, we hope he won't worry so much about being banished that he rules with too heavy a hand. We shall see."

"I expect Herod Antipas will tighten his grip, fearful of the same fate as his brother," Joseph said. "It is hard to know which is worse: the foreign rulers or our leaders who govern in their shadow."

When they completed the repairs, the trader paid what Joseph asked, and offered him the promise of assistance if he ever needed it as he passed through Samaria. "Your people and my people don't always get along." His nod met Joseph's. "May my brothers be blessed to break an axle in Nazareth!"

"May your brothers have your patience," Joseph replied.

When the man went on his way, Yeshua asked, "Poppa, what does that mean, that Herod Antipas fears a fate like his brother's?"

Joseph said, "He fears being banished like his brother. We might pity such a man, both fearful and powerful, but we steer clear of him."

THE HILLS around Nazareth provided the setting for Yeshua

to grow under Joseph and Mary's guidance. The oak trees offered shade for birds' nests and later hard wood for the carpenter's shop; the tallest juniper grew up under Yeshua's gaze. "Will it one day reach the sky, Poppa?"

"If we can see the top of the tree, it still has room to grow."

The doves played their game of 'follow me, follow you,' cooing to mark the quiet interludes. A larger bird, with wings spread wide, soared toward the sun, hovering high above and then sped toward them, only to reverse course and soar again.

"Is it watching us, Poppa?"

"Not us; it is searching for a meal for its brood."

Then, as if to illustrate, the great bird dashed down, straight to its scrambling prey. A rabbit darted into its hole, forcing the flying hunter to pull up and search once more. The screams of hungry chicks in a nearby nest filled the air.

"How many times will it have to catch something, Poppa?"

"Until it has fed all its babies."

Half a dozen vultures with up-swept wings flew in uncoordinated circles. They took turns swooping down and returning to their loose formation. "They're not fast like the other one, Poppa. Why do they fly down and up?"

"The great hunter is swift so it can catch its running prey. These vultures wait for the prey to die before they claim it."

Yeshua pointed to the dark birds floating above him. "What are they waiting for?" He looked around, a worried look on his face. "What's going to die, Poppa?"

"Come, Yeshua. Let's find out." Seeing the area the vultures focused on, Joseph led Yeshua into thick brush between two small hills, where turpentine and mustard trees seemed to sprout from layers of brambles, vines and myrtle. As Joseph and Yeshua penetrated the undergrowth they came upon a lamb, caught in the thicket, bloodied from pulling against the needles and briers, now lying on its side resigned to die there, not even bleating from fear or for respite.

"Are the big birds waiting for the lamb to die, Poppa?"

"Yes, they are but you and I are going to spoil their day." Joseph opened the leather sheath that hung from his belt and pulled out his carpenter's knife.

Yeshua grabbed for the knife. Joseph pulled it back. "A little more practice at carving and shaving and then you can handle a sharp blade. We want to make sure the blade doesn't slip and hurt the little lamb." *Or hurt you.* Yeshua drew back.

Joseph hacked the weeds and vines, and pulled away the flowering chains of capers until his hands were raw. The lamb, seemingly free, lifted its head. It did not attempt to stand.

"Why doesn't he get up, Poppa?" Yeshua reached for the lamb, stroked its head and put a hand under it. "He's stuck, Poppa, underneath." Yeshua withdrew his hand, pocked with the blood of the lamb.

Joseph slid one hand under the lamb and with the blade in the other hand cut the briers that held the small animal captive. He eased the lamb up from the brush. He and Yeshua plucked the thorns from his coat and barbs from its skin. They carried it to a stream and fed it drops of water on their fingertips until it was able to drink from their cupped palms.

The dark birds above them shouted their anger at the rescue.

"Let's take him home, Poppa. Joses will know what to do for him."

"Good idea, Yeshua. Joses can add him to his woolly flock."

"I'll ask Joses to name him, 'Rescued.'"

VISITS between the cousins became regular occurrences. By the time they reached their eleventh year, as soon as one arrived at the other's house, they were off to explore hills and caves, rivers and groves, and the people who lived among them. John retained a fascination with exploration and discovery as well as physical superiority: taller, broader, stronger, faster.

On one such visit to Nain Yeshua followed John up a hill and came upon a group of boys John's size but who seemed two or three years older. Joseph followed at a distance, busying himself with searching for wild berries and wondering if John ever joined this little pack in his wandering. The boys were throwing small stones at the remnants of a basket that hung from a tree thirty feet away. Yeshua and John watched, until all of sudden John picked up a stone, reared back, let it go and struck the basket. Yeshua joined the older boys as they cheered for the direct hit, all but one boy.

That one, taller than the others, came up to John. "A sling is the real way to deliver a blow. Anyone can throw a stone."

John neither stepped back nor answered him, but watched and waited.

"Watch me, little boy." The tall one reached into his cloth

belt that drooped around his hips, and took out a sling. He held it up for John to see: a thin leather strip a mite longer than his arm, with a small loop on one end and a knot on the other, and a little leather pouch attached to the middle. He picked up several stones and selected one of them. Holding the knot between the thumb and index finger of his right hand, he put the stone into the leather pouch, and placed the loop around his middle finger. The other boys stepped back, anticipating his next move. John stepped back with the other boys and Yeshua followed. The tall boy spun the sling, winding and rewinding his arm in a great arc until the sling hummed, its pitch rising with the speed of the stone. As the stone sped forward he let go of the knot, releasing the stone. It missed the basket but tore a chunk of bark from the tree. No one cheered.

"Here you try," said the boy.

John imitated what the tall boy had done. As he spun the sling he hesitated, and the sling went slack and the stone fell from its pouch.

The boys laughed.

Joseph stepped behind a tree to be sure the boys would not see him, but continued watching and listening.

"Better stick to throwing, little boy," said the tall boy as he returned the sling to his belt.

"Would you take it out again and let me see it?" John pointed toward the now hidden sling.

"Why should I do that? You're too little to do anything with it."

"Maybe I am but I'd still like to see it. Or are you so afraid that you keep it hidden?"

The boy stiffened, and then coiled as if to strike.

Yeshua spoke up. "I know it's your sling. You don't have to show it to anyone if you want to keep it to yourself."

The boy relaxed and nodded. "Maybe you'd like to see it," he said to Yeshua.

"Yes, sure, I'd like to see it."

The boy handed him the sling.

Yeshua looked closely at the leather and the little pouch. "Did you make this?"

"Yeah. What's wrong with it?"

"This is the finest sling I've ever seen. You have every right not to show it to anyone."

Joseph laughed to himself. Not only the finest but also the first sling Yeshua had ever seen.

The tall boy responded only by throwing his shoulders back and cocking his head.

"It's finer than any my cousin has ever seen, too," said Yeshua.

"I didn't know he's your cousin. You can show it to him if you want."

Yeshua held the sling up to his eye level. John examined the stretched out leather as if calculating, but did not attempt to take it from him. Yeshua returned it to the tall boy.

The cousins turned back when the pack ran farther up the hill, hopping from one boulder to the next. On the way down the hill the cousins talked about the sling. John said, "You surprised me Yeshua, the way you got him to show it to me. I saw how it is made and now I'm going to make a sling just like it."

"So you can hit the basket?" asked Yeshua.

"I don't care about the basket. I care about hunting."

"Hunting? What for?"

"Locusts. Hunting them will give me plenty of practice because it takes a lot to make a meal."

~

A NEW JOB at Tabor held great promise for Joseph, not only for the work itself but also because it marked the first time Yeshua would work beside him on a job away from Nazareth. He looked forward to reliving the experience he had had with his Poppa, when as a ten-year old he accompanied him to Sepphoris. There they met Anna and Joachim and he fell in love with Little Mary. What might Yeshua experience over the next week?

They followed the familiar way down the hills southeast of Nazareth. The road branched, one side continuing south to Nain and the other turning east on the Plain of Esdraelon to Tabor. Where the road split a crowd had formed. Shouts reached Joseph and Yeshua before they could see the cause of the commotion. As they came within sight of the center of the crowd, a man wearing a white tunic and prayer shawl raised a stone above his shoulders and brought it down hard on the back of a kneeling woman's head. The woman fell to the ground, bloodied and motionless. The crowd pelted her with stones of their own, the last ones striking a lifeless body. It ended almost as soon as it had started.

Joseph, too late, grabbed Yeshua and turned him to himself. "I am sorry, my son. You did not need to see that."

"Why, Poppa?" Yeshua pulled himself from Joseph's grip, hid his face in his hands, shuddering. He cried out, "Why did they do that? What bad thing could she have done that a Pharisee would start such a thing?" He sobbed into Joseph's chest.

Joseph held Yeshua until the sobs ebbed. He lifted the small face toward his, and looked at him, eye to eye. "It is the law, Yeshua. A harsh law, yes, but it is the law."

"What law could bring this to anyone?" In spite of tears

and sobs, he spoke with an anger Joseph had never seen in him. Yeshua's tears rolled down his cheeks; his reddened face reflected his rage and his sorrow.

"If she lied to her new husband and said she had not been with another man, the law says she is to be stoned." Joseph again embraced Yeshua, held him close, and did not let him pull back. "I am sorry your young eyes witnessed such a thing."

"Poppa, the rabbis in our synagogue told us of this. They spoke of the Law and the requirement of stoning an unfaithful woman. When they spoke, it sounded clean and just and wise, but that is not what it looks like." He turned and surveyed the crowd, now dispersing to their homes and markets and synagogue. Two women tended to their dead neighbor. "I will go home and tell the rabbis what the Law looks like." He paused and looked to Joseph. "What about 'merciful and gracious is the Lord' that David sang about? When does that happen? 'Slow to anger, the Lord puts our sins as far away as east is from west.' Why do they ignore that?"

At first they had not been close enough to see the face of the woman but Joseph now saw she had dark eyes and hair like Mary's, so dark it turned black in the shadows. He shuddered at the thought of Mary's plight if he had followed his first reading of the Law after learning of her pregnancy. "Yeshua, our people have lived this way for generations of generations. You will find another way. You must."

CHAPTER 11

*N*ow approaching twelve years of age Yeshua
received permission from his Poppa and Mama
to take the six-mile walk alone to Nain to spend three days
with his cousins.

Mary sent two large round loaves she had baked:
double-ground wheat flour leavened with barley yeast and
flavored with mulberries, finely chopped figs, cinnamon
and honey. She rubbed each with oil flavored with pomegranate, "to keep the inside moist and the crust tender," just
as Anna had taught her. She wrapped them in clean cloths
and tied them them to Yeshua's back. "When my son runs,
everything leaps to the ground," she said. Along with the
loaves, Yeshua would deliver love and blessings from
cousins to cousins.

When Yeshua returned home he had much to tell Joseph
and Mary, complete with all the excitement and details of
his adventures. As soon as he greeted Zechariah and gave
him Mary's gift, John pulled him away and led him through
densely treed hills to the Jezreel Valley where a brook grew

and flowed southeast to the Jordan River twenty miles away. "We will save that trip for another day," said John.

A mile's run south along the growing stream brought them to a clearing where the fast flowing water gurgled and slowed on the flatter landscape, forming a clear quiet pool. John grabbed Yeshua's arm. "Slow, quiet." Yeshua welcomed the pause to take a breath and wipe his brow while John's forehead was bone dry. John pointed to the pool. "This is the water of the spirit."

Yeshua looked at him, wanting to ask but unable to form a question.

"The spirit comes to us with the clarity of water, cleansing and invigorating." He grabbed Yeshua's arm again. "Shhh."

His gaze flitted from Yeshua to one corner of the pool and then to another. "They frighten easily," he whispered, as fish darted about. In a second his outer tunic dropped to the ground, as John stuffed the hem of his inner tunic into his belt. He picked up several pointed stones and eased himself into the thigh-high water while he drew a sling from a sack that hung behind him. Yeshua watched in amazement as his cousin moved with the grace of the fish around him. John loaded the sling, spun it above his head and sent a stone flying to the water. A fish quivered and then went still. John reached for it and pulled it up. As he walked out of the water, he took a knife from his belt and killed and dressed the fish.

"Come, eat." John handed the first piece of boneless fish to Yeshua.

"Shouldn't we cook it?" Yeshua could not believe what he had seen.

"If we eat it right away it won't need baking."

Yeshua took the piece of white translucent fish. Sweeter

than any fish he had tasted, it needed neither salt nor onion. They sat, eating, enjoying each other's company, not having to fill the time with words. After they finished, John took the scraps and tossed them into the bushes. "The birds and the bugs will take care of that."

Yeshua followed John's lead as they washed their hands in the pool. "I remember the boy with the sling and the basket tied to a tree."

John nodded at the recollection. "An interesting game, but still a game. The sling serves more than child's play."

"I remember the story of how David used the sling as anything but a toy."

"David knew what he was doing." John handed the sling to Yeshua. "Here, you try." He pointed at large rocks away from the water.

Yeshua took the sling, loaded it with a stone, spun it and released the stone. It landed beside the rocks. He tried again and got closer to the target.

John said, "A few days of practice and you'll be ready to hunt for your supper."

The boys spent another hour near the stream, exploring caves that appeared from nowhere and finding wild berries that grew out of crevices. They enjoyed walking home at a slower pace, out of the Valley of Jezreel and through the hills south of Nain. John told Yeshua about Judah, the man from their own Galilee who preached with great zeal, exhorting the people to ignore the foreigners' tax assessment.

"How do you know about all this?" Yeshua asked.

"I listen. Whenever I see or hear a preacher, I go closer and listen. I keep hoping one of them will encourage the people to recognize their own wrong-doing and ask for God's mercy. I haven't heard any mention of it. They are all about power and independence, as if nothing else matters."

They talked of the stories of the Torah, of the wicked cities, of Lot and of his wife whom the Lord turned into a pillar of salt.

"Do you believe what the rabbis teach us?" asked Yeshua.

"The Torah provides the ribs of the stories; the rabbis add the flesh, each from his own imagination," John said.

"They try to make the covenant come alive," Yeshua said.

"The covenant is alive. It does not need a teacher or preacher to turn it into mush. One teacher in our village never speaks of repentance because he says the Lord of the covenant tires of forgiving us. 'As long as I did not confess my sins, I moaned in misery; but when I declared my sin to the Lord, he took away my guilt.'"

"As far away as east from west," added Yeshua.

"The Lord never tires of forgiving, and if a man confesses and repents he knows which sin is forgiven."

They walked on, sometimes rapt in each other's sayings, sometimes content to be quiet. Yeshua was about to tell John about the stoning he had witnessed when their conversation stopped in mid-thought just outside John's village. A crowd of several dozen men were listening to two others who stood high above them on a rock ledge. Yeshua and John stopped and stood nearby. The two men on the rock spoke of the coming tax collection period and exhorted the crowd to refuse to pay.

The exhortation hit a responsive chord in the gathering. Most of Galilee supported their families through farming and shepherding. They resented that in addition to contributing to the upkeep of the temple, they were forced to pay taxes on farm products and the land itself, with a portion going to the Romans and more to Herod Antipas's building program. Antipas's rule followed his father's strategy of keeping the Jewish people in a kind of economic slavery while placating them by expanding the Great Temple in Jerusalem and hiring them as craftsmen and laborers.

"By hard work you earn what you have. Don't let the foreigners take it from you," said one of the speakers, a young man, much younger than Yeshua's Poppa. He was clothed in beggar's rags.

Every now and then he paused in his speech and the other man, younger still and also in rags or what might have once been a large sack, shouted out, "No drachma for the foreigner, no mite for the pretender." He sang out in rhythm, repeated the refrain, and then stopped for his comrade to continue preaching.

Someone in the crowd shouted back at them. "What about tithes and temple taxes?"

The preacher implored them. "Nothing! Give them nothing! Herod the Pretender steals your tithes for his whoring and misery making. Give him nothing." He surveyed the throng, looked his audience in the eye and continued in a stronger voice, "Your land taxes go to the pretender and the foreigner. Give them nothing!"

"No drachma for the foreigner, no mite for the pretender! No drachma for the foreigner, no mite for the pretender!" The shouter increased the tempo.

The crowd now took up the refrain. "No drachma for the foreigner, no mite for the pretender!" Over and over they shouted as their thrusting arms increased the intensity of the chant.

As the crowd got worked up, out of the wooded hills came a band of horsemen. The thunder of the hooves brought the shouting to an abrupt halt.

John whispered to Yeshua, "Soldiers." He strained to look more closely. "Some kind of soldiers."

"What are they going to do?" Yeshua said.

"Let's go up closer so we can see."

"No, John. This is close enough."

"Don't worry." John pointed to a small passageway in Nain's wall. "Be ready to run through the eye of the needle. A soldier on horseback won't fit through and by the time he goes around through the gate we'll be safely home."

Yeshua followed John's lead.

The riders galloped through the crowd, knocking a man to the ground. He covered his head with his arms and hands. One horse rose up and his hooves fell hard on the man's chest. A shriek filled the air. The soldier spurred his horse to rise up and crash down again. Blood flowed out of the fallen man's quieted mouth. The rest of the crowd scattered, stopping just far enough away so they could see what would happen. Three soldiers chased after the speakers, trapping them between themselves, the main band of soldiers and the higher steeper rocks. Two horsemen dismounted and grabbed for the speakers. The younger one spun out of the grasp and scampered up the rocks. The soldiers did not give chase, but threw the captured one to the ground.

"Hang him on the gibbet," shouted one of the mounted soldiers.

"Do that and you'll be next on your gibbet," bellowed the soldier with the fanciest uniform to the one threatening crucifixion.

A dismounted soldier held down the captive. "Hear that, the gibbet," he said. "Give thanks for your lucky day. If we were soldiers from the Empire you'd be hanging on a cross for preaching insurrection."

The crowd that had scattered now realized the soldiers had no interest in them so they went closer. Women who had stood at the outer edges of the crowd and had been the first to run now eased closer to the violence.

"What have I done? Talk. I've done nothing more than talk." The captive, now kneeling, looked from the soldier who held him down to the others. They had dismounted and were coming closer, picking up stones as they approached.

"Sedition, we call it," said his captor. "That's what you've done."

One of the mounted soldiers turned his horse and shouted to the crowd. "Sedition! Blasphemy! If anyone else feels the same way as this wretch, you can be next."

The silent crowd cowered.

The captor walked behind the kneeling man, picked up a large stone and smashed it down on the back of his head. He keeled over in a lump. The rest of the soldiers pounded the man with stones until nothing would be gained by another stone. They remounted and rode through the again dispersing crowd.

John pulled Yeshua by the tunic. "Come. Home is not far."

"Wait. Wait to see if anyone takes care of the dead man."

Several minutes passed. Those who had run now drifted away. A man and a woman walked to the fallen man whose preaching partner had come out of hiding.

John again pulled at Yeshua who went with him this time.

"What an awful occurrence! To take a man's life so easily, like blowing the dust off a sill." Yeshua shook his head.

"The hills around Nain will be quiet for months to come.

That's the way Herod likes it and why the soldiers do this terrible deed. The worst part is that they are not foreigners."

"How did they get that way?" he asked. "And what will they do next?"

~

YESHUA RETURNED to Nazareth even faster than he had run to Nain. He told Joseph and Mary of his visit and of John's comfort in living off whatever he came upon. "The fish tasted sweet and tender. We ate it right beside the river." Joseph and Mary felt Yeshua's excitement.

"You must show me how he did it," Joseph said.

"Better that John teach you. He has the strength of a farmer's ox and moves with the grace of a splendid fish. Oh, you should see him sling a stone." He feigned spinning the sling and letting the stone fly. "John can do anything he decides to do."

Joseph and Mary exchanged glances, choosing not to interrupt Yeshua's tale.

Mary said, "I'm glad you enjoyed your visit, Yeshua. You haven't told us of Zechariah."

"He loved the cakes. 'Baked with the flavor of affection,' he said. We had some with black tea. That old man never changes. He'll enjoy living as long as Methusaleh!" He tilted his head and looked up at his mother through the shadow of his brows. "Half the time he has no idea whether John is in bed or on the other side of the Jordan."

Mary gave a little laugh. "The older you get, Yeshua, the more you remind me of my father. I'm glad you all enjoyed the loaves." She shifted her gaze to Joseph. "I do worry about our cousins, one more than the other. John is so ready to take risks and if anything happened to him I can't imagine what would become of his father."

"We will keep close to John but that will calm us more than him," Joseph said.

Yeshua nodded, started to say something and then changed his mind.

His parents waited, giving him a chance to start again.

Finally Joseph said, "What is it, Yeshua? Something bothers you."

Yeshua's eyes filled. He lowered his gaze. "We saw a man stoned." He looked to Joseph. "Like the woman we saw near Tabor."

Mary drew a breath, loud enough for Joseph and Yeshua to turn toward her. "Oh, my son, my poor son." She put her arms around him and held him.

"Soldiers came while two men were preaching to a crowd. Right outside Nain, not far from Cousin Zechariah's house."

"We should not have let you travel alone." Mary turned from Yeshua to Joseph. "How could we let our son go into such danger?"

Joseph extended his arms, and put one around Mary and one around Yeshua. He held them for a moment. "I'm sorry, Mary. Yeshua, let us thank God you came back safely."

Yeshua pulled back. "We were never in any danger, John and I. The soldiers showed no interest in the crowd either. Just in one of the preachers. It wouldn't have mattered which one they grabbed." He paused. "'Sedition,' the soldiers said. 'And Blasphemy'. They killed him for talking to a crowd that wasn't all that big. It was Nain, Poppa, not Jerusalem!"

"Sedition?" Joseph shook his head. "What were the men talking about? And whose soldiers were they?"

"The two men told the crowd not to pay their taxes. They said Herod and the foreigners should not be allowed to take what the people work hard for."

Mary looked to Joseph, her eyes asking if he knew anything about this.

"Zealots," Joseph said. "Judah and others preach independence and exhort the people to hold back the tax payments." He asked Yeshua, "Did the soldiers have an eagle medallion on their uniform?"

"I don't think so. Everything happened so fast I'm not sure." He paused again, squinting in thought. "The soldiers told the man he was lucky because if the soldiers from the Empire had him he would be looking down from a cross." He threw up his hands. "I don't know what that meant. How could he be lucky?"

Mary said, "I hope you never witness such cruelty again."

Joseph said, "It means that the soldiers you saw were Herod's. Foreigners would have crucified the man for speaking against the Emperor or the Empire."

Yeshua looked from Mary to Joseph, bewildered by what he had shared with them. "Why did they say he was lucky if they were about to kill him?"

Joseph drew Yeshua closer to him. "For the poor wretch the stoning ends in an instant. Death on a cross takes hours."

JOSEPH'S FRIEND Efron approached him one day. "Your James must be past his twenty-first year. I hear the fishermen in Capernaum bring their damaged boats to him, and if they don't have a boat he builds one for them." James had followed his inclination and moved to Capernaum where he worked as a boat carpenter as many hours a day as the sun permitted.

Joseph nodded.

"Chava said it is time for our Leah to find a man as good as the man Mary found, Mary the youngest daughter of Rabbi Joachim. I think Chava is right."

With all his work keeping the Capernaum fishermen fishing, James had not approached Joseph for guidance in finding a wife.

Joseph said, "Leah is a devoted daughter. I see her with Chava. She would make a fine wife for any man, including James."

"I will talk to my daughter about her future."

Joseph understood Efron's desire to have his daughter married and his hope that she be the mother of the Messiah. He could not tell his friend that God had already made his choice.

Before Joseph responded to his friend, Efron added, "Chava's sister lives in Capernaum."

"I will talk to James when I see him, which won't be soon."

"Unlike her mother, Leah is in no rush."

"Perhaps I will send word to him."

A YEAR AFTER THEIR BETROTHAL, James and Leah were married in Nazareth.

Joses, as a shepherd in quiet Nazareth, spent his time tending his sheep and wandering the hills in search of strays. Yeshua often wandered with him. After walking the fields with Joses one day, Yeshua told Joseph and Mary they had come upon a stray from Joses' own flock. "I called to it and it did not budge. I went closer and called to it again but the sheep kept foraging."

Joseph sensed the reluctant animal had frustrated Yeshua. He was about to help Yeshua understand when Yeshua continued.

"And then Joses spoke to it, almost like a song. The sheep stopped eating and ran to him."

Joseph put an arm around the boy's shoulders. "The sheep know Joses just as he knows them. When they get to know you, they will come to you, too."

THE COMING of another spring brought the promise of another Passover in Jerusalem and the hope they would meet Mary and Salome and their husbands as well as James and Leah. As an unmarried man, Joses would travel with Joseph and Mary, leaving his now sizable sheep flock in the care of Simon and his sons.

In the days leading up to the trip, Mary prepared food for the first two or three days of travel. Joseph made sure his purse would provide for the journey, the festival and their return. As they expected, on the day they chose to start the sojourn they joined a caravan that had started north of Sepphoris and took them past Nain where they met up with Zechariah and John. The growing column then went east toward the Jordan River. For the first time in years the caravan did not cross the Jordan but traveled south to Jerusalem on the west side of the River. With mad Archeleus gone and Coponius as prefect over Samaria and Judea, Passover pilgrims now believed they could travel through the region with a greater sense of safety.

As each day wore on, the men drifted toward the front

of the procession, with the women and some older men behind them. Young boys and all the girls traveled with their mothers while older boys like Yeshua and John moved from one group to the other and often disappeared from either. The caravan trekking not far from the Jordan River provided great diversion for youngsters who chose to run a mile or more from the caravan. They explored and fished and hunted, and then found their way back to their families for an evening meal in the camp. Since Mary and the other women could prepare the meal only after the day's march, meal time was less regular than at home, and some family members did not arrive until others had eaten.

Zechariah gave a blessing, praising God and giving thanks that the two families, now including James and Leah, were sharing a meal in the days before the great feast.

As soon as Zechariah finished, John said, "We saw the preacher, the partner of the one that was stoned outside our city."

Mary let a loaf of bread drop. "Where?"

"By the river," Yeshua answered.

Reading concern on Mary's face, Joseph said, "It could have been anyone; you could be mistaken."

John said, "I'll never forget his beard, all full of curls and twigs. Besides, he wore the same sack."

"I hope his presence and others like him does not bring the prefect down on us. We hoped travel in Samaria would be easier now," said Joseph.

"Samaria is Samaria," said Zechariah. He reached for some olives and the piece of bread Mary had set in front of him.

Mary asked, "What does all this mean for our caravan and our Passover?"

John answered with his usual enthusiasm. "It means we live in exciting times."

Zachary said, "Excitement! What excitement is there in a beggar in rags telling us, 'Do this, don't do that.' I'll tell you excitement..." He looked around as if hoping someone would finish his thought.

Joseph said, "Excitement turns to drudgery if the foreigners become less tolerant and can't find a scapegoat, or if Herod grows more fearful of losing control. Other pilgrims report that Judah the Zealot is nearby calling on the people to overthrow the prefect and the foreign yoke he represents."

What had started as a meal of family joy ended with mounting anxiety.

DURING THE PASSOVER festival the population of Jerusalem increased tenfold, raising tensions on many levels. Leaving Joses with Mary and Yeshua and the rest of the family at the entrance to an inn, Joseph and James entered. Like every other inn in Jerusalem, the courtyard had become a sprawling campsite. Two men turned from haggling with the innkeeper to arguing with each other.

"I claimed this spot before this intruder brought his pack animal." He looked in the direction of the man's wife. They had no pack animal.

The second man's eyes narrowed, his nostrils flared. "May the Lord turn your lambs to swine." He spat in his rival's face. As his arms went up ready to bring entwined fists down on the first man, out of nowhere came two soldiers who stepped between them. Before they drew a weapon or said a word, the two men fled. The soldiers walked on.

Taking his purse from his inner tunic, Joseph asked the keeper, "Why are the soldiers so close at hand?"

"You are from Galilee, am I right?" He did not wait for a response. "Your ruler is visiting our fine city. Where he goes, his legions go." He put out his hand, intent more on payment than conversation.

Joseph paid the innkeeper for the last large area in the courtyard, where he, his extended family, and their donkey would spend several nights.

In this context Joseph, Mary, Joses and Yeshua, James and Leah, Zechariah and John, commemorated the exodus of the Israelites from Egypt and the angel of death sparing every Israelite home that had the blood of the lamb smeared on its lintel. Early in the afternoon on the eve of the Feast, Joseph went with James, Joses, Yeshua and John to the temple. They entered the Court of Gentiles where tables of the money changers let the faithful trade for the coins they were required to use to purchase sacrificial animals. Not far from them a chaotic collection of animal sellers stood behind tables or stacks of cages.

"The perfect lamb, ready for an offering and a blessed meal," said a seller wearing a bloodied apron.

Joses gulped, took a breath, and lifted the lamb, peering into its eyes, opening its mouth and turning it over, revealing scars and a heavy rash covering its belly.

He looked at Joseph, and then turned to the seller. "*Perfect* lamb, did you say?"

The merchant took the lamb from Joses without a word, handed it to a bloodied-apron partner, picked up another lamb from a pen full of them, and faced Joseph, ignoring Joses. "I made a mistake. This is the perfect lamb."

Joses picked up the animal and repeated the examination, and nodded to Joseph.

"We will take this lamb. But first you must gave the sick lamb to my son. He will take care of it."

"No," the seller shouted. "We are not here to give away the animals. What difference does it make? You're going to slit its throat anyway."

"Keep it then," Joseph said as he turned from the man. "I will speak with the Temple priests and then you will sell no animals."

"Wait." He spoke in quiet tones now. "I have traveled far with the lambs." He held the first lamb out for Joseph. "You can have both animals, my gift to a faithful family."

Yeshua said to the seller, "Our ritual calls for an unblemished lamb and you would deceive us?" His voice rose. "You not only profit by it but you cheat us out of our observance as well." He looked ready to jump up on the table.

James wrapped his arms around Yeshua and quieted him.

John shouted at the animal seller. "You desecrate the Temple courtyard with your lying and cheating."

Other sellers and traders came running to the commotion, took the pens and the lambs from behind the tables and disappeared into the crowds.

Two priests came running, shawls and robes flying, hands rubbing against each other. They stopped. One said to Joseph, "This is the Temple of God. What are you doing to it?"

John stepped in front of Joseph. "This seller is cheating our people who have come to worship and keep holy the Passover."

The seller looked at the priests, head lowered at an angle of respect, his hands behind his back. "Your holinesses, I have nothing to sell." He gestured to the empty spaces behind his table. "How can I cheat?"

The priests looked from him to Joseph, to the young men and then to each other.

Joseph said to them, "This boy speaks the truth. This seller sought to defile the sacrificial altar by selling a blemished lamb."

The priests shrugged in helplessness. One of them said, "Without an unclean animal to reject, we can do nothing." The priests headed to the Court of Women and the courts inside.

Joseph said to the boys, "Passover will still come and we still need a lamb." He stepped to another table and made a purchase with Joses' approval.

Joses carried the lamb as they all walked through the Court of Women into the Court of Men and stopped at the entrance to the Court of Priests. There a priest accepted the lamb. After it was slaughtered, portions of it and two loaves of unleavened barley bread that Mary had baked became the family's offering. They accepted the portion of the lamb they were to roast and eat.

AFTER THE MEAL Zechariah went to the Temple for priestly duties on this day of sacrifice and prayer.

Mary said to Joseph, "I have an uneasy feeling, like I have when you are away or when Yeshua is out with John. Yet I know you are all here and I should let nothing worry me."

Joseph said, "I share your sense of ..., of ..., I don't know what. Jerusalem is our spiritual home, yet I am anxious to go home to Nazareth."

"Joseph, are we not trusting as we should. We have every

reason to rejoice in this time of intimacy with our God, but I cannot rid myself of this feeling that wine is about to burst from its skin."

"I worry that Yeshua will bolt off with his cousin in the way the ox drives against the yoke, head down, with no thought of where to go. God has delivered our people, he guided us and the son of God away from the baby killer, and he will deliver us yet again. Mary, let us put ourselves in the warmth of his wings. You and I are feeling the unease of all we have heard this last week, the unrest, the conflict, ..."

"And the fear of a terror we neither see nor know," Mary said.

"For twelve years we have guided the son of God toward whatever his Father has ordained. Our need for faith has not ended."

"HEAR ME, Lord; listen to me sighing. At dawn you will hear me cry; at dawn I will plead before you and wait." Joseph led his family out from the camp, as did the heads of the other families. In a short time this collection of individual families again became a caravan.

As the sun rose higher so did Joseph's spirit. Each additional mile from Jerusalem felt like two miles closer to home. The first long day brought the pilgrimage eastward past Jericho to a camp within a few miles of the Jordan River.

Joseph, James and Joses worked their way back from the men's section of the caravan and found Mary, Leah and Zechariah and together they set up a site for the family. Mary spread out a large cloth and brushed off sand and blades of grass that always found their way onto the food cloth. In the center of the cloth she arranged the food she had brought for the first day's meal.

"I have not seen Yeshua since early this morning," Mary said.

Joseph said, "He and John spent an hour with the men and then drifted back in the caravan."

They both looked toward Zechariah. He said, "I have not seen John all day."

"They probably went to the River," said James. "I'll look for them."

"Yes, do," said Mary. "They will soon arrive with a sack of fish." Joseph knew her words were intended to calm any worriers among them. She looked in every direction and at every family group setting up a similar meal site.

They sat on the outer edges of the cloth but food held no interest for any of them.

Joseph stood up. "I will search among our friends before it gets dark. Those two boys are quite capable of going anywhere and doing anything, but we should look in the obvious places first."

"No, Joseph, go to the River. I'll look among our friends," Mary said.

They parted and searched, and recruited others to search with them. Along the banks of the Jordan, Joseph investigated every shape, every movement and every pile of rocks that might capture the attention of two twelve-year-old boys. To no avail he inquired of a group of men who had come to wash away the dust of the journey. The fading light that follows the sunset disappeared and with it all hope of finding anyone in or near the river.

By the time he returned to the family site, James and Joses had also returned from their looking. He saw disappointment flush on Mary's face. He went to her side.

"No one remembers seeing either of them all day," Mary said. "No other boys are missing. A band of traders going to Jerusalem said they would watch for them." She took Joseph's arm. "Joseph, what are we going to do? All the talk about Zealots and rabble-rousers, and the impatience of the authorities have me unnerved. What has happened to the boys?" Fear permeated her every word, like the deep anxiety that comes when a child's fever refuses to break.

Joseph recalled Abraham and the trust he had at his worst moment. He calmed his own fears and held his voice steady in order to calm hers. "Mary, the God of our ancestors has entrusted his son to you and me."

"And we have lost him."

CHAPTER 12

*C*amp site fires glowed around Joseph and Mary. James sat on the meal cloth beside Zechariah, passing food to him from Mary's abundance—barley bread, dried fish, and a sack of figs, the new spring figs, juicy and sweet, that she had bought in Jericho as the caravan passed the markets.

"John will find us when he learns we have Passover figs." James looked up at Mary. "Nothing will keep him away. Yeshua will return with him, you will see."

Mary wrapped her arms around herself; her gaze fell to the ground. All of a sudden she shook her head as if shaking off a web that had caught on her face. She said to Joseph, "Whether we are in the mood to rejoice or lament, our God remains steadfast. We must as well. 'My heart exults in the Lord. There is no rock like the Lord.' If Yeshua is to find us, we can wait right here. If we are to find him, we must go to wherever he is. We do not go alone for 'He will guard the footsteps of his faithful ones.'"

Joseph said, "He is not lost. He is somewhere we don't

know. Yeshua has come unscathed through his twelfth year while many see their sons not live through their sixth. We will find him. I will return to Jericho, and if he is not there I will go to Jerusalem."

"I am going with you," Mary said.

"Our donkey will not move after walking all day. I will go faster alone."

"I am going with you if I have to run." Her look of determination conveyed confidence and trust and a need to protect rather than arrogance or fear.

Joseph nodded consent, knowing nothing would be gained by a prolonged discussion. "The donkey will carry you as far as Jericho. There we will leave him with the herdsman and rent another for the rest of the journey to Jerusalem. Come, we will go now."

In the five miles to Jericho they met only a few stragglers on a quest to catch up with the caravan. Night travel meant slow travel. Joseph walked in front of the donkey, clearing the path of stones and branches that might lead to an injured animal or, worse, a fallen Mary. They stopped to search at every inn and caravansary along the way as well as in and around Jericho, all to no avail. Midnight came and the gates of every caravansary closed. A gatekeeper shouted to the couple, "Traveling at this hour means you're seeking either trouble or a child."

Joseph had to restrain the rented donkey that was eager to trot, perhaps after many days of confinement. "At least he'll make us hurry to Jerusalem," Joseph said with a burst of new energy.

"If he doesn't kill you trying to keep up with him." Mary reached into a sack every now and then and gave Joseph a chunk of bread, a couple of olives or one of the new figs. "With no sleep you need food."

In spite of Mary's best efforts to ward off hunger, the lack of sleep and hours of walking a dozen miles uphill from the Jordan to the hills east of Jerusalem led to near exhaustion for Joseph. "If you die you'll leave me to raise Yeshua by myself. The Lord did not choose us for this kind of ending. We must rest." She drew Joseph's attention to the remnants of a fire pit at the mouth of a cave.

Joseph tethered the donkey to a tree and used his flint to light a fire in the pit. He explored the cave with a lighted branch until he was satisfied they had no unwanted companions, either human or beast. He spread out their blankets at the edge of the cave and arranged Mary's tunic as she lay back. With two fork-shaped boughs he lifted a heated stone and set it closer to Mary's blanket.

It seemed that he had just lowered his head onto a bundle of cloth when the rising sun awakened him. He looked up to find Mary sitting, watching him. She smiled as he struggled to adapt to the morning brilliance.

"Did you not sleep, Mary?"

"While I lay sleeping my heart kept vigil. As I slept I sought him whom my heart loves but I could not find him."

Joseph reached toward her and took her hand. "We will find him."

"I know why the Lord chose you for this journey even if I don't understand why he chose me. My dear husband, your strength carries me and your love warms me more than the fire stone. That's how I get to anywhere from here." She rubbed his feet with oil. "If only I had some soothing balm to bathe your busy feet."

"You could not use it because I would use it first on yours." He smiled and let his eyes close for a moment. "Thank you, God of our father Abraham, for my wife, the mother of God's son."

He sat up. "We will rise and go about the city, in the streets and crossings we will seek him whom we love."

While the day before had demanded a steady climb out of the Jordan Valley, this morning required steep ups and downs as they wound their way through the hills. When they stopped in mid-morning to buy food at a village market and fill their skins at a well, further inquiry produced the same disappointing result.

"God himself will provide," said Joseph. "I sometimes wonder whether I believe it or I'm talking myself into it."

"We believe it," said Mary. "It's hard to feel it in here." She struck her heart.

With the sun well past its highest point, and the donkey now content to walk, Joseph and Mary arrived in Jerusalem. They went first to the inn where they had stayed, thinking that if Yeshua and John had returned to Jerusalem, they would expect his parents to look for him in a familiar place. From there the couple went to the markets where they had purchased provisions during their stay, and then to the home of rabbis who were friends of Zechariah.

"They could not have disappeared but no one has seen a hair of their heads," said Joseph.

"It gets harder to think of where to look for them. Soon it will be dark and the looking will get harder."

They returned to the inn they first visited, took a room and prepared a meal.

"We have missed some place that should be obvious to us. When we think of it, we will find the two boys and wonder at our foolishness for not going there first," Joseph said.

"Where might that be, Joseph?"

"I don't know but it will be obvious."

They nibbled at their food and sipped from their replenished water skins. "Where have we not thought to look?"

They reflected in silence, each offering a prayer to accompany their empty thoughts.

"Mary, do you think they could have gone ahead to Nain? They could easily have run ahead along the banks of the River, explored and fished the way John fishes, and afterward returned to a caravan well ahead of ours."

"Nain and Nazareth are obvious in a way, and it's well known that some caravans set a much faster pace. They could be almost there by now and wondering if they're in front of us or behind us."

"If only we knew."

"We can't send a message."

"We'd arrive at the same time as a messenger," Joseph said.

They searched each other's eyes for some unspoken hint of what to do next. They could abandon Jerusalem and return north. If the boys had gone ahead, they would find them in Nain or Nazareth and all would be well. If the boys had not gone to Nain or Nazareth, then where might Joseph and Mary look?

"We can't return. Not yet. Not until we give up hope of finding them in Jerusalem," said Joseph. "Nazareth and Nain are far from Jerusalem and we will have to come back here if they are not there."

They returned to quiet deliberation.

"Bethlehem," Mary shouted. "They might have gone to Bethlehem, knowing it was David's city and Yeshua's birthplace. Or just to have somewhere to go."

"Yes. If either of them came up with the idea of going to Bethlehem, two or three hours would have them there."

"And now where have they gone? They could still be

there or on the way back or have already left and be on their way to ...." She hesitated. "To where?"

Joseph shook his head. "It was easier when they were little."

Mary laughed. "Much easier. Unfortunately thinking that won't find them."

"It is late, Mary. We have thought of some obvious places. Tomorrow we can think of more and look there."

He checked the fire, tucked the blanket around Mary and lay down. He wondered if Yeshua had begun to realize he had a mission. Caring for him was easier when he was little, but now he must grow into what he is called to become.

MORNING BROUGHT a new determination to their search. After several hours of looking in inns they had not already visited, Joseph said, "When the boys went to the Temple with me, the money changers and the buyers and sellers upset Yeshua. He did not want to wait with us to accept portions of our lamb for roasting so I had to persuade him."

"The Temple! Why did we not think of the Temple before? Yeshua felt drawn to the Temple, at least before the experience you speak of. John, too, caught the spirit of worship there, although he criticized much of what he heard."

"How could it have escaped us? We will go to the Temple and if they are not there, we will go on to Bethlehem."

She looked at him with her knowing look. "We have found the *obvious*. He's there, I know it." She struck her breast. "In here I know it."

As Joseph and Mary entered the Court of Women they

first saw John standing at the fringe of a gathering of rabbis and teachers who were excited over whatever was happening in their midst. The couple moved closer, Mary behind Joseph. He stopped abruptly; she bumped into him. Both fixed their gaze on their son, a mere ten feet away, carrying on a discussion with those around him.

Joseph shouted loud enough for all to stop their talking and buzzing. "Yeshua!"

Mary spoke louder than Joseph had ever heard her, "Why have you done this to us? We have looked all over for you."

Yeshua responded to them with a look of disbelief. "Why were you looking for me?"

Mary's look of astonishment matched her son's. "We thought we had lost you."

"Your mother is frantic with worry. You could have told us or at least told someone in the caravan you were coming here." Joseph looked from Yeshua to John. "Was it your idea or your cousin's?"

Not giving either Yeshua or John a chance to answer, Mary said, "Your father and I have searched Jericho and Jerusalem and everywhere in between."

Yeshua stared at Mary. "My Father?" He turned and directed his words at Joseph. "My Father searching for me? I don't understand what you mean." He looked back to Mary. "It is because of my Father that I am here. Did you not realize that I must tend to my Father's house?"

The rabbis looked from Yeshua to the couple and back to one another.

"Father's house?" asked one of the rabbis.

"Does he not know where he is?" asked another.

"Or does he not know this man is his father?" posed a third.

"I told you there was something odd about him," said the first.

Mary, pale with shock, turned to Joseph. "What is he saying?"

Joseph tried to read Yeshua's face. He whispered to Mary, "He feels a pull that he does not yet understand. The heart of his Father speaks to Yeshua's heart in a language we do not know and Yeshua is just learning." Joseph felt trust and confidence grow within his own heart. He extended his arm toward Yeshua and whispered to Mary. "Reach out to him, Mary. He will come with us."

She did.

He did.

CHAPTER 13

*T*he next several years saw change in Nazareth and other villages of Galilee. Zealots preaching the overthrow of the foreigners became more willing to bear the punishment that came with capture, whether from Herod's soldiers or the Emperor's. Banditry grew, making travel more dangerous and less frequent.

After Zechariah's death, John responded to Joseph's invitation to live with them in Nazareth with a polite "maybe after Passover" without specifying whether Passover in that year or the next or some later year. Both knew his sense of independence required him to stay on his own. He visited Nazareth often. This met with mixed feelings in Joseph and Mary as it meant Yeshua had less need to travel to Nain, but then Yeshua spent more time with his risk-taking cousin.

"John has a way of disappearing in the hills," Yeshua told his parents. "Or in the desert for that matter," he added. "No one can catch him, or sometimes even see him."

Yeshua's skill at carpentry and masonry exceeded his interest in the crafts although he enjoyed the forays to other cities and villages with Joseph. Mary missed them then but worried less than when Yeshua roamed Judea with John.

Years earlier Jacob and Joseph had spent weeks and months journeying to Sepphoris to help build that city and its theater during the first Herod's administration. During the unrest that followed Herod's death, Judah, the son of Hezekiah the bandit, attacked Sepphoris, plundered its treasury and armed his followers. In response Varus, the Roman Governor of Syria to the north, destroyed much of what remained of Sepphoris. Now Joseph and Yeshua made the same journey to rebuild that city under Herod Antipas's mandate that Sepphoris become the 'Ornament of Galilee.' Traveling to Sepphoris posed less risk than to other cities because of a Roman century of eighty soldiers and a full company of Herod's army garrisoned there. Officers in either army sometimes maintained their family in a home within easy reach of their garrison.

As they left Sepphoris for the trek home one day, Yeshua said to Joseph "Herod's kingdom seems to be all around us. Where is your kingdom, Poppa?"

Baffled for a moment Joseph finally said, "Our home is my kingdom; you and Mary are my kingdom." He thought of all the messages from his familiar stranger; of finding, then losing, then finding Mary; of their betrothal, his doubt, and their marriage; of their travels to Bethlehem, Egypt and back to Nazareth. "My kingdom is not a place."

"I understand you more than a lot of what I hear and see."

A budding tekton, Yeshua earned not only a wage but also a reputation for intricate stone design and careful application of the full array of chisels, blades and saws. Poppa and his son and the other Nazarene workers started each day's trip in groups of four or six or eight talking and praying psalms, and ended in one's and two's, just as they had a generation earlier. A constant fear of subversion forced Herod Antipas to continue his father's prohibition of even small crowds.

One day when Joseph and Yeshua had gone more than halfway home, they saw a horse rear up and throw a small child riding with a soldier. The child's scream pierced the quiet evening, a cry of pain and confusion. The soldier who had sat behind the child climbed down from the saddle, steadied the animal and knelt at the child's side. Joseph and Yeshua ran to his side.

Strong looking and several years younger than Joseph, the soldier now appeared to be frightened himself. With one hand he cradled the child in his lap; the child held tightly to his other arm.

Without looking up, the soldier said, "Run and get the village physician." His tone said he was accustomed to giving orders. He nodded toward Nazareth.

Before Joseph could respond the soldier said, "I fear the arm is broken." Now more a father than a soldier, he looked up at Joseph. "He is my son." The child was not more than four years old.

Joseph knelt beside the soldier, examining the child's forearm, already red and swollen, but not bleeding. "We have no physician in our village."

"No physician? I thought your laws forbade you to live in a village without one. One of your teachers told me that."

Joseph said, "That is an old rabbi's tale. We have a midwife in our village, no physician."

"The trip back to Sepphoris will cause him much pain and perhaps make the injury worse. On the battlefield I would wrap a soldier's broken right arm and put his sword in his left hand."

"This is not a battlefield." Joseph pulled out a small sack hidden in the folds of his inner tunic. From it he took several strips of white linen and a tiny clay vessel. From that he removed a cork stopper and poured a few drops of amber liquid onto a cloth.

The soldier looked with amazement at him. "A magic potion, is it?"

"Not at all, lavender and jasmine oil. It will reduce the pain and the swelling." He held the child's arm, humming as he did so. The child looked up at him, focusing on the hum, and stopped crying.

"I did not expect one of your people to help me, a foreigner." The soldier's eyes had questions he did not pose. He looked at Yeshua and then back to Joseph. "You have a son, too. Is that why you stopped to help us?"

"Why would I not stop?" Joseph pointed to the soldier's belt. "May I use that sheath?"

The soldier undid his belt and slid off the knife sheath. He removed the knife and slid it into another sheath on the horse's saddle. "How do you know what to do?"

"We are tektons who suffer the perils of our craft. It is not as dangerous as yours but perhaps we earn injuries less severe but more frequent." He and the soldier exchanged looks of understanding.

Joseph took the sheath, pressed it against the child's wrist and forearm and wrapped it with the linen cloths, rendering the child's arm immobile. From his tunic sack he removed a small leather pouch and handed it to the soldier. "Put a sprinkle of this cumin powder into water and give it to your son. It will control the fever until you get him to your physician."

Joseph turned to the child. "You look old enough to stand up."

The child looked up at his father who smiled, nodded encouragement and offered his hand. The child took it and stood.

The soldier lifted his son onto his horse and turned to Joseph. "You have shown a great kindness to my son. I must repay you."

"No you mustn't."

"Someday perhaps there will be an occasion. What is your name?"

"Joseph. They call me Joseph the Tekton. We live in Nazareth. Take care of your son."

"I will." He mounted his horse. "I am Caelus from Sicily." He clicked his tongue and the horse broke into a trot toward Sepphoris.

"Poppa, I'm glad we stopped. I must learn some of your healing methods."

"Your Grandpoppa Jacob taught them to me. Your Grandmama Rachel made the special mixture."

They walked toward their home and talked of the soldier and his gratitude, and his love for his son.

"Is Sicily far from Sepphoris?" Yeshua asked.

After thinking for a moment, Joseph said, "I never heard of it before."

"If you never heard of it, it must be far away." They walked for a while. Yeshua said, "Caelus wanted to repay you. Do you think there will ever be such an occasion?"

"A soldier repay me? I don't see how."

RAUCOUS and troubled gatherings became more frequent in the neighborhoods and on the outskirts of every village and city. Outside Sepphoris Joseph and Yeshua saw a crowd gathered halfway up a hill about fifty paces from the road. A woman's wail filled the air even at that distance.

Yeshua said, "They might need your help like the soldier did a year ago. Do you have Grandmama's mixture in your tunic sack?"

Joseph pointed inside his tunic and nodded.

Seeing no one gathering stones, Joseph motioned to Yeshua to walk up the hill with him.

A detail of ten Roman soldiers, half of them mounted, covered the face of the hill. Three of them were tying a man, squealing and struggling, to a wooden cross piece, a five-foot length of roughhewn timber. Yeshua grabbed Joseph's arm; his face blanched. "What will they do with him?"

"We will go back down. We should not have come up. Your mother is baking the sweetened wheat bread that you like."

"No, Poppa. I am eighteen years old. I am as tall as you, almost. I must see what happens to him."

"It will not be pleasant."

They stayed.

The man, as large and as strong as any stone carrier, now lying on the crosspiece, kept wriggling and pulling his arm out of the rope. One of the soldiers knelt on the man's forearm, frustration written in the soldier's every move, while another picked up a heavy hammer and a nail, its coarse edges catching the low sun. He jabbed the nail into the palm of the man's hand and struck the hammer a blow; the man pulled his arm away, leaving a chunk of his hand under the nail. The man let out a violent yell and fell unconscious. The soldier grabbed his dangling arm, set it on the cross piece and hammered a nail between the two bones of the wrist. Another soldier took a rope and tied his other arm to the opposite end of the cross piece. The man awoke and screeched again his heart-piercing scream.

"You there," a soldier barked at two of the bigger men in the crowd. The two men's expressions changed: fear replaced curiosity and hate remained. A soldier commanded them to lift the cross piece with the man attached and drag it across one end of a longer piece, the post. The soldier with the hammer drove two long iron rods through holes in the cross piece and into the post. They tied ropes around the two pieces to reinforce the cross. Two soldiers and the two helpers lifted the cross piece, and maneuvered it until the opposite end of the post dropped into a hole in the ground. Every clumsy motion, every straining lift, every pull of the rope and the final jolting drop, brought new blood-curdling screams from the crucified. Dried blood on the cross piece, deep grooves on the post, and disturbed earth around the hole – all gave witness to the frequency of this excruciating ritual. One of the soldiers tied the man's feet to a bloodied block of wood bolted to the post. The crucified man pressed his feet against the block and pulled up with what remained of his arms. He drew loud gasping breaths. When his arms tired, the downward pull of his limp body stopped his lungs from drawing another breath. Almost unconscious, he lifted himself once more, air flooding in again, screams escaping. Up and down he would continue for hours, until exhaustion brought an airless death.

One soldier stayed at the site to keep the crowd from rescuing the condemned; the others, their work done, left in two columns, one on foot, the other on horseback.

Still holding the hammer, the soldier who had nailed the man to the cross withdrew from the others and led his horse down the hill alone. As he approached Joseph and

Yeshua, he stopped, looked at them, and dropped to one knee. His hands shook, his shoulders and head quivered, as if throwing off an invisible rat that had sunk teeth into his skin and claws into his hair.

Joseph knelt on one knee facing the familiar soldier. Yeshua stood beside his father.

"I can't do this anymore," said Caelus of Sicily. He took a deep breath, gained control of the shaking and stood up. He turned toward his horse, leaning on the saddle.

"How is your son?" Yeshua asked.

He turned around toward Yeshua. "He has recovered." He looked to Joseph. "Our physician said you missed your calling; you should have become a physician."

"He is kind to say that."

"He said my son's arm will heal but he will never be a soldier. At first I grieved for him at that loss." He turned and looked up the hill where the crucified man endured the suffering in periods of silence punctuated by screams and gasps. "Now, I am not sure it is a loss."

Joseph, too, looked up at the crucified man. "What did he do to deserve such a fate?"

"Little enough. A common thief. If he had practiced his craft among your people—he was one of you—he would not have even gotten our attention. He made the mistake of robbing a messenger of the emperor."

Joseph pondered the sin of the bandit and the punishment not for what he had done but for choosing the wrong victim.

"I must tell you something," said the soldier.

Joseph stepped closer, wary of the horse's wandering hooves.

"I appreciate what you did for me, what you did for my son." He hesitated, looked around and then continued.

"When I was assigned to the crucifixion detail, our cohort leader taught us how to think of what we do. He told us, 'A great bird swoops down and its talons snatch a squealing rabbit. The next day it returns to the same spot and, by Jove, not only does it see another rabbit but it looks like yesterday's dinner. Thus it is with these Jews: there's one to replace every one you snatch.' After what you did for my son, I saw things differently. So today I oversaw my last crucifixion. I have paid for a new duty."

"No wonder you choose not to do this." He shifted from understanding to puzzlement. "Do you mean you pay for your assignment?" Joseph asked.

"Not according to the rules, but the cohort leader makes the assignments and, like every soldier with a wife, he needs more money than he earns."

Soldiers gave the appearance they were in charge of the life they led, but they were as much subjects as those they commanded.

"My record will show a duty deferred and before I retire I will have to complete the crucifixion assignment." Having regained his composure, he mounted his horse. "With Fortuna's blessing my death will intervene."

❧

"MY DEAR SON, I wish you had not seen all that," Mary replied when Yeshua related to her every detail of his and Poppa's encounter with crucifixion.

"Mama, I am no longer a child. Poppa has taught me about the savagery that comes from the desolation in men's hearts. He has also shown me the joy of turning one heart."

"We see more wickedness today than when I was a young girl and you will see even more I fear. If you have to witness the wretched deeds man does, better that you see them with your Poppa."

"The first time we met the soldier, I saw Poppa heal the child. Today I learned he also healed the child's father. 'He who pardons our sins also heals our ills.'"

"'And he surrounds you with love and compassion.' Yeshua, you may no longer be a child in your own eyes, and those of our neighbors, but you are our child. It can be no other way," said Mary.

"Friends my age are married. Do their parents still think of them as children?"

Mary gave Joseph a silent message, more a question: Has Yeshua spoken to you of marriage?

Joseph gave his head a brief shake. He said to Yeshua, "It is the same for other parents as for us. We think of you not as *a* child but as *our* child."

Mary said, "If I had any doubt that you are no longer a child, it vanished with all the stitches your new tunic requires. You are as tall as Poppa." She raised her eyebrows in a loving gesture to Joseph. "But slimmer."

"Poppa, can I stand beside you?"

Joseph stood. Yeshua's eyes widened.

"You are right, Mama. I didn't realize." He thought for a moment and then said, "Even more reason then, you must let me see the blessed and the not so blessed."

AT THE DEATH of Caesar Augustus, Roman Emperor for forty-one years, uncertainty and increased fear took hold throughout Judea. The uncertainty dissipated rapidly as the people realized that the new Emperor, Tiberius, would rule the Empire with a harsh hand but not concentrate it on them. In Galilee fear of Herod Antipas outweighed fear of the Romans.

Not caught up in the fear of either, John continued to take Yeshua on his exploring adventures, eastward through the hills to Tabor, or northeast to Magdala and then north along the Sea of Galilee as far as Capernaum, and other times westward to Mt. Carmel and up through Syria to the Great Sea.

"Some days we find more teachers at a crossroad than in the synagogue," John said to Mary and Joseph before he and Yeshua set off to visit James and Leah in Capernaum.

Joseph asked, "What do these teachers teach?"

"Some pretend they know what's in the Torah or the Writings. Most like to hear themselves talk," John said.

"John is well able to keep up with them: he challenges them," Yeshua said. As the cousins had matured, Yeshua had grown broader and several inches taller than John, who remained more wiry and agile.

"After they talk about Moses or Abraham or our father David, they get to the same old message, pushing the people to withhold their taxes—even after Judah and his followers were quashed—and get ready for the great uprising. A few in the crowd follow them until soldiers run them off."

Mary's hands would not be still, one knitting the other. "Be careful not to arouse them or, worse, get the attention of the authorities." She picked up a bundle wrapped in cloths and handed it to Yeshua. "Give this to James. He and his family will enjoy it with their evening meal." She turned to John. "You'll be in Capernaum by evening?"

John nodded and he and his cousin departed.

After they left Mary confided to her husband. "After all their excursions I should have more confidence in them but John now can't seem to listen without debating, even provoking. He worries me, the way he flings his words as straight and keen as he slings a stone."

"Words and stones both can hurt, but his words will hurt him more than anyone else," Joseph said. "Yeshua has a calming effect on him."

Mary said, "It's the effect that John has on Yeshua that bothers me."

∾

BEFORE NIGHT FELL ON NAZARETH, Joses ran into the courtyard and then through the rear entry into the house. "Joseph," he called in a whisper.

Joseph got up from a chair in the main room and went to him.

"They've taken him." His whisper rose so it wound up as a raspy yell. "The soldiers have taken Yeshua." He paused and took a breath. "They took him and several other men as prisoners."

"Who has taken him? Where?" Mary asked as she rushed into the courtyard.

Joses looked from Joseph to Mary, annoyed at himself for being so loud. "Soldiers on horseback. They led Yeshua and others away, tied with a rope."

Joseph said. "Joses, calm, now. Tell us everything you know. When did this happen?"

"Today, in the afternoon. We were leading my sheep to the lee side of the hills a few miles beyond Garis. A boy from our village was helping me. I had a plain view of the road that goes to the Sea of Galilee and I watched two men climb up to the face of a cave there and they started to speak, getting louder and louder but I was too far away to hear the words and then I saw Yeshua and cousin John so I ran toward them and my sheep ran after me but then I remembered that the young ones, our five new lambs, could not keep up and might wander off and a wolf or a great bird would snatch them so I turned back and got all the sheep together." He paused, took a breath, then another, and let his shoulders sag.

Joseph said, "Wise choice to come to us."

"I thought you would not want Mary to hear, I mean until we knew more."

"I wish neither of us had to hear any of this but we must," Joseph said.

"You are a messenger of the Lord, Joses," Mary said. "Tell us, did you see soldiers beat Yeshua and John? Could you tell where they took them?"

"No, they didn't beat any of them. They didn't take John, just Yeshua."

Joseph looked from Joses to Mary just as she directed her puzzlement at him.

"They took Yeshua but not John," Joses repeated.

"Where did John go? What about the two men who were preaching? Did the soldiers take them away?"

"They ran off. When the soldiers galloped in from the wooded hillside—not far from where my sheep were grazing—most of the crowd ran. I saw them but couldn't understand them. I then saw everyone start running. The two rabble-rousers ran up from the rocks they were standing on, up and across the ledges, and then I couldn't see them. John and Yeshua were on the edge of the crowd, not even trying to get close. Then John pulled Yeshua after him as he, too, ran toward the caves and rocks. There are many caves on that side of the hills. A woman fell and Yeshua stopped to help her get up. Then she ran after the others to the hills. The soldiers grabbed anyone they could. There were six soldiers so they grabbed six men."

Mary sat at their table, her face ashen. Joseph sat opposite her and motioned to Joses to sit as well. All were silent for several minutes, pondering what Joses had told them.

Where was John? Where did the soldiers take the prisoners? People had recounted tales of Herod's soldiers leading prisoners off and killing them rather than having to present charges against them. The foreigners sometimes had a more humane approach to dealing with the people of Galilee.

"What kind of soldiers were they?" asked Joseph.

"Horse soldiers," Joses said.

That won't help us.

"We must find out where he is and we must go to him," said Mary.

"Joses, could you tell where the soldiers were leading the prisoners?" asked Joseph.

"They went around the hills on the cold side, not back to Nazareth. I've gone through the hills up there and the fields lead toward Sepphoris. There is no road from there but the soldiers were walking them across the plain, all tied together."

"That makes sense. Both Herod's soldiers and the foreigners have garrisons there, probably prisons as well," said Joseph.

"We will go to Sepphoris. You've been there ten thousand times, Joseph. Let's not delay."

"I'll get your donkey ready," said Joses.

Mary gathered whatever bread and fruit were in their bowls.

Joseph said, "When we lost Yeshua eight years ago I did not trust as our father Abraham trusted. You reminded me we must trust especially when we don't know."

"No, Joseph, we reminded each other. We both grew in faith as we searched."

"When we found him in the Temple, I decided if we ever lost sight of him again we would go to where he is to be found: the Temple." Joseph shook his head, finding it hard to believe all they had heard. "Today we will not find him in the Temple but in a prison." *We will seek our son, a man who has done no wrong, in a prison. What are we to think of us who were charged with his safety?* "O Lord, replenish our strength; guide us along the right path. Guide us to see that even when we walk through the darkness, we fear no harm for you are at our side."

Mary said, "In Jerusalem we were able to search and as long as we could search we were sure we would find him. I never imagined we would neglect our Yeshua to the point of his becoming a prisoner." She waited in thought. "John is the one. John's venturing spirit has always frightened me. I feared it would put them both at risk. Never did I imagine peril such as this."

CHAPTER 14

"In all your trips to Sepphoris you never contemplated one like this," Mary said as she and Joseph started on the Sepphoris road from Nazareth.

A half hour after they left, wind from the Great Sea brought rain that flew more than fell. The wool tunics Mary had squeezed into the sack now became their protection. Brief pauses in the rain allowed limited conversation that buoyed their spirits.

"Happy were all those trips, first beside my Poppa and then beside our son. First I, then Yeshua, learned of life in Galilee beyond Nazareth. The grandeur of Sepphoris stood in such contrast to our little village. Sepphoris was magnificent with its palace and theater and water works." He looked up at Mary on their donkey. "More splendid than its physical beauty was a baby named Little Mary."

She adjusted the tunic covering his head and shoulders as the donkey plodded along. "You had no way of knowing that with Little Mary you would travel from Nazareth to Bethlehem to Egypt and back to Nazareth."

"And now to Sepphoris, where we began. Whatever we find in Sepphoris this day we will trust in the Lord. 'Lead him out of his prison and we will give thanks to your name.'"

Joseph recalled the visitor in the cloudless blue tunic and the years that had intervened since their last encounter. "Where are our messengers?"

"What do you ... oh, yes, my breeze and your friendly stranger. It must mean the Lord has no need for a messenger. We will trust that we will know what he wants of us when we get there."

The rain and wind stopped as abruptly as it had started. They reached the last mile, the portion of the road that was now paved. As Sepphoris came into view, someone ran out of the pre-dawn mist toward them.

"Cousin Joseph, Cousin Mary," John shouted as he approached them.

"John, why are you running?" Joseph looked beyond him to see if anyone was chasing him.

John came up to them and stopped, bent over with his hands on his knees, gasping for air. He still had the bundle Mary had given him for James. After a minute he stood up straight. "Did you hear what happened to Yeshua? Yesterday?"

Mary climbed off the donkey and put her arms around John. "We know what Joses told us last night. Are you all right? Have you seen Yeshua?"

"I am not hurt but I fear for Yeshua."

Mary drew an audible breath and stood motionless. "Tell me."

"I followed the band of soldiers with the six men in tow, tied hand to hand. I stayed well behind them on the plain and above them through the hills. They brought them to a prison in the garrison inside the city." He nodded toward Sepphoris. "They did not beat the men, at least not so far."

Joseph asked, "In which garrison are they held?"

"The prison inside Herod's garrison. People say it holds so many prisoners they are like fish in a net. I would have stayed to watch what happens today but I wanted you to know about Yeshua."

"Does it matter which garrison holds him? He is a captive either way," said Mary.

John looked up to Joseph, waiting.

Joseph said, "Neither is the right place for Yeshua. The foreigners would bring charges against each man and would release him if they had none."

"And Herod?" she asked.

"He does not concern himself with such legal structure. If he chooses to detain one, he detains him. For as long as he wants," Joseph said.

"I must go to him. Even if I cannot see him I must get close to him." Mary mounted the donkey and the three set off again for the city and the prison.

Joseph asked John, "Why did the soldiers take captives? Joses did not talk about a disturbance of any kind."

"There was no trouble, just talk. Too much talk. Two men spoke out about the fraud in our own Temple taxes and tithes. It was nothing new. I don't believe they knew what they were talking about but a small crowd gathered. Herod's soldiers sometimes like to make an example of a few easy targets. Yeshua and I stood at the back of the gathering. Yeshua had not said a word. When soldiers came at a gallop, people ran in different directions. It was chaos. Yeshua was running behind me when three women in front of us ran into each other and fell in a heap. Yeshua stopped to help them get up. As soon as the women ran off, the soldiers grabbed him. He's always doing that sort of thing with no regard for his own safety. All the men they took are strong looking, like Yeshua."

"What do they do to them to make them examples?" Joseph asked.

"The example comes in capturing them. They think it will keep people away from the Zealots and other rabble-rousers. Once they seize them, they put them to work. They paved this road we're walking on. Prisoners are slaves and road building requires many laborers. That's why the prison bulges with sturdy men."

Mary thought and hoped aloud. "Maybe they won't mistreat him since they need his labor."

THE GATES of Sepphoris stood open all day and much of the night as the city had become an attraction. Joseph, Mary and John entered freely. Both Joseph and John knew the city well so they walked directly to Herod's army garrison. Behind it stood their prison, and beyond it were the plains that stretched north toward the distant Province of Syria. What had been a modest prison had grown, with an open prison courtyard used to house extra men. Men held in the unwalled courtyard were tied together with six or eight feet of rope between each man and the next. Joseph peered into the courtyard as the three eased past.

"I don't see Yeshua in there," said Mary, who had done her own looking. "What does that mean? Where is he?"

John said, "Last night this courtyard was filled. They must have gone to a work site." John looked past the court-yard toward the plains. "Either within the city or perhaps on the road to Magdala. Herod is determined to pave every road that leads to Sepphoris."

They chose to search within the city first. If all the captured men were of Yeshua's size, they would be easy to find. They went neighborhood by neighborhood, often skipping a section that showed no sign of construction. They dared not inquire of anyone.

As they passed Herod's renovated theater, Joseph said, "You were too young for you to remember, but your family's house stood right there." He pointed to the remnants of a street that had become part of a sprawling market. "Another time we will come back with Yeshua and share a story or two."

"That sounds like a man reinforcing his trust." Mary nodded agreement. "Yes, we will return *with* Yeshua."

By noon they had scoured all the building sites they could see. They paused for food and a brief rest and set off on the newly paved road toward Magdala on the shore of the Sea of Galilee.

The road began northeastward and within two miles turned more eastward around a hilly interlude. The sounds of banging and hammering reached them before they came out from behind sandy mounds and saw a work-site not fifty yards in front of them. From that distance it looked like a small army wandering around, but as they came nearer a division of tasks became clear. Each team of workers did one thing. They unearthed great stones from the hills, transported the stones to a cutting station, cut the stones into usable rectangular pieces or pavers, dug and leveled the ground to receive a layer of pavers, and laid the pavers in straight rows.

The three walked forward. No one questioned them.

"The Romans have a hand in this." Joseph pointed to

designs within the brickwork, such as an arc of pavers set within a rectangular frame of stones of a contrasting color. "That's their style more than ours. Yeshua and I have both laid stones like this. The way the work is organized far surpasses anything Herod's men could manage." He looked at other scrolls and swirls in the roadway. "He'll be right at home here."

Mary looked at him, eyebrows raised, head tilted. "What did you say?"

Joseph understood her question and realized what he said was not what he meant. "If they see what he is able to do, he might not have to break his back with digging and lifting."

"Cousins, look" John said, nodding in the direction of a crew of prisoners setting down the pavers.

Yeshua worked with four other men, setting stones and sprinkling fine sand between them. The men, untied, walked freely from stone pile to road, placing and replacing the pavers until each section met their satisfaction. Travelers heading one way or the other walked around the workers, gawking as they passed.

Joseph, Mary and John did as the other travelers did until Joseph bade them stop. He helped Mary from the donkey, took a file from a saddle sack and pretended to check the animal's hoof.

They looked around in every direction, catching glimpses of Yeshua on each turn.

"Can we give him the sweet loaf you sent for James?" John asked his cousins.

Mary smiled at him and shrugged her shoulders. Her look reflected all their uncertainty.

"I ate some of it last night. It tasted as wonderful as I expected," said John.

"I'm glad you still had it with you. We never know what a morsel of bread will do. 'You fed your people with the food of angels and furnished them bread from heaven, ready at hand, untoiled for.' In this case, John, I think you toiled for it." She looked from John to Joseph. "How can we get it to Yeshua?"

Joseph said, "I will walk over and give it to him. What can they do, take it away from him? He will give most of it away anyway."

"No, Joseph, I'll go. The soldiers are less likely to wonder at a woman who shows a little kindness. I will want to speak to him but I will not say a word."

She took the loaf from John, opened the cloth wrapping and walked back to the men placing the stones. With her head low, she bent and handed the loaf to her son. The smell of the sweat from his tunic assaulted her; she thought of the sweet scent of her baby son not long ago as he nuzzled against her. The cuts in his fingers from handling the sharp-edged stones forced out the tears she had managed to hold back. She turned to hide them as they dropped to her face. Yeshua took the wrapped bread and set it on the ground. As she walked away from him, she heard him hum a song they had often sung together. "Praise the Lord from the heavens; give praise in the heights."

"You there! Stop." A soldier standing near where she had left Joseph and John shouted at her.

She did so.

"Come here. Now."

Mary walked to him, eyes cast down.

"What did you give to that prisoner?"

"Some bread for the workers." She looked up at the soldier. "And for the men who protect them. Enjoy it."

The soldier did not respond but nodded his head to the

side, directing her to move on. She returned to Joseph and John.

The soldier walked to the stone setters, picked up the loaf, broke off a piece, ate it and then broke off another chunk. He threw the rest of the loaf on the pile of sand the setters used to tighten the contacts between the pavers. "You'll like the gritty texture." He laughed and walked back to his station.

A worker beside Yeshua picked up the bread, tore off a wedge and passed it on to another prisoner. As Yeshua kept working, the loaf shrunk until the last morsel wound its way to him. He closed his eyes for a moment before he ate it.

"He knows we have found him. That alone will sustain him," Joseph said.

The three continued to walk toward Magdala until they were out of sight of the prison crew. They waited until a large contingent of travelers going toward Sepphoris reached them. They spread out among the others and again walked past Yeshua. A supervisor or engineer looked closely at the work the men had done. His non-military attire, complete with upswept tunic tucked into a broad leather belt, indicated he was a Roman but not a soldier; long calipers hanging from his belt, where soldiers carried a blade, showed his status as an engineer. Pointing to different sections of the roadway, he conversed with the prisoners, not barking as the soldiers did. Yeshua's co-workers pointed to him in response to something the engineer said or asked. After a few minutes, the engineer walked away and the prisoners continued working.

Not wanting to draw attention to themselves, Joseph, Mary and John stayed with the throng until it dispersed on arrival in Sepphoris. As they walked together through the city, John recognized three men who had been in the crowd when the soldiers captured Yeshua. He went up to them and asked where he might get a meal.

The man and his companions explained they were not from this city and they, too, were looking for food.

One of two women standing behind the men recognized John. "You were listening to the tithe-protesters on the road to Magdala yesterday."

One of the men grabbed her arm. "Lower your voice."

Another of the men said, "Better you say nothing at all."

She looked around at passers-by and those standing in doorways and continued in a subdued tone. "Your friend helped me get up."

The other woman, more a girl than a woman, stepped forward and said, "Me too. I'm sorry he bothered because the soldiers wouldn't have taken us. If they can't get the rousers they take any strong men within reach."

"You've seen this before, have you?" asked John.

The first man looked uneasy. "What is it to you?"

"It's nothing to me. My friend and I were on our way to Capernaum when we came upon the rousers, as you called them. They're nothing to us either."

The younger woman said, "They took my brother. They have him out digging rocks for the Magdala road, better off there than rotting in the courtyard."

"Do you know how long they'll keep him."

"As long as they want. If we ask at the garrison, they'll declare a charge and neither we nor my brother will like the declaration."

John looked to Joseph and Mary who had pulled back at what the woman said.

"What will you do?" asked Joseph.

"*Wait* is what we'll do. It'll take more patience than I have but without the money it's the only way."

"What does money have to do with it?" asked Joseph.

The women looked at the men, sheepish like, as if they had said something they should not have.

The talkative man said, "The soldiers don't care which man is the prisoner and which isn't as long as they have enough laborers so they don't have to lift a shovel themselves. And they're not beyond a bribe."

The young woman said, "If we had a hundred shekels my brother would be a free man and the soldiers would snatch another man tomorrow."

D<small>AYS</small> <small>TURNED</small> <small>TO</small> <small>WEEKS</small>, and daily treks to Sepphoris became more strenuous, but not as exhausting as seeing Yeshua shape stones and lay pavers day after day while they did not yet have the money to free him. That goal prompted them to save all they could of Joseph's earnings.

They had learned that in the late evening the soldiers at the courtyard allowed prisoners' friends to bring food for prisoners and soldiers alike, provided the food met the soldiers' liking. While each evening saw different soldiers on courtyard duty, every one of them bartered for food. Joseph and Mary made their visit after the sun set each day and then returned the five miles to Nazareth afterward. Their evening prayer became a prayer on foot: "'My God, my god, why have you abandoned us? We call by day but you do not answer; by night and we have no relief. In you our ancestors trusted and you rescued them.' Father Abraham, help us to trust like them and like you."

Mary made sure they had bread with olive relish or fruit

compote, and grapes or pears. When they could they bought either goat cheese or salted fish, which Mary soaked in goat's milk as she had in Egypt. They had to balance saving enough to free Yeshua with spending enough to provide satisfying meals. The soldiers rewarded their special efforts by ignoring their son, far preferable to routine malicious treatment.

At the end of the fourth week, they came to the garrison prison courtyard as they had done each day. They did not see Yeshua.

As they walked the perimeter of the prison, a soldier, whom they had fed several times, came to them.

"You are looking for someone. That is not allowed."

"Where is Yeshua?" Joseph asked.

"That is not your concern. Nor is it mine, for I don't care to know the offenders' names."

"Please, tell us where our son, Yeshua, has gone," Mary said.

The soldier looked tired, tired from a long day of work, tired of his surroundings, and tired of dealing with people he wasn't paid to deal with. His uniform said he had spent much of the day on dusty, sandy roads.

"You must be hungry, my friend. Mary, have we something to share with this man?" Joseph handed her the sack.

Mary removed a pottery bowl from the food sack and handed it to the soldier. He took it without a word. She unwrapped the loaf, broke off a double serving and gave it to him. He took it and pulled off a small piece.

The soldier looked around at the other soldiers stationed in the courtyard. He held the hunk of bread in front of his mouth and spoke in a murmur. "The Romans took a tall prisoner this morning. I don't know his name but he had a reputation for saying little and executing fine stone work."

"Where did they take him?" asked Mary.

"That's all I know." He looked from Joseph to Mary and back to Joseph. "If I knew more I would tell you."

"A blessing," said Joseph.

Joseph started walking, with Mary right behind him. After they walked some distance away from the prison, Mary said, "I don't know where to go but I know we must find him."

~

SEPPHORIS HAD no temple but did have several synagogues. "Unfortunately we do not have to look there," Joseph said.

"Agreed."

He read anxiety on her face, and she must have seen the same on his. "We will not lose trust," Mary said.

"The foreigners will send him where they need his skills." *What did it matter if his Poppa taught him all he knew about working with stone and wood? About the hills and wells in all of Galilee? Of little Nazareth that lives a hidden life while Sepphoris's every breath is on display? To what end did Mary and he make sure Yeshua knew the stories of their people, the perseverance of Moses, the trust of Abraham, the songs of David, the resilience of Joseph? Why did the Lord send his messenger to Joseph if any man could bring the son of God to his destiny? It was Joseph's work, to preserve his son for what he is to do!*

"...far away?" Mary was talking to him. *Yes, he was far away.*

"I'm sorry, Mary. What did you say?"

"What do you mean they will send him wherever they need his skills? Do you think they will send him far away?"

"The emperor's lands are vast, Mary. It seems that roads, palaces, theaters, homes, whole cities spring up everywhere. But they don't *spring up*; someone builds them."

They walked across Sepphoris, past remnants of the city wall that reminded them of the city's growth under Herod Antipas. The Roman garrison faced the setting sun and the Great Sea with its ships and ports that brought in what the local economy could not provide. Workers, stripped to the waist, carried, dragged, and carted loads of stone, lengths of lumber, and mounds of sand in through the garrison portals. Joseph and Mary stood nearby, watching and looking for Yeshua.

After some time Mary said, "He is not among them."

"I would not expect them to make him a porter. If he is here, he is using his skills."

"Joseph, they would be breaking his back now if you had not taught him your craft."

He wondered if Mary had read his thoughts, the temptation to wish it all away. *Abraham, I need you.* "God will provide," he said.

"Even as we walk in ignorance of what is to come, God is providing."

They saw him exit through the garrison portal beside the foreign engineer who had examined his work weeks earlier. The two men stopped and turned back, taking turns pointing up at the garrison, pantomiming walls, windows and turrets.

"He has the same dirty tunic. He never before had to wear such a garment." Mary's concern for her son went beyond his safety.

"Wait. Let's see where they go."

The couple waited and watched. After some time Yeshua saw them. When it seemed that his discussion with the engineer had ended, he appeared to ask something. The engineer nodded, looked toward Joseph and Mary and signaled them to approach. Yeshua stepped behind a stack of timbers.

The engineer said to Yeshua, "Be quick or we will both lose our jobs or our heads."

Yeshua embraced his Mama and Poppa. "Do not fret for me. I am treated well."

The filth on his skin and tunic belied his claim.

Mary pulled back from him, her expression proclaiming she had a plan. "Joseph, undo your tunic. You, too, Yeshua."

They did as Mary said.

"Now switch tunics, swiftly." She looked across the busy work area where everyone had a task.

The engineer stood to one side without letting his gaze leave either the son or his parents. After Joseph and Yeshua switched their clothing the engineer said to Joseph, "If this one learned his craft from you, you did well. If you also taught him what put him in here, not so well. Now, be on your way." Yeshua disappeared inside the garrison beside the engineer. Joseph and Mary walked on.

Mary rolled up Yeshua's tunic as they set off for Nazareth and home. Herod's garrison offered regular contact with their son. They had to continue their routine of walking each day to and from Sepphoris if they wanted to continue to see him.

"It is good Yeshua has grown to be your size. You could never wear a tunic the size of John's."

Joseph smiled at his wife's simple optimism. "God provides for his son in ways we could not arrange. We have no choice but to trust. 'God himself will provide.'"

"So I will wash his tunic and we will trust."

Their trip again became an occasion for their evening

prayer. Afterward they became quiet amid the sounds of the night: the scurrying as prey evaded the predator, the rustling as the breeze disturbed the branches and the chirping as locusts called and replied.

Joseph broke the silence. "Whatever the foreigners are building inside, it won't take forever. We will watch for what happens next."

~

A WEEK after Mary made Joseph and Yeshua switch tunics, they saw the engineer climb into a coach drawn by two powerful white horses. Arrayed behind the carriage, three columns of soldiers stood ready to ride. Others stood in front of and beside the coach.

Joseph walked as close to the carriage as he dared. Although he did not understand the language spoken by the soldiers, he heard one of their leaders say "Caesarea" and "Rome." These he knew of and wondered if they had become Yeshua's destinations. Thirty miles from Sepphoris, the port city of Caesarea on the Great Sea served as the gateway to Rome and Athens and other places that the people of Galilee had only heard about.

"Let us wait here to see if the engineer requires Yeshua to go with him," Joseph said to Mary after he rejoined her. They found themselves beside a group of several women on the edge of a small crowd that had gathered.

Within minutes of the engineer getting into the carriage, a driver cracked the whip and the horses broke into a trot. Some mounted soldiers led, some surrounded and most followed the coach as the formation rode west.

No prisoners had gone as part of the company. "I wonder if Yeshua's prison life will change now," Mary said.

One of the women, dressed in reds and purples unlike what most women wore on the streets of Sepphoris, said, "If you've got a man inside, you can be sure everything will change."

The women with her as well as Mary and Joseph looked at her, confused at what she might mean.

"The change of duty always brings new routines for the prisoners, some bad, some worse. I've seen it for years." She sounded like someone who knew what happened inside the garrison, or at least the prison section of it. She turned to Mary and in a softer voice said, "I heard what you said so I thought I'd let you know how it is."

Mary held her gaze, wanting to know more but not wanting to bring attention to Joseph and her or to Yeshua. "Many soldiers just left the prison. Who guards the men inside until the soldiers come back?"

"That half century will ride to Caesarea and board a ship for Rome. Another half will ride the horses back here later today. In the meantime a reduced force will keep the prisoners busy."

Joseph wondered how she knew so much of prison practices. If he had the chance he would ask Mary to find out.

Mary looked at him with her look of knowing. She turned to the woman, touched her arm and said, "You must love someone inside very much to prompt you to give of yourself."

The woman looked at her, taken aback. "What do you ..."

Mary continued, "Standing, watching, waiting day after day is a great gift, often the only one we can give."

The woman lowered her head a little and her voice, too. "They took my son. Our own people came to my house and took my son." She raised her head and clutched at Mary's arms. "They told the soldiers my son had spoken against the Emperor. He would never do that." She cried, pulled her hands from Mary and wiped her face in her own robe. "Here they scourged him. In order to go inside to care for him I have to give the guards the only thing I have to give." Her voice rose in spite of her efforts to control it. "I hate them." She took one deep breath and then another. "But I love him." She dropped her hands to her side. "So tonight I must find a new soldier willing to trade."

"You have great courage," Mary said to the woman, "and great love." She looked from the woman to Joseph. "Would I have the courage to give what this woman gives in order to care for a son? My son, our son?" Her lips formed the words for Joseph's eyes alone: "The son of God?"

Joseph looked from Mary to the woman to the garrison prison. Two foreign soldiers led Yeshua and a dozen other men out through the portal, and walked them toward the paving project where Yeshua first encountered the engineer. Joseph wondered why Herod's soldiers roped the prisoners together, but the foreign soldiers did not.

Before Joseph and Mary left the woman to follow the prisoners, she said to them, "I think you, too, have a son." She nodded toward the line of prisoners. "Get him out if you can; at any cost get him out. The last commanders were more concerned with getting work done than in keeping track of the prisoners or the charges against them. The new half century might want to keep track. Get him out before it comes to that." She turned and walked away from them and the line of prisoners, to resume her watching and waiting and bartering.

~

"WHAT DO you have in our food sack?"

"Are you hungry, Joseph? It is not yet noon. Are you ill?"

"Mary, listen." They had just left the synagogue, Joseph from the men's side and Mary from the women's. "That woman told us what we must do for our son, and she does not know he is the son of God."

Mary nodded to him.

"That poor woman does what she does out of love for her son, but she cannot get him out of this hell. We must get Yeshua out of there, and we must do it before they make a charge against him, a charge that may stand for years. Years, Mary."

"We do not have the hundred shekels to get him out. What can we do?"

"We must get him out *today!*" He let the 'today' sink in. He had said it; now he must see it through.

"What does the food sack have to do with this? What do you have in mind?" She opened their sack, and showed him a round wheat bread, a hunk of hard cheese, two pears and a handful of roasted chestnuts.

He eyed the chestnuts, picked one up and put it into his mouth, rolled it around inside and then spit it into his hand. He gripped it, rolled it back and forth between both hands and looked at his palms. Brown, dark brown. "That's it," he said with enthusiasm.

"Joseph, what are you talking about? You have eaten hundreds of chestnuts and you know you must peel them first."

"When you made me trade tunics with Yeshua, what did you say?"

She thought back for a moment. "I said his was so full of sweat, washing it turned the stream to a sewer."

"Not that. When you said I could switch tunics with Yeshua, what else did you say?"

"Joseph, I don't feel like guessing. Tell me."

"You said it was a good thing I didn't have to switch tunics with John because his tunic ..."

"Was too small for you," she finished his thought. "Yes, it was fortunate you and Yeshua are both tall and broad." Her brows rose. "Joseph, are you thinking ..."

"Yes, I am. We must do it today before the new soldiers get to know him. We have never seen the soldiers that led him and the others out today so perhaps they are not familiar with the prisoners. Yeshua and I are the same size, we have the same skills, ..."

"His hair is dark like mine while yours is light brown and ..." She smiled at him, gripping his arm. "Light brown with a little silver." She eyed it more closely. "More silver than we have ever had in our purse." A shared laugh brought a relaxed moment.

Joseph put three chestnuts into his mouth, puffing out his cheeks.

Their son was still a prisoner but the air had lightened. Their talk took on a sense of purpose. "I'll keep my head down and not let the two soldiers see the skin of many years," he mumbled.

"Joseph, what if it doesn't work? What if the soldiers at the road site do know him? You both will be prisoners. Or worse than prisoners."

"It will work, Mary. This is how the Lord is providing. Now, take these chestnuts and let them soak inside your mouth." He handed her two chestnuts. "Water will make them wet but won't loosen their dye."

They rolled the chestnuts around in their mouths. After

a couple of minutes Mary took hers out and stroked Joseph's hair with them.

Joseph said, "His tunic reeks of sweat and worse; I will switch his for mine while you take the bread and cheese to the soldiers. Keep them busy. They long for the company of a woman even for the few moments they allow. I will put on Yeshua's tunic and then you will walk away with the man with the clean tunic."

Mary looked at him. Hope took its place beside the worry in her eyes

"Afterward shall Yeshua and I return to Sepphoris and then go home to Nazareth?"

"No. Continue walking in the same direction. When you reach Magdala go north along the shore to Capernaum. James will welcome you. Yeshua knows where to find him."

"We will come back to you, to make sure you are fed and well."

"No you won't. Yeshua is not to return to Sepphoris, ever. Someone might recognize him. And you, Mary, let forty days pass before you return here. When you do return, remember to call me, 'Yeshua.'"

She took in all Joseph said, tilting her head as her father did when he was pondering something.

Joseph said, "The name Yeshua fits him, not me." He recalled the stranger in the cloudless blue tunic and his instruction: *You will name him "Yeshua" because he will save his people.* "I am not a savior."

"You are *his* savior, Joseph." Tears filled her eyes.

"None of that, Mary. We have a son to save."

Mary took the chestnuts from Joseph's mouth and continued to rub his hair until the last chestnut shared its rich color with Joseph's fading locks.

~

ONE OF THE soldier guards said, "Hard cheese needs fruit."

Joseph handed a pear to each of them, keeping his head down and saying nothing.

Mary said, "Take a bite of the pear with each bite of cheese." She tore off half the bread for the two soldiers and handed Joseph the remainder to bring to the four prisoners. Accustomed to this exchange, the soldiers neither objected nor hindered Joseph.

"She thinks we have never eaten hard cheese before," one of the soldiers teased.

Mary laughed with them and drew their attention away from the prisoners and toward the east and the gravel road that wound around the hills, thinning in the distance. "How far does the road go?" she asked, pointing.

They turned to look with her. "All the way to Magdala on the lake. Setting stones will keep us busy for many months," replied one soldier.

The other soldier laughed. "Keep *them* busy, you mean."

She continued to engage them with talk and questions.

By the time Joseph could no longer hear them, he had reached the prisoners who were on their knees. Yeshua and another man placed stones, the third filled the spaces with fine sand, and the fourth tamped it down with soft firm strokes. Joseph got down beside Yeshua, making a display of tearing chunks from the bread.

The prisoners hesitated, glancing back to the soldiers.

"They know I'm giving you this. Eat."

They took it eagerly.

Joseph whispered, "Your mother said to slip out of your tunic and put on mine."

Joseph and his son undid the belts around their tunics,

pulled them over their heads and exchanged them. As he passed him his tunic, Joseph handed the rest of the bread to Yeshua.

"Stand up, take this bread, break it, and give each of us a piece," Joseph told Yeshua.

Yeshua did as Poppa told him.

"Go to your mother and walk toward Magdala with her. Do not say a word to her or to the soldiers. Stay on the unpaved road."

He obeyed.

Mary started walking before Yeshua reached her. As he passed her, she stepped behind him and walked until they were out of sight of the work team.

His fellow prisoners finished eating and picked up a stone or a scoopful of sand or a trowel or a mallet. Joseph placed the next paver and the process continued, the sand road reluctantly giving way to another achievement for Herod.

As the sun set, prisoners and soldiers walked back to the garrison prison and entered a roofless yard surrounded by a stone wall where another fifty or more prisoners stood, or sat on the ground, or lay against the wall, their voices creating a collective murmur. Even in this open courtyard the stench of sweat, urine and feces forced Joseph to cover his face with his tunic; its scent brought Yeshua to him. An evening meal consisted of earthen bowls filled with a watery gruel and four flats of stale bread. The men snatched the bowls and the bread from one another, each clutching at them in turn. No wonder Mary's daily offerings to the prisoners had met with ravenous glee.

As night approached, the prisoners wandered to either assigned or accustomed spots. Waiting until the others had settled themselves, Joseph found an unclaimed spot and sat against the wall. "I will keep your teachings always, for all time and forever; let Yeshua and Mary walk freely for they, too, cherish your precepts." He pulled his tunic tight around himself, rested his head on his arm and lay sleepless, remembering the past month of nights when concern over Yeshua kept sleep at bay. As he did then, he passed this night thinking of Abraham preparing to sacrifice Isaac while knowing—not hoping or believing or trusting, but knowing deep within himself—that the Lord will provide. He thought of David, little David compared to the great king, armed with just a sling. A sling! John's sling had become his constant companion. Might he be using it this very minute to provide a meal for himself? Or for protection from the marauders of the night, human or animal, malicious or simply wild? If he came upon Yeshua in Capernaum, would Mary be able to persuade Yeshua to stay close and not risk another arrest for being part of a crowd attracted to another messiah? Galilee had seen enough messiahs over the past twenty years. Their people had grown weary of them and ready to surrender any who did not fit their expectations, just as they had relinquished any hope of relief from the oppression imposed by their own leaders as well as the foreigners.

The next day more stones, more sand, more bloodied finger tips prodded the paved marvel farther east. No kind woman appeared with bread as the sun climbed, baked the prisoners and set. The return trip to the prison began with tunics soaked with sweat and embedded with sand, and ended with chilled damp skin forming a bond with the same tunic that would cover them at night. Joseph learned that the evening meal was also the first of the day.

One of the men who laid pavers beside him approached

him as he sat in his place at the wall. "I don't know who you are."

Joseph looked up at him. "Like you I am a tekton. You are a man of considerable skill."

"Whoever you are, I know who you are not."

Joseph stood up, not wanting others to hear.

"The new cohort arrived yesterday. They neither know who we are nor care. You chose the day as wisely as you select stones."

"We have little to select; we do as we are told."

"I do not know why you traded places with another man, but you did. The soldiers will not look kindly on you if someone were to inform them."

"Why might someone tell tales?"

"Someone who wants a clean tunic and half a visitor's cake might or might not share what he knows."

Joseph promised the prisoner that when Mary returned she would get him a clean tunic and a whole cake of his choice. Joseph hoped that others did not know what this man knew. How desperate this poor man had become, to threaten another prisoner for a bit of food and clean clothes. In time would he wind up the same?

CHAPTER 15

In the weeks that followed, the road pushed toward Magdala. The work site had grown to eight crews of four men each to lay and tighten the pavers, with additional men to carry sand and split stones. Travelers passed them almost every day, with a rare offer of food. New soldiers, like the old, allowed this intrusion if they, too, shared the gift.

When he looked into the distance, as he did several times a day, Joseph hoped to see his wife. One day he did, with a man walking beside her. *Dear God, do not let Yeshua come here.* The men who had worked with Yeshua remained on the road crew and one of them would surely recognize him. The man who still waited for his reward for keeping silence knew him and would speak out unless some simple luxuries persuaded him otherwise.

As the pair came close to the work site, Joseph saw James with Mary. They approached the soldiers with their several bundles. After the usual examination and appropriation of their share, the soldiers permitted Mary and James to proceed to the men working with Joseph. Mary opened the sacks of food and spread it among the men. One bundle held a clean tunic.

Joseph could not fathom the feeling that overcame him. He wanted to hold her, to tell her all that had happened or not happened, and how he missed her and Yeshua and James and Joses, how the hardest part of each day was enduring the separation from them and not knowing if the separation would ever end. The soldiers permitted the food and tunic but only the briefest conversation.

As Mary handed Joseph the tunic, he nodded toward the man next to him. Mary looked at Joseph, then at the other man, and back to Joseph, her face in a frown of mystery. She did as Joseph indicated.

So much he wanted to tell her but he wished to listen more. He whispered, "How is Yeshua? How are you?" He thought of James and his family, and turned to him. "And you, dear James?"

Yeshua and Mary found Capernaum as busy as Nazareth was quiet. Boats and nets and fish odors had become part of their life. James's business had blossomed, building and repairing boats all over the northern end of the Sea of Galilee, while his family had grown with a third son. Cousin John visited often, disappearing as seamlessly as he reappeared, and growing more fervent. "Galilee's itinerant preachers have plenty of ardor but they should persuade the people to repent not rebel," he had repeated to Mary and Yeshua. Yeshua still yearned to accompany his cousin but so far had done as Mary asked. The two cousins spoke constantly of a way for one of them to trade places with Joseph. Mary had sent word to Joses to make their Nazareth home his own. While busying herself with sacks and bundles, Mary bent to Joseph's ear and asked, "Have you heard how long you must stay here?"

When Joseph looked at her he caught her looking at the stripes on the back of his neck.

The soldiers shouted for the visitors to move along. They had finished eating, so everyone else had to do the same.

Joseph pointed to the lacerations. "They're from the lash." He saw the look of horror on Mary's face and added, "Only once have I felt its sting." He stepped closer to her and whispered, "Not one prisoner has left since I came in. Rumors say Herod plans to pave every road in Galilee and Perea, right up to the wilderness." He chose not to say he expected to be a prisoner for many years.

EACH MONTHLY VISIT reminded him of Mary's lavish love for him. In their few minutes together he learned of James and his family and boat business; of John, and of Yeshua becoming more like John. While Mary never said so, he sensed Yeshua was growing restless. Few men in their twenties remained unmarried and lived with their mother. Yeshua must have felt the pull to get on with his life. As Joseph had this thought, he wondered if Yeshua had yet glimpsed what sort of life lay before him.

Mary had gotten word to Joses so he, too, walked the two hours to steal a minute with Poppa Joseph.

"Nazareth is not the same without its tekton," Joses said to Joseph.

"Nazareth has many fine tektons. Dedicated shepherds, not so many," Joseph said.

Because this and all unofficial visits could end at the

whim of the guards, Joseph urged Joses along. "Tell me about Joses."

"Poppa Joseph, I have come to ask your blessing. Do you remember Sarah, Simon's granddaughter?"

"I remember her. 'Sarah, the girl with the goats,' you used to say."

Joses laughed with Joseph. "She still prefers goats. For their cheese, she says. Simon says we will have two herds."

"You have my blessing, Joses. The Lord will be your shepherd; nothing shall you lack. Be a kind husband and tell Simon he has a fine granddaughter and she is a blessing to him." Simon and his wife had raised Sarah. Her mother, their daughter, had died at her birth and a year later her father had traveled to Jerusalem for the holy days and never returned.

"On your way," shouted a guard.

"Go, graze in green pastures," said Joseph as Joses left him.

Yeshua had grown up with James and Joses as his brothers. Now they had given him two sisters.

MARY TOLD JOSEPH ABOUT JOSES' wedding, a year later of his new daughter whom he named Hannah and later of his son. "They named him, 'Joseph.' Joses said the new Joseph would be just and kind and strong like his Grandpoppa Joseph."

Joseph smiled at the news of the growing family.

"Yeshua insists on coming to see you. Joseph, you must relent and let him come. Surely he can't be in danger after all these years."

As long as she brought gifts for them, the soldier guards permitted her to visit. Joseph no longer laid stones on the road to Magdala or anywhere else. Now permanently bent at the waist, his work was restricted to carpentry within the garrison. "Thank God I am still able to carve and shape furniture for the garrison that grows each year. If not for that I fear I would be left to rot in a desert dungeon," he told Mary.

"If he doesn't come soon, I am afraid he will not know his Poppa. You have become so thin, my love, that if you stand sideways you disappear."

"The way Little Mary disappeared?"

"I didn't disappear."

"As far as young Joseph was concerned, you might as well have."

They laughed together.

Joseph said, "Remember how Yeshua used to ask if he would ever be 'as big as my Poppa.' We used to tell him, 'soon, be patient.' Patient or not it came too soon."

"James has taught him about keels and oars, about boats and fishermen. He gets restless, more so after Cousin John visits. I hear them talking of how they will soon take the place of Galilee's preachers and zealots and of the people's need for something to enliven their faith. They say they will let our people see there is more to life than complaining about the foreign yoke on our necks. Joseph, maybe you can slow him down when he comes."

Joseph said, "Slowing him down will work only until he starts to do whatever he is going to do. He called it the Father's business; that put a name on it but didn't help me understand. You are right, Mary, danger to him has passed since none of the soldiers here know him. The prisoners he laid stones with are now held in Magdala where the paving will soon end and start somewhere else. I have lived through the darkest night without him, darker still without you. Bring him when you come in a month's time."

~

"A BEARD of silver wool does not hide a father's eyes." He snarled his words. "Nor does a sweet cake protect a fugitive son."

Joseph recognized the hate in the man's voice and looked up from his place against the wall. "Come closer, my friend. My eyes work neither well nor far."

"Lucky you are to have two eyes." Putting his back against the wall, the prisoner slid down and squatted beside Joseph.

Joseph saw one eye sealed shut, a jagged scar running across it. "Paver chips and sand find our eyes like flies find the candle," Joseph said.

"No stone bits or sand took my eye. Strong hands and a vicious heart leave deep scars." He paused long enough for two prisoners to walk past them. "But enough of me."

"I've not seen you in here before. But then there's plenty I don't see," Joseph said, hoping his visitor would end it there.

"I worked close enough to your son to know the difference between him and you. Until I ran off."

"You were released?"

"Released, hah. One day we were on our knees paving the way to Magdala and a couple of preaching zealots gathered a crowd nearby. Years ago. Our guards paid closer attention to them when the crowd started chanting and jeering the way they do. One of the men in the crowd – no bigger than a boy, his head full of fiery curls – debated with the zealots, and when the crowd started to cheer for him, the soldiers must have feared a riot for they tore after him, leaving us with our pavers and mallets. I ran. For years I ran. Running taught me something: there's always someone who remembers. Someone was happy to share what he remembered. Someone got a lush reward for turning me in."

"I'm sorry you are back here," Joseph said.

"You'll be sorrier soon enough. You and your fugitive son will earn me *my* lush reward." He got up. "A reward far greater than a clean tunic." He walked away, talking to himself.

A day earlier Joseph could not wait for Yeshua to come. Now the thought of his visit sickened him.

"YOU DO NOT LOOK like the Yeshua bar Joseph that I knew." The voice came from the opposite side of a work table where Joseph transformed raw cypress into fine planks for a garrison refectory table.

Joseph kept his head down, focusing on his task and stealing a glance at the speaker's feet. They were clad in soldiers' sandals with straps that crisscrossed his lower legs. He could not place the voice, but then he would not recognize the voices of many soldiers except his present keepers and they had never guarded Yeshua. Perhaps the engineer had returned as a soldier.

"You there, I spoke to you." The firm voice carried a hint of respect.

Joseph strained to look up at the speaker. A closer look might jog his memory.

The soldier took two steps closer and they stood face to face. "Do you not remember me, *Yeshua?*" Without giving

Joseph a chance to answer, he whispered, "Or should I say, 'Joseph'"?

He urged his weak memory. This man, too, knew him and Yeshua. Either this man of authority or the prisoner of desperation might finger the unsuspecting Yeshua. Yeshua's first visit in years would alter his life in the way Joseph and Mary sought to avoid. Joseph now had no way to keep Yeshua away from Sepphoris. The stranger in the cloudless blue tunic had brought messages to him; perhaps he would deliver one from Joseph to Mary, if only Joseph knew where to find him.

He and Mary had kept Yeshua safe for more years than he could count, preparing him for his Father's business. Did a man's purpose vanish when he could no longer pursue it? Did the years of raising the son of God come to naught if a desperate man intervened? Did he count as waste the years of trusting? He had no answers. He did not know.

That phrase!

Did not know.

Especially when you do not know.

Trust, especially when you do not know.

Father Abraham, help me believe. Help me to trust as you trusted.

The soldier stepped back. "My son recovered nicely and now serves the Empire as a physician."

He remembered. "Caelus!"

"I have learned that good people wind up in bad places so it came as no shock when I saw 'Yeshua bar Joseph, Nazareth' on the prisoner docket. Unless your village has grown in my absence, there can't be more than one with that name."

"Nazareth remains a small village," Joseph said.

"Seeing you rather than him does surprise me. How did that come about?"

Joseph prayed for guidance to answer without giving anything away. He raised his head as far as he could.

The soldier's look said he realized Joseph could no longer straighten up. "I am sure you have a long explanation so we will save it for another time. How long have you been in this hellhole?" His demeanor matched the one Joseph now recalled, that of a man who had come to understand that those who suffered and died at the hands of the foreigners were individual people not faceless creatures.

"Four years." Counting years had once meant counting Passovers, each distinguished by where he and his family had celebrated – in Jerusalem, in Nazareth or in Egypt; and whether James and Joses, and Zechariah and John, had joined them. Now each Passover mimicked the one before and the one before that. "Maybe more than four."

"The prisoner docket shows your son's name with no release date."

During his prison years no one had ever mentioned a release date or lack of one. "What does that mean?"

Joseph and Caelus exchanged looks of helplessness.

"I wish it were otherwise," Caelus said, "but without a date on the docket, you will be here for the rest of your life."

CHAPTER 16

While carving intricate patterns into smooth boards that would become the face of a cabinet demanded complete concentration, planing and sanding planks required a familiar rhythm that allowed the mind and heart to read scrolls from memory, to reflect on their meaning, and to remember the joys of his life with his wife and his boys.

For several weeks after each of Mary's visits he relived their few moments together; for the next few weeks he took solace in the anticipation of her next visit. This month moved more painfully than all the others for at its end Mary would come with Yeshua. He would look the same, or would he? Time alters a face, a smile, even hands. Did it change Yeshua's heart or hopes? What were his hopes? Joseph never knew with any assurance. Did Yeshua know any more than he did? Now Joseph feared Yeshua would not survive the short visit, one that would offer no chance to learn all he wanted to know about his grown son. And about the business of his heavenly Father.

In spite of longing to see Yeshua, he hoped something would keep him away from Sepphoris and the prisoner determined to harm him.

"Yeshua bar Joseph," a loud voice shouted over the din of the early morning workroom.

Having grown accustomed to answering to his son's name, Joseph looked up toward the crier.

The crier stood atop a low platform. On rare occasions a prison crier would announce an event that would alter life in the prison. More often he shouted the name of one or more prisoners. The named prisoners usually disappeared from the prison, while the others never learned why. Occasionally such a named prisoner returned, his clothes bloodied and stuck to his body. Whatever sympathy his fellow captives offered was the only care he received. Scourged prisoners did not live long. Witnessing how a scourged prisoner spent his final days or weeks taught his fellow captives the value of good behavior.

"Yeshua," Joseph shouted back, acknowledging the crier. When he first took Yeshua's place he hoped to get through a week, then a month, then through the next change of cohort; each milestone gave him greater assurance that his and Mary's fraud had succeeded. Now he doubted.

Joseph followed a guard to a cell where there were two huge prisoners. Joseph had seen them before, carrying great baskets of sand for the road pavers and fighting with other prisoners or each other in the crowded courtyard where they spent each night.

The larger of the two prisoners shouted as soon as the guard shoved Joseph into the cell. "You! You're a tekton. Why are you in here? Doing something nasty, were you?"

Joseph faced the man who spoke, remembering the beating these two had given a fellow prisoner who did not answer them. "They worked me as a tekton. You were a carrier alongside me."

"Not alongside you, beneath you. The soldier devils treated me like I was your slave." As he spoke he seemed to be remembering; the more he recalled, the redder his face became and the louder his voice grew. "Now you're in here with me." He shoved Joseph across the cell. "And you will be my slave."

The second prisoner grabbed Joseph by the throat and threw him to the ground. "You had a pretty visitor." He pulled Joseph's hair. "I never got one of *them*." He kicked Joseph in the stomach. Joseph doubled over, gasping for air. He had steeled himself against betrayal by a desperate man. He had not expected to face death staring at the feet of cellmates.

The bigger man pulled off his sandals and pushed them into Joseph's face, twisting them so the straps drew blood from his lips and tore at his eyes. The smell from the sweat-rotted leather turned his stomach with the same vicious force as the kick.

Joseph pulled back but the small cell offered no room to retreat. He leaned against the wall as he stood up, holding his stomach with one hand and protecting his face with the other. His cell mates let him get up. They moved from side to side, tightened their fists, prepared for another onslaught.

"Have you nothing for us, old man?"

"I have a promise for you." Mary would bring something on her next visit.

The shorter man grabbed for Joseph's tunic, pulled it open and again threw Joseph to the ground. "He has something for us," he shouted. Finding nothing in Joseph's tunic stoked his fury. He raised both arms, clenched his hands together, ready to bring them down like a sledge on Joseph's head.

"Stop," the guard yelled.

The prisoner lowered his hands rolled into bony balls.

Joseph tightened his tunic around himself.

The guard's scream brought a soldier. "Who instigated this?"

The guard said, "These two were quiet," -- he pointed to the large prisoners -- "until we put the third one in with them. They have history together. These people all do. If we didn't need their labor we could slaughter them and be done with it."

"Open the cell," the soldier commanded.

When the guard turned the key, the soldier Joseph knew pulled open the door, reached in and grabbed Joseph by the back of the neck.

"The lash will settle him," said the guard.

"I won't waste my energy with the lash. I'll finish this one." He slipped a noose around Joseph's neck, tied his hands behind his back, and left with Joseph in tow. "A walk in the desert will solve our problem."

Joseph would not believe Caelus would repay him like this. *Isaac only appeared to be in jeopardy. Abraham trusted: God himself will provide.* Joseph searched for trust. Caelus led him to the stable side of the garrison, mounted his waiting horse and walked through the gate toward the roadless coastal plain to the northwest with Joseph in tow.

After a mile that felt like four, the soldier stopped, dismounted and stepped back to Joseph. "It had to be that way." He looked at Joseph, wincing at the sight of the bruises on his face. "I knew those two would cause a ruckus and have at you but I didn't think they would inflict such punishment so fast." He untied the loop from around

Joseph's hands and lifted the noose from his head. "I couldn't let my son's savior rot in there." He took a skin of water from the saddle strap and handed it to Joseph.

"The God of our fathers will bless you," said Joseph.

"*The* god? You have only one? It must be a powerful god and a busy one."

Joseph smiled. "Yes, we keep him busy." He winced as the smile ignited the welts there.

The soldier pointed toward the southeast. "Stay off the paved road from Sepphoris toward Nazareth. One of the patrols might recognize you and neither one of us wants that to happen." He shifted his extended arm to the southwest. "Keep the high sun on your left until you reach the hills. From there you will know the way."

O, how he knew the way to Nazareth! Once there, he would have to get word to Mary. Joses could go to Capernaum to tell Mary to stay there. No, Mary could bring Yeshua to him in Nazareth.

No, no. Mary and Yeshua might have already started on the road to Sepphoris. They would go to the prison where someone would tell them Joseph had died or escaped or was executed. Worse, the one-eyed inmate would report Yeshua. Their years of safeguarding and of trusting would fly like sand in the wind.

"Yes, I know the way. May God bless you twice," said Joseph.

The soldier mounted his horse ready to ride off.

"Wait. If my wife comes with Yeshua..."

"If I see them, I will tell them." He spurred his horse.

～

CAPERNAUM LAY MORE than twenty miles away. The usual

route from Sepphoris meant traveling on the newly paved road to Magdala and then north along the Sea of Galilee, an unwise choice for an escaped prisoner. Better that he go north to Cana where he could rest, perhaps even visit the synagogue he had repaired all those years ago with Poppa— or was it James or Yeshua? Had the roof held through the rains and winds? Unless the Lord build the house …. Could he walk as far as Cana, much less Capernaum? If he did he would have no chance of intercepting Mary and Yeshua for they would not come to Sepphoris by way of Cana. He had no choice but to go to Nazareth.

"Poppa! Poppa, look at you," cried Joses when Joseph struggled into his house. He wrapped his arms around him and held him. "Come, you must lie down. I will wash you. What happened?"

Joseph kissed his boy Joses. The sun so low in the sky meant he had spent the whole day walking the five miles from Sepphoris. "I thought I would never see this house again. Let me look at you." He had all he could do to raise his head to see Joses.

Joses brought towels and a basin of water. He bathed Joseph's feet and hands and arms and face, and soothed his cuts and welts with oil bearing the scent of healing lavender. Rachel's restorative recipe had stayed with the family!

A woman came into the room.

"Poppa, this is Sarah, my wife."

She smiled to Joseph. "You are welcome in our home." She thought for a moment. "In your house." She handed a clean tunic to Joses and left the room.

Sarah brought tea and honey, bread and cheese, and a bowl of dark berries. With her help Joseph sipped the tea.

"Ah, berries. I get them only when Mary brings them." He realized that Joses and Sarah knew little of his life over the past years.

With stops and starts he explained to Joses and Sarah how Caelus had freed him but now he feared the awful price Yeshua and Caelus would pay if Yeshua were recognized in Sepphoris.

Joses said, "Caelus. I remember that name. Yeshua told us how you set his arm in a sling."

"It was his son we helped years ago. Caelus repaid me when I most needed him. The seeds we sow..."

"...can take years to bear fruit." Joses finished the thought.

Joseph said, "We must get word to Mary that I am safe here." How easy it had been for the messenger in cloudless blue to deliver messages *to* Joseph.

"None of our neighbors is going to Capernaum anytime soon. I would have heard if they were." Joses said.

"I will go," said Joseph. "We cannot risk Yeshua returning to prison."

"No, Poppa. It is three days to Capernaum, four if the walking is slow."

"I know how far it is, Joses. I walked here from Sepphoris with no trouble." *A little trouble perhaps.* "Before the sun rises I will start. If you want to come with me, your brothers in Capernaum will rejoice to see you."

JOSEPH SENSED that someone had come to him. It was not Joses, who had returned from the sheepfold in the middle of the night and went to spend the rest of the night in Sarah's room, allowing Joseph the freedom to stretch his aching back and to move about without fear of waking anyone. Perhaps Joses would awaken in a few hours to go with Joseph to Capernaum.

Silver light that wandered through the curtains Mary had made years earlier let him see he was indeed alone. He rolled onto his stomach, got to his knees and pushed himself up from his mat. Contradictions they were, the certainty that someone was here and the clear view that he was alone. He limped out into the courtyard, careful not to disturb the couple or wake the sleeping children. If this were six months earlier or later, it would make a perfect Passover night. Even with the moon at its brightest, every star sought to be seen, as numerous as the sons of Abraham. The sleepless enjoyed this quiet time of night, too early for the warming earth to bring the breezes from the Great Sea and too late for the cooling ground to send them back. For the first time in years he relished his courtyard and wondered who now lived in the houses around it. If he went to Capernaum, he might never find out.

"Your workbench is bare."

Joseph turned toward the voice. The silver light played on the stranger's tunic, dyeing the cloudless blue a pale purple like the grape before its time. "I had a feeling you were here."

"I see no gnarled grape vines or table planks to be sanded."

"Gone is the time for vines and cypress," Joseph said. The messenger knew all that, or did he? "Did you give Mary a message?"

"Joseph, the Lord is well pleased with you. You have done what he asked and gone where he led."

"Where do I go next?" A fatigue overtook Joseph. He moved a bench away from the worktable and sat on it.

The messenger sat across from him. "You and Mary have brought the son of God to the beginning of a journey."

"What do you mean, the *beginning* of a journey? He is not still a child."

"His journey must end in a way you would not allow."

Joseph shook his head. "No, don't say I have failed to keep him from harm."

"You endured blows meant for him. You hungered in his stead. If he is to save his people, he must be permitted to know the stripes that will afflict his body and the hatred that will sear his soul."

Joseph's friendly stranger had always brought messages of joy, not foreboding, and of endurance, not torment. "If you mean Yeshua is to bear the stripes in Sepphoris, then I will return and save him."

"Mary, not you, will suffer with Yeshua but she will not draw him from the Father's will."

"No. Not my Mary. I must bear the burden with Yeshua."

"You are to remain in Nazareth. Your time is close at hand. Read the writings of the great prophet before your visitors arrive to enjoy the evening meal with you today."

Joseph let his head fall onto his folded arms.

～

"Poppa, the sun has risen. We must go." Joses stood beside Joseph who lay sprawled on the workbench.

Joseph sat up and looked around even though he did not expect to see his visitor. Never had breathing required such effort.

Joseph recalled what the messenger had told him. He

thought of the baby he had held, of the swaddling he had wrapped around him, of the boy excited to share their journey to Sepphoris with the other Nazarene workers, of a young Yeshua amazing the rabbis in the Temple in Jerusalem and his puzzling reference to the work of his Father. Now his son would soon know scourging and loathing. On their journeys they had witnessed messiahs encouraging the people, the same people who turned on them, bringing stoning and, if the foreigners were involved, crucifixion. *God of our fathers, save my son, your son, from this fate.*

"We will stay here, Joses."

"What about telling Mary you are here?"

Joseph looked into Joses' eyes. There he saw love and concern, but no knowledge of what had come about. He felt his own eyes fill.

"Poppa, you are ill. You must not travel. I will go to Capernaum."

Joseph did not know how Mary would learn he was in Nazareth. *Trust, especially when you do not know.*

"We will stay here, Joses. Pick out your finest lamb for Sarah to prepare for our visitors and bring me the scroll of the great prophet."

MANY TIMES he had read the scroll with the tattered edges. When he and Mary first became husband and wife they read, "The virgin shall be pregnant and bear a son and name him 'God with us.'" Their hearts knew the writing referred to Mary, to her son, to them, to their family and to their people. "A child is born to us, a son given to us," met their joyous belief. Uncertain of the details, they rejoiced in their calling: to bring the son of God to the brink of his mission.

He became more convinced, more elated, that the words of the great prophet applied to their son, more assured than ever. Long ago he had read the scroll for the first time with Poppa Jacob. Now he heard Poppa's voice, "Read the whole scroll."

He continued reading. "I give my back to those who beat me, my cheeks to those who pluck my beard; my face I do not shield from blows and spitting." Joseph had felt the beating, the insults and the blows in prison; Yeshua had already lived through some of the same. *God of Abraham, let that be the last of it.*

He had rejoiced in the earlier words of the great prophet. The later ones turned that pleasure to pain.

He could read no more. He closed the scroll.

Again he heard Poppa's voice: *Read the whole.* He unrolled the scroll once more.

"It is our infirmities he bears; our sufferings he endures. For our offenses he is pierced; by his stripes we are healed. Not opening his mouth, he is led like a lamb to the slaughter." A vague recollection of the rest of the writings came to him. He wanted to stop reading before he reached what he knew was there, but dared not. The words struck him as never before. "He will surrender himself to death; by this he shall take away our sins and win pardon for our offenses."

Lord of Abraham, you guided me to replace Yeshua in prison; let me now suffer in his place. "Show me favor; hear my prayer."

~

"Poppa, they are here." Joses knelt beside Joseph's mat. "Mary has come with Yeshua and James and Cousin John."

Joseph struggled to open his eyes, heavier now than his largest hammer. He reached for Joses. Instead he grasped a smaller hand, one that had comforted him during their years together. A smile consumed his face.

"Joseph, my husband, for weeks I have seen you with my heart, now I see you with my eyes." Mary bent and kissed him and caressed his face and head.

"Poppa, my savior." Yeshua took Joseph's hands in his own.

"Yeshua, my son." With great effort he rested his hand on Yeshua's head. "May you have the strength to accept your father's blessing. Too late do I know your heavenly Father's business."

"Poppa, you suffered in my place and saved me."

The suffering he had endured was like a drop of rain in the Great Sea. Yeshua's turn was coming and Joseph could not hold it back.

Joseph reached up and took Yeshua's face and pulled him to himself. "Now I understand."

Yeshua gave no sign that he understood.

As Joseph released him, he reached for his older boys, his hands carrying his blessing from one head to the next.

"James, builder of boats! Stay strong for Yeshua, keep his bark strong and his feet dry."

"Joses, Nazareth's good shepherd! Feed your lambs as they feed us."

For the first time he noticed John among them. The same blend of worry and excitement that John always aroused in him now engulfed him. John bent to him, taking his turn for a blessing. Joseph said, "As your father blessed you, so I bless you. The meaning of his words is clear now."

He lifted John's face to his. "You and your cousin are destined to be more than playmates: you will share his mission to your final breath."

John's shoulders drew back. He nodded. "It was you who taught me to trust. Pray I will."

The hardest burden lay in knowing and being unable to intervene. *Trust.*

Joseph motioned Mary to bend close to him. He said, "My messenger came." The words came in halting spurts. "Unless I dreamed it."

Mary adjusted the blanket under his head. "Just because you dreamed it doesn't mean it didn't happen." They shared a soft laugh.

Joseph's laugh became a smile and then a sob. "He spoke of Yeshua starting his journey. I did not like what he said of him or of you."

"What did he tell you?"

"He reminded me of the old man in the Temple when we presented Yeshua." He kissed one hand, then the other. "Your suffering, too, has not yet begun."

She pulled one hand from him and struck her breast, as if stabbed by the words of the prophet.

He felt himself sliding on a long slope, with no hand rails to grip, no footholds to grab and, most painful of all, no one with him. Where would the hill end? He was falling up, not down, ever higher. Who would be there to hold him? How long would he wait for his Little Mary to join him? Would she?

Then he saw them all, as clearly as he had seen the stranger in the cloudless blue tunic. James and Joses were young boys; Poppa Jacob, with a hammer and a scroll, reached for him; Mama Rachel summoned him with harp and song. Cousin John stood alone, off to the side, eyes anxious as they sought Yeshua. Mary stood above him, drawing him to herself and extending her arms to him and to all who would follow. Yeshua rose behind her, arms spread wide to receive his Poppa.

THE END

ABOUT THE AUTHOR

Chris and his wife, Kathy, have raised four sons, two adopted from Vietnam. They have 11 grandchildren, some adopted from South Korea, Liberia, Haiti and The United States.

The couple has lived in Pennsylvania, Virginia and Barbados, and currently make their home in Palm Coast, Florida and Frederick, Maryland. In Pennsylvania and more recently in Florida, they taught religious education and led discussions on scripture in parish programs.

While a professor at Penn State – Harrisburg, Chris taught statistics and related courses, and authored a Quantitative Methods book (McGraw-Hill, 1980). He earned degrees in Mathematics at Iona College, The University of Notre Dame and New York University, and traces his interest in bible studies to Good Shepherd School in upper Manhattan.

Readers may reach him at ckmck@earthlink.net and on Facebook (Chris K. McKenna).